ANGELS
IN HEAVEN

DAVID M PIERCE

ANGELS IN HEAVEN

THE MYSTERIOUS PRESS
New York · Tokyo · Sweden
Published by Warner Books

A Time Warner Company

Once again I willingly take the blame for the invention of all the characters herein, plus many of the bars, streets, businesses, and so on. I do not, however, accept any blame whatsoever for the inventions of Hollywood and the San Fernando Valley.

Mysterious Press books are published by
Warner Books, Inc., 1271 Avenue of the Americas, New York, NY 10020

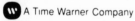 A Time Warner Company

Printed in the United States of America

First printing: August 1992

10 9 8 7 6 5 4 3 2 1

Library of Congress Cataloging in Publication Data

Pierce, David M.
    Angels in heaven / David M. Pierce.
        p.   cm.
    ISBN 0-89296-483-9
    I. Title.
PR9199.3.P486A84   1992
813'.54—dc20

91-50827
CIP

For Rick

ANGELS
IN HEAVEN

CHAPTER ONE

I once read on a lavatory wall the word *pitiful* described as the "state of an enemy after an imaginary encounter with oneself."

I have another description of *pitiful*—the state of one V. Daniel (me) as I sat slumped over my secondhand desk in my God-knows-how-many-hand office on a certain Monday morning late in September, in the year 1987.

And the fact that this office was in that scurvy part of California known as the San Fernando Valley, where smog is as common as dandruff on a bible salesman's collar and just about as chewy—well, that wasn't a big boost to my morale either.

Pitiful was putting it mildly. Pitiful was something to look forward to when I felt better, a lot better.

And from whence derived this emotional prostration?

Not from, say, a trifle like a fortieth birthday. That had come and gone four years ago. Not from, say, the mere death of a loved one or some other petty excuse, such as the old family doctor telling me that I had but one more month to live before dying in excruciating agony from a parlay of leprosy of the balls and cancer of everywhere else. Nay, nothing so shabby, so one-horse, so niggardly.

No, the cause of V. Daniel's degrading gloom lay right there

1

on the peeling veneer in front of me. The items in question had, two days previously (a windy Saturday), cost me altogether just over one hundred dollars. And although commonly referred to as "they," they were really only one item and came in a fake leather case, or small sheath.

I took them out reluctantly, polished them on the flimsy bit of rag the optician had generously included, and put them on. True, I could see better. True, I no longer had to bend over and peer at my computer screen from a distance of six inches. True, I could probably thread a needle now after, say, ten tries instead of a hundred, but how many needles does a macho guy like me thread in one lifetime, not very many, and who cares anyway?

I got up and went back to the small washroom at the rear of the office and looked at myself in the streaky mirror for the tenth time that hour. Arthur Miller wore glasses; who laughed? But Woody Allen wore glasses and everyone laughed at him. And Clark Kent. And Sergeant Bilko. And Hirohito.

The phone rang. I went back into the office proper and picked it up.

"Hello?"

"Eh, hello," said a deeply resonant male voice. "With whom am I conversin'?"

"With Victor Daniel," I said, adding somewhat bitterly, "now known to one and all as Four-Eyes."

"Yeah, well," the man said. He hesitated a minute. "Eh, see, it's like this, you were referred to me by my agent."

"By name of?"

"Oh, yeah, Bobby Seburn? The one you once did a job for? Him."

"Ah yes," I said. "I remember it well." I had indeed once done a job for Mr. Robert Seburn, who was the type of recently invented combination agent and personal manager who handled sports people—golfers in silly footwear, petulant tennis players, basketball players, baseball players, and others of that overpaid subspecies. Mr. Seburn had wanted to divorce his wife and suspected that sufficient grounds existed. Not being averse to taking on such demeaning chores, I had agreed to look into it. It turned out that his wife was involved with someone else, all right—one of her girl friends—but like the man said, that is another story, and anyway it's already been told.

"Would you be a sportsman, sir?" I asked my mystery caller.

"You could say that," he said cautiously. "Eh, how's by you if I drop by sometime later today? I'm cool up till two-thirty."

"You name it," I said. "I'll be here."

We settled on one-thirty and hung up on each other. Hmm, I thought. Wonder what his story is. A sportsman, you could say. Sounded to be a black man. Statistically highly unlikely to be a golfer—there were only about two blacks on the professional circuit. He might be a designated hitter for the New York Yankees; he sounded worried enough. Well, I would just have to wait and see, wouldn't I?

As it was then just after ten o'clock, that left me three and a half hours to fill, time enough to do a chore that I'd been putting off for no good reason but sloth, for a lawyer friend who had an office downtown near MacArthur Park. I wouldn't have to drag my weary but otherwise gorgeous bod all the way down there, though, as the work involved was more or less in my part of town, which was more or less Studio City.

The chore was: to prove that one of my shyster pal Mel "The Swell" Evans' clients, a seventeen-year-old Latino whose given name was Ronaldo Isidro but whose gang name was—appropriately, according to Mel—Blades, could not possibly have gotten from point A, his abode on Roscoe, to point B, the scene of the crime (a stabbing), Tony's beer bar down on Lankershim Boulevard, in fifteen minutes. There were witnesses galore who swore Blades was in his *casa* ("house," to you illiterates) till seven forty-five the night in question, and another set of witnesses galore who swore the stabbing (in the lower tummy) happened at eight o'clock precisely, as some TV show they were all waiting for had just started. The assailant had not been identified by any one of the roomful of witnesses, unsurprisingly, but the cops had arrested Blades because (1) he was a member of a rival gang of the dead youth's, (2) these gangs hated each other, (3) Blades had been heard to say often, loudly, and publically that he (the slain youth) was already dead but just didn't know it yet, and (4) Blades wasn't called Blades because he shaved a lot.

For those, like yours truly, who did the occasional job for those like Mel who weren't big enough to have a handy chap like me on their payroll full-time, alibi checking was a common and routine assignment most of the time. One had to be careful, though, to leave no conceivable loophole in one's statement, not even a hint of one, not even a mistake in syntax. So I got out my trusty memo pad, courtesy of M. Martel, Stationer, and neatly listed all the possible ways for a young, virile (overlooking such afflictions as undernourishment, lack of vitamins, drug addiction, and the like) male to get from point A to point B.

Car. Bike. Motorcycle. Roller skates/skateboard. Foot. Plane. Boat. Helicopter. Train. Subway. Bus. Goodyear blimp. Flying carpet. Levitation. That seemed to about cover it.

Rule out the fantastic. Rule out plane and helicopter. Likewise trains, as there weren't any. Likewise subway, as there wasn't one. Likewise boat, as the one river in the neighborhood had only a foot of water in it most of the time, and anyway, it ran the wrong way. That left car, foot, bus, bike, motorcycle, roller skates/skateboard. Method, attention to detail, logic—such are the attributes of the superior man.

Car—well, that I could cover. I did have a car after all, a beauty too, I may add—a pink and blue Nash Metropolitan in perfect condition except for the shocks and plugs. Foot—that unfortunately meant running, which left me out. But was my landlord Elroy not a jogger and did he not owe me one?

4

Bus—that was me again. Bike . . . now who did I know who was crazy enough to ride a bike in L.A. My brother Tony's two kids had bikes, but I never saw them use them and I sure wasn't going to ride around on one of those wobbly things. Someone once said, When in doubt, ask a woman. I think it was a woman. So I called up one, my woman, if I may put it so grossly. She was working but, I felt, not displeased to be disturbed for a few minutes by her wandering boy.

"Evonne, sweetheart, don't get me wrong," I said, "but do you know anyone who rides a bike and who is young, male, and fit?"

"Only a million," she said, naturally enough, as she worked as personal assistant to the vice-principal of a large high school that was only a few blocks away from my office.

"Could you possibly have two of them present themselves at my office complete with bikes this lunchtime for a short but well-paid assignment?"

"Sure, sweet pea," Evonne said. "What's it all about?"

So I told her what it was all about, and then the conversation drifted into other, more intimate areas that frankly are too sensational to detail here. After blowing her a deeply felt kiss, I rang up Elroy, my office landlord, who not only owned the small cluster of one-story buildings that included my place of work but also a good deal of other real estate in and around Studio City.

"My man, my main man!" he exclaimed after I'd explained my humble needs to him. "Consider it done. I'll see you anon. Sooner than anon."

Then I took a deep breath and called up Sara Silvetti, a young female of my acquaintance who occasionally, when I had no other option, served me as a sort of girl Friday, only in her case it was more like Monday.

"Sara? It's me, your main man," I said when she'd finally answered the phone. "Hope I'm not disturbing you in the middle of something important, like writing an ode to your mistress's eyebrow." I should mention here that Sara, if you took her word for it, was a poetess, but as far as I was concerned, the rubbish she wrote made "Queen for a Day" seem intellectually stimulating.

"Rock on, Pops," the twerp said. "Sooner or later you'll come to the point, and I hope it's sooner 'cause I got more important things to do than shoot the breeze with grumpy old has-beens like you."

"Like what?" I scoffed.

"Like putting garbage down the chute, like washing some tights, like eating some roughage, like a million things."

"Well, pardon me ever so," I said. "I did not know we were going through an active phase. Listen, gruesome, want a job?"

"Doing what, Pops?" she said suspiciously. "Risking my life again for peanuts?"

"I merely want you to roller-skate, or skateboard—the choice is yours, they are roughly equal means of transportation—from point A to point B. Then I want you to go back to point A and skate to point B again. Is that so much to ask?"

"Depends where points A and B are, don't it, master mind?" she said. " 'Cause if point A is in South Dakota and point B is in Tasmania, you can forget it."

"Grow up, for God's sake," I said wearily.

"You grow up," she said. "What do you want to be when you grow up, anyway?"

"The opposite of you," I said. "A kindly grandmother. And points A and B are only a few minutes away from each other, so get over here, will you?"

"I'll think about it," she said and hung up on me. Was I worried? Not a whit. She'd come all right, she was probably already out the door. If there was one thing she loved more than racking her feeble adolescent brain for rhymes for *surf-board; uppers; gross; like, man; weed; pot; far out; yeccch;* and the few other words that formed the basis of both her vocabulary and her poems, it was what she called "sleuthing" for me.

Sleuthing? I ask you. I've never sleuthed in my life.

I had one more call to make to complete the list, and that was to Willing Boy, another kid I let rob me blind from time to time for doing some simple task. This one worked for the delivery/message service I used regularly. So I called the service and the lady dispatcher there informed me that Willing Boy was available and then added, as she always did, that he was already on his way, although I knew full well he was still lounging in the back room, combing his hair and looking at pictures of Evel Knievel in *Motorcycle Monthly*.

Within fifteen minutes or so, all my troops had gathered, including of course Sara, who was the first to arrive. Did I mention she was, as well as being a poetess, a punk? Sara was a punk like the pope was you know what, like I liked chili dogs heavy on the grease, and like they didn't like me.

That September morn she waltzed into my office seemingly straight from a cast party of the *Rocky Horror Picture Show*— her yellow hair sprayed up into points in the new, daring, porcupine look; her skinny frame draped in an old herring net worn over an orange body stocking with so many holes, locusts must have wintered in it. On her feet were an elegant pair of wedgies—too bad they were different colors. She had a pair of roller skates slung over one bony shoulder, and strapped on her back was a stuffed elephant with a zipper in it, so apparently it doubled both as a pet and a backpack. Her lipstick was black. Her fingernail polish was white. On one cheek she had drawn with an eyebrow pencil a crisscrossed hatching effect that presumably represented a scar.

"I say!" she said as soon as she'd come in. "Get the prof! What are those specs for, Prof, you in disguise?"

I'd actually forgotten I had the damn things on, so I whipped them off and hurriedly tucked them away in a pocket.

"I am, as a matter of fact," I said. "I occasionally do have to look like I have an IQ of more than fifty, unlike some I could mention. And I adore your hair like that. It is hair, I presume, not just one of Bozo the Clown's fright wigs." That one was rather neat, I thought.

"Now I know what to get for your birthday, Prof," she said, snapping her beringed fingers in a phony air of discovery, as if she'd been up nights thinking about it. "A year's supply of Sight-Savers."

I was just preparing my withering retort when Willing Boy pulled up outside on his beloved Yamaha, cut the motor, and then gave us a wave through the reinforced glass of my front picture window, which I noticed still needed washing. He'd no sooner come in when Elroy went jogging past, disappeared out of sight, then came back again, looked in the window, did a take, disappeared again, then reappeared again running backward. I don't know—some days everyone thinks he's a comic.

After he'd finally come in, I introduced everyone to everyone and asked them to kindly settle down so we could get on with it. Sara perched by my shoulder on the corner of the desk, as was her wont, but not mine. Elroy took the spare chair facing me, and Willing Boy propped his lanky frame against the wall and tried to appear attentive, which was difficult with the amount of leg, albeit spindly, that Sara was showing.

Willing Boy was a tall, tanned, handsome youth with shoulder-length blond hair that he was addicted to coiffing with a foot-long plastic affair he kept tucked in the back pocket of his leathers. He had done many a chore for me in the past, some of them legal.

The ponytailed Elroy was not much older than Willing Boy. He'd come into his real estate empire some years before, when his parents, two uncles, and an aunt or two died in a horrific car crash one rainy night outside Riverside. To everyone's amazement but his own (since he had a well-founded reputation for being a total space cadet), he had done extremely well. He too was a good-looking young man, although not the knockout that Willing Boy was. Despite his riches, it was Elroy's fancy to dress down, way down, usually in torn cutoffs, $1.99 K-mart T-shirts, and the cheapest flip-flops on the market, but that day he had for jogging purposes put on a disgraceful pair of tattered sneakers instead.

I looked them over—ah, my brave boys and my bonny tomboy lass—once more into the breach we go.

"Everyone got a watch?" I said.

Everyone did but Sara. I sighed and lent her mine.

"Please ensure that all your timepieces are in working order."

They all did.

"Everyone know where the corner of Roscoe and Lankershim is?"

Everyone knew but Sara. I sighed, got out my Rand McNally, and pointed it out to her.

"Point A," I said, "is an apartment building at 11167½Roscoe. Point B is a Mexican beer bar called Tony's at 52005 Lankershim. We will proceed in convoy to point A, me and Sara and Elroy in my car, Willing Boy on that death trap of his. When I say go, we all head for Tony's in our various ways and means, making a precise note of the time we get there. Everyone got a pen and paper?"

Everyone did but Elroy. I sighed and handed them over.

"Then we go back to point A and do it all over again as a double check. All clear so far, troops, any questions?"

"I got one, Prof," said Sara, lighting up a long, thin, nasty-looking cheroot with a kitchen match. "Why?"

I told them why.

Then Sara said, "How much?"

I told them how much. Sara said I had to be joking. Willing Boy said OK by him. Elroy said as far as he was concerned, he was insulted by the question—what were friends for after all? And anyway, he ran an hour a day, so who cared where?

"Thank you, Elroy," I said with dignity. "According to the map, the shortest way is east on Roscoe and then south on Lankershim, but keep your eyes open for anything that might save you time on the rerun—an alley, or cutting through a gas station, or whatever—as what we are after is the fastest possible time one of us can get from A to B."

"Does that mean running the lights?" Willing Boy asked with poorly concealed eagerness.

"It does not," I said sternly. "This isn't a case of a guy who is sitting at home suddenly deciding to kill some other guy he hates, so much so that he leaps up and tears out and burns up the macadam to get to the place where the other guy is. According to the cops, this is a case of a guy who went out in a normal way to go to a bar and meet his pals and have a beer or two, and then the trouble started. But let us not dawdle, either, Sara, let us not stop for a joint or two and a peanut butter and red currant jelly sandwich and a large Cherry Coke."

"Ha-ha," said Sara. "Prof."

I had them all sign blank sheets of paper, on which I would later type their statements; then I locked up and off we went. We made our way to point A, then off we went to point B, with no problems except that, because I didn't have a watch and I'd forgotten to bring the stopwatch from my desk, I had to ask a kindly lady for the time when I arrived at Tony's, since I had beaten both Elroy running and Sara on her skates, while Willing Boy had already clocked in and started back to point A. We repeated the process, again with no problems; then I forked over an exorbitant amount of money and dismissed the troops, after remembering to retrieve my watch. Elroy jogged off happily into the smog, and Willing Boy happily gave Sara a lift back where she lived with her adoptive parents, or at least that's where they told me they were going.

I did entertain a slight doubt as they took off in completely the opposite direction.

I was parked across the street from Tony's. I made sure the car was well locked up, caught a bus north, waited on Roscoe for a crosstown bus, descended at point A, then reversed the process, descended at point B, noted the times, and then made my way back to the office. From this sort of thing you make a living? you might query. From this sort of thing and other sorts of things, I might respond. How do you make your living? Selling roach poison or meat packing, perchance?

I retrieved my typewriter from the huge safe in the rear bathroom in which I stored everything of value when I was out, and started on the paperwork. By the time the two kids on bikes came by, I was just signing my own statement, which was identical to the three others except in means of transportation and the times involved, saying in appropriate officialese that on such and such a day, one of us did such and such a thing twice, which took us so long on the average, and that our timepieces had been checked for accuracy before and after, and that none of us had any prior knowledge of or prior commitment to the accused, and so on.

As soon as I'd explained the mission to the two high school kids and they had zoomed off on their ten-speeds, I strolled around the corner to Fred's Deli for a late breakfast of two onion rolls liberally smeared with cream cheese and two glasses of buttermilk and also to pick up my winnings from the ball game the night before, when the Dodgers had humiliated the Giants. Tim, the house bookie, an old-timer who more or less lived in the first booth to the left as you went in, paid me my twelve bucks cheerfully.

By the time I got back to the office, the boys were already there waiting for me. We settled up; they signed their John Hancocks; then I typed up their statements, made out an expense voucher, and took the whole lot around the corner to Mrs. Martel's stationery store for copying and notarizing.

Then I divided everything into two, mailed Mel his half, and when I'd gotten back to the office, stowed away my half in the safe. I was entering the financial details into Betsy, my adorable Apple II computer, when my mystery caller knocked once on the front door and then came in, right on the dot of one-thirty. I stood up to greet him, partly out of politeness and partly to show him I was no shorty either, although he must have been at least three inches taller than my six foot seven and a quarter. At least I now knew what his sport was, and it wasn't miniature golf or riding to hounds.

CHAPTER TWO

My mystery caller was not what you would call handsome, but when you are his height and weigh in at about 240, you don't have to be. He was attired in what was his idea of natty (although it was far from being my idea)—a no-lapel green lightweight jacket worn over a chocolate brown shirt that was buttoned all the way up to the neck; dark, sort of forest green cuffless slacks; and either snakeskin or alligator half boots. His pockmarked face was square in design, and so was his hair, which was trimmed in that box-shaped straight-sided look that was commencing to be popular amongst the Sepia sporting set. I was attired in a sleeveless Hawaiian shirt featuring a motif of tropical birds, also cream cords and moccasins. My face was not square, and neither was what was left of my graying locks.

He introduced himself as James Jefferson ("J. J.") Hill. I introduced myself as V. (for Victor) Daniel. We sat down; I switched off the computer.

"You know how to use one of them things?" he said.

I nodded modestly. I didn't bother telling him it had taken me years to get the hang of it and I was still making mistakes so basic sometimes it laughed at me.

"J. J. Hill," I said. "Milwaukee Bucks. Power forward."

He nodded, pleased. "Maybe the Lakers this year," he said. "It all depends."

"On what?"

"On what happens the next few weeks," he said. "I'm out here like on trial so Coach Riley can get a good look at me and see how I fit in before the season starts."

"When is that, Mr. Hill?"

"Shee-it," he said, waving one big paw. "I'm J. J. to everyone, including my kids. Not till November, but we're workin' out already, sort of like spring training, you dig?"

I said I dug. Then I said, "Well, I hope you make it, J. J. They are one hell of a team."

"Only the world champs," he said, "is all. I figure I got a chance if I lose a few pounds and polish up my de-fense. You ever play?" He took out a pack of Juicy Fruit and popped two sticks into his mouth.

"A little," I said. A little is right. I played a couple of years at high school, but then I changed schools, and as the one I changed to was in the Illinois State Juvenile Correctional System and it only had one netless hoop, that was about it.

"I'd have a better chance," J. J. said around the gum, "if I didn't have this other thing on my mind."

He seemed disinclined to go on, so I said, "Hell, J.J., out with it. I can't help you if I don't know what it's all about."

"Ain't that the truth," he said, taking a deep breath. "Well, here 'tis." He took a postcard out of his pocket and tossed it on the desk in front of me. "I got this last week."

I looked it over. On one side was a stock shot of cars on an L.A. freeway at night, taken with a long exposure so all the car lights showed up as streaks of color. On the reverse it said, on one side, "Mr. J. J. Hill, c/o The Lakers, The Forum, Inglewood, L.A., Cal.," and on the other scrawled with a ball-point, "Congrats, J. J. Hope you make the team. Yore old pal, Pete."

"So what's the problem in some old pal wishing you well?"
I said.

"The problem is," J.J. said, "if it's the Pete I think it is, he
is not an old pal, he is a fucking bookmaker I once was fool
enough to do business with in my younger days."

"What kind of business?"

"Point shaving," said J.J. "When I was at college."

"Ah," I said. "That kind of business. Where was this?"

He told me. To protect the institute of higher learning
involved and also my own ass, as there are such legal niceties
as slander, defamation of character, and the like, I will only
say that J.J.'s old university was somewhere between three-
quarters of an hour and an hour from my door if you went
southwest via the Golden State, Ventura, and San Diego free-
ways.

"Who else was involved, J.J.?" I got out my memo pad
again.

"You gotta know? I don't want to get them involved after
all this time."

"Highly unlikely," I said. "But sooner or later I'll have to
have a word or two with your old pal Pete, and the more I
know about it the better."

He told me the names of three other teammates who had
also been involved. "But hell, I haven't seen any of them for
years."

"How many years?"

"I been out of college three years. Since then."

"Tell me about Pete," I said. "Pete who?"

"Pete Berry," he said. "They usta call him Goose. Little guy
who was always around. He ran a book and had something to
do with fruit machines or something, I don't recall exactly."

"What was your cut?"

"Five hundred bucks a game," he said. "Shee-it. Can you
believe it. But don't get me wrong—we never blew a game,
just kept inside the spread."

"Local guy obviously," I said. "The card was posted from here and you never heard from him in Milwaukee, but as soon as you show up back here, the postman comes a-calling. What do you figure he's after?"

"B-R-E-A-D," said J. J.

"Well of course bread," I said, "but how? Does he want you to do the same thing again, holding your past misdemeanors over your head as a threat, or does he just want a payoff or he'll write another souvenir postcard, this time to Coach Riley?"

"Either way," he said, "who needs it? Just the thought of that jive-ass running around loose out there is startin' to get to me." His face brightened briefly. "But what if he's bluffing, man? What if he ain't got no proof and is just trying it on?"

"Oh, he's probably got proof of some kind," I said. "He'd think he was just being clever, having a little insurance. Hell, he could even have movies. But like you say, even if he doesn't, he's a threat as long as he's running around loose."

"Do you think you can do something to get him off my ass?"

"Yes, I do think so," I said.

"Like what?"

"Like I don't know yet," I said, "because I don't know enough about the Goose. If he's a nickel-and-dimer, I'd approach him one way. If he's Al Capone, I'd approach him another way, like with extreme caution."

J. J. smiled, revealing a lot of expensive enamel. "I hear ya talkin'," he said. "So how do you find out which he is?"

"Oh, I have a connection or two," I said. "I'll probably start by getting someone downtown to pull his sheet and see what that tells us."

"Talkin' of bread," he said. "What's all this gonna set me back?"

I thought for a moment, came up with a figure, then thought for another minute of the difference in salaries between a power forward for the Milwaukee Bucks and a power private investigator in Studio City who was late again with the rent, and then doubled my original figure.

"Whatever," J. J. said expansively, making me wish I'd tripled it.

"How do I get in touch with you, J. J.?"

He gave me the name of his hotel and said I could also drop him a note anytime the next few weeks, care of the Lakers. And if it all went well and he caught on and stayed in town, front row tickets at the Fabulous Forum anytime, man.

"Thank you, J. J." I said. "I'll be in touch." We stood up, shook on it, and I ushered him out. His car, which looked like a rental, was parked down the line in front of Mr. Amoyan's shoe repair establishment. I watched him take off and merge into the traffic on the main road.

All right, I thought. I like it. I'll get to drop in at afternoon practices and watch Magic and Kareem playing Horse, pass the time of day with Byron and Coop, and sit right behind the bench with Evonne at home games, and maybe go out for a beer and some barbecue with the boys afterward and have long talks with Kareem late into the *noche* about the problems of being giants in a world of Pygmies. . . .

Yes, for once the future looked rosy. It still looked rosy after I'd partaken of lunch at Mrs. Morales' Taco-Burger stand three doors along from me. As per usual, her combination plate lacked a certain everything, but it did have an abundance of lettuce, which was Chinese cabbage.

Back at the office, I phoned my brother Tony, who had the rank of lieutenant in the Los Angeles Police Department and who toiled downtown one desk over from a testy little shaver known to one and all as Sneezy. The cop on the switchboard told me that Tony had stepped out of the building for a moment, which was probably just as well, since Tony and I didn't see eye to eye on a great many things, including—if not heading the list—outsiders using police facilities.

"Sneezy!" I said when the switchboard had passed me on to him. "Just the bloke I wanted a word with. It's your old pal Vic."

"I have no old pals," Sneezy said. "I had one once. His name was Curly. He was a cocker spaniel and he was run over by a Wonder Bread truck when I was six."

"Now I know what to get you for Christmas," I said. "A little puppy dog with a kink in its tail."

"Well, if that's all you called to tell me," he said, "consider it told."

"There was one other trifle," I said. "Punch up the sheet on a local called Peter Berry, aka Goose, for me, will you? It won't take but a jiffy with that electronic marvel you operate so brilliantly."

"Anything to get rid of you, Daniel," he said. "Hang on."

I hung on. Thirty seconds later he said, "How much do you want?"

"How much is there?"

"Not a lot," he said.

"All I really want to know, is he small-time or big-time, his last known, and maybe the name and station of the arresting officer the last time he got done."

"Is that all?" Sneezy said sarcastically. "Sure you don't want to know his jockstrap size too? Peter Melvin Berry, aka Goose, Goosie. Looks small-time to me. Some racetrack con. Destruction of property. Illegal book. Last known address, 224 East Street, that's the one in Anaheim. Arresting officer—Lt. L. Carstairs . . . hang on . . . South Station. Good-bye." He hung up.

"Good-bye and thank you ever so," I said to the dial tone.

It was getting on to four, almost time to close up, so I figured I'd leave Lt. Carstairs for another day, and do just that—close up.

As soon as I got the car started, I realized that by a strange, almost eerie coincidence, Evonne got off work about then and that if I stepped on it, I might just be able to catch her before she left St. Stephen's High School, where she worked.

I caught her in the rapidly emptying parking lot, as it happened, accepted her offer of something cooling, and followed her back to her place, which was a white frame two-story cottage not that far away. She liked it there because the ground-floor apartment (hers) included a garden out back, where she grew tomatoes, parsley, lettuces, cucumbers, and various other uninteresting rabbit foods. We went in the back way, I made us a couple of drinks while she did what women call "freshen up," whatever that means, then she plumped herself down beside me on the couch, gave me a short but satisfying kiss right on the old smacker, and said, "Let's talk."

"A wonderful idea," I said mendaciously, not liking the sound of it at all. "Your bed or mine?"

She pushed back a strand of blond hair behind one shell-like ear with one hand and took a sip of her gin and tonic with the other. Sometimes I thought she looked like Blondie in the movies. Sometimes I thought she looked like Marie Wilson in the movies. She was so pretty, even with hayfever she was pretty. I adored her. Mind you, she wasn't perfect, who is? Max Factor she wasn't when it came to makeup; a distaff Mario Andretti she wasn't behind the wheel (but look who's talking); she always left the skins on when she made french-fried potatoes; and I could list other faults, but why cavil?

"I've been offered a job," she said, "and I'm thinking of taking it."

I liked the sound of that even less—rightly, as it soon turned out.

"A promotion, more money, less work," she said. "But it's in San Diego."

"Oh, shit," I said.

"Yeah," she said, giving my cheek a brisk pat. "Oh, shit."

"Lots more money?" I said.

"Lots."

"A promotion?" I said.

"Up two grades."

"Two grades!"

"Don't be sarcastic," she said.

"I won't," I said. "San Diego, eh."

"Yeah," she said. "There's the rub."

"I'm glad to hear there is one," I said. "I was getting worried for a while."

"I'm still worried," she said. "But that's not what I want to talk to you about."

"Jesus," I said. "You mean that's the good news?"

"Not exactly," she said. "I want to talk to you about Sara."

"Sara?" That one came out of left field. "Do you mean Safety Pin Sara, the Elizabeth Browning of the punks?"

"None other, dear," Evonne said. "I don't think you're treating her right."

"God Almighty," I said, not knowing what else to say.

"Do you know she looks up to you? Do you know she talks about you a lot?"

"No, I didn't," I said. "And when have you two been doing all this getting together anyway? I didn't know you were seeing each other. Want another drink?"

"Later," she said firmly. "You're not sneaking off to the kitchen now."

"The very idea," I said. "I am a grown man after all. So go on, I can take it."

"She was over here Sunday, if you must know," Evonne said. "When you were busy moving your mom. Do you know why she's a poet?"

"I've never even thought about it," I said.

"Well, think," she said.

I thought. "I think she's a poet because it's easier than working," I said. "It gives you an excuse to hang around the house all day and raid the icebox, and it also gives you something to tell your friends you are that they're not."

"Be serious, can't you, unless you are," Evonne said crossly. "Sara is an orphan, as you know."

"I ought to," I said, "it was only me who found out who her real parents were—and for nothing, may I add."

"Yeah," she said. "Good old big-hearted Vic, we all know."

I thought that low blow was rather uncalled for, but I let it pass for the time being.

"Do you know what she told me orphans do a lot?"

I could think of a few things I would do a lot if I was an orphan, like run away, like sneak into the girls' dorm, but I said (perhaps wisely), "No."

"Daydream," Evonne said. "Daydream."

"Shee-it," I said.

"Yeah," said my beloved. "Is the penny starting to drop?"

I hung my battered, empty head.

"And it is not too difficult, is it, to trace some kind of connection between daydreams and writing poetry?"

"All right," I said. "All right."

"Another thing, big boy," Evonne said. "Why do you think she's a punk?"

"Well, that one's easy," I said, desperately trying to think of some answer that wouldn't get me killed. What I thought was, she was a punk mainly if not entirely to irritate the shit out of me and the other adults in her ken, but what I said was some rubbish about peer pressure and adolescent role playing and the necessity of overthrowing the previous generation's values and standards.

"Oh, that," my darling said with a dismissive wave. "That might be why she became one in the first place, but the reason she still is one now is she doesn't know how to stop without looking like she's chickening out."

"Oh," I said.

"So all you have to do is come up with a good reason for her to stop," Evonne said, giving my hair a tousle. "You're a bright lad, occasionally. That shouldn't be too hard."

"No, no," I said. "But it won't be too easy, either, knowing what a stubborn nerd she can be." Evonne gave me a look, so I added hastily, "But I'll try, I'll seriously try, if you seriously try to put even the idea of San Diego out of your mind forever." I looked at Evonne's guileless countenance, then a chilling thought came to me. "If I thought," I said, "if I even suspected you cooked up this whole San Diego fantasy just to soften me up about Sara . . ."

"Why, sweetikins," Evonne said. "Perish the thought and get us another drink, and then maybe I'll be strong enough to see what you look like in your brand-new glasses that I know you got on Saturday and I can see right there in your shirt pocket and you've been too scared to put on before now."

"As long as you don't call me 'Prof,' " I said. "One in the family is enough."

CHAPTER
THREE

What with one thing and another and then the first
thing again, I didn't get back to my place till seven-thirty or
so that evening, and when I did, I couldn't help noticing the
LAPD squad car, complete with Mickey Mouse ears on top,
parked in my driveway (right where I usually parked) waiting
for someone. I hoped it was Godot, but I wasn't about to bet
on it.

I parked out in the street so I wouldn't have to move the
car later to let the cops out, while I frantically tried to figure
out what the dickens they wanted with me this time. I cannot
deny there were one or two trifling matters they might con-
ceivably want to run over with me, and one matter not so
trifling they might want to run over with me downtown while
a very strong light shone on my face. Who of us has not some
minor peccadillo to hide, especially in my kind of work?
Although I seldom did repos anymore, I had recently, with
the aid of a pal to do the steering, repossessed a Chris-Craft
down Huntington Harbor way to oblige another pal—without
sticking too closely to the letter of the law of the land or the
sea. And there had been that slight fracas a while back when
I had to get mildly violent with a senior citizen who was
about four foot six in all directions and had more chins than
the Shanghai phone book and the Hong Kong yellow pages

put together, and who wouldn't cough up the $999.95 she owed me for a new set of locks plus a burglar alarm system I'd installed in her apartment in West Hollywood.

And all right, if you must know, I'd had the mildest of altercations the week before with a drunken yokel who threatened he'd bring charges against me for grievous bodily harm, emotional distress, inciting to riot, and unlawful assembly when all I'd done was give him a few playful taps in the men's room over at the Two-Two-Two. It wasn't my fault he lost his balance and the condom dispenser fell on his head. It was his fault for being loud and obnoxious to a couple of Jim's patrons, two well-dressed, quiet young chaps who were sitting on the sofa in the corner minding their own business, sharing a brandy Alexander and holding hands.

The only other thing I thought it might be, in May I'd been involved in a particularly sloppy divorce case—one that made the Seburns', with all its twists and turns, seem like a stroll in the park on a midsummer's eve. Things had finally gotten so messy that three of the people involved had vowed havoc would descend on poor little me one way or the other, and what was a cop car in my driveway but potential havoc?

But deep down I knew the boys in blue were there for another reason. I could see it writ large and clear.

One of the cops, the one on the driver's side, got out when he saw me approaching.

"Victor Daniel?"

"That's right. Is it about my mother?"

"I'm afraid so," the cop said. "Mrs. . . . Miner—would that be her name?—reported her missing a few hours ago, at four forty-two actually. Normally we wouldn't even be called in on something like this until at least twenty-four hours had passed, but someone must know someone, because we got a call an hour ago to look into it."

"My brother," I said. "He knows someone. A. Daniel, Lieutenant, LAPD, currently assigned to Records Division down-

town. Mrs. Miner would have called him when she couldn't
get me."

"Gotcha." The cop nodded. "Frank figured it was something
like that," he said, indicating his partner, an older cop who
was still in the car, reading.

"However it happened, thanks for coming," I said. "I appreciate it. So what's the story? Is Mrs. Miner around?"

Mrs. Phoebe ("Call me Feeb") Miner was a tough old duck
who was the landlady of the apartment I shared with Mom
three weeks on and then three weeks off, when she went to
Tony's. Feeb lived under us and was my mom's best friend.

"She's out looking," the cop said. "She'll be back in a while,
she's been checking in every hour just in case. I said she'd do
better staying by the phone, but she had her own ideas."

"She usually does," I said.

"We hung around because we didn't want there to be no
one here when you showed up."

"That I appreciate too," I said. "Who are you two thoughtful
gentlemen anyway?"

He introduced himself, then the older cop, Frank, who was
still getting on with his reading. Then he said, "I understand
your mother's taken off before."

"Fourth time this year," I said. "She's usually back in a few
hours, but once it was two days."

"Where did she go that time?"

"She couldn't remember," I said. "She's got a version of
something called Alzheimer's disease. It can make you forget
things."

"It can also make you forget how to do things you've done
all your life, like light a cigarette or take a bus," the cop in
the car called out. "You forget the names of things too—
anomia that's called. Sometimes you repeat things people say
to you. That one is called exholalia or something like that."

The younger cop looked at his partner with pride and told
me, "He does that all the time."

"It's called reading a book once in a while instead of looking at beaver," the other cop said mildly.

A few minutes later they took off, after assuring me that a description of my mom and what she was wearing, according to Feeb, was already out and a lot of fuzz all over town were already keeping their eyes peeled for her. Frank roused himself sufficiently from his literature to suggest again that one of us stay by the phone in case. I said one of us would and thanked them again.

Well, Feeb showed up in her old rattletrap about a quarter of an hour later, greatly distressed, her electric blue hair all over the place, and wanting to take all the blame, as she was more or less Mom's keeper when I wasn't around. They were supposed to be continually in touch with a simple beeper system I'd rigged up, but Mom forgot to wear her end of it sometimes and mislaid it sometimes and didn't wear it on purpose sometimes.

Anyway, Mom finally turned up over at my brother's in a taxi just after three A.M., unharmed, unmugged, and otherwise fine. Tony's wife, Gaye, told me over the phone Mom even seemed a little elated by her escapade. I had a glass of buttermilk to settle my tummy and went to bed and ran over in my mind the whole sorry story one more time.

Tony and me were at our wits' ends trying to figure out what to do. We couldn't keep Mom with us much longer; it was getting impossible—and getting riskier to leave her alone even for a few minutes. We weren't about to put her in some state or county charity facility; nuff sed. The best we could do would be to get her into a first-class home somewhere near, and I'd actually gone to look at one in Glendale that was possible. What wasn't possible was for me and Tony to come up with ten thousand dollars a year from his LAPD salary and my pittance. With a wife, two kids, a cat, and a mortgage, Tony was stuck in his job, so that left it up to me, V. (for Victor) Daniel. It was Mel Evans who'd suggested the possibility. He had departed from a huge law firm—one of those with senior partners and junior partners and accountants and paralegals and legal secretaries and all the rest—to start up on his own a while back, and he'd heard that his ex-company's one-man (plus secretary) investigation department was about to lose its one man.

The job paid thirty-seven thousand, plus the usual side benefits like stolen paperclips and Christmas parties, and one call from Mel could set up an interview with the company prez. Mel figured I'd probably land the job too—what with my expertise, his rave recommendation, plus the fact that he was like that with his old prez.

And it wouldn't be so bad.

Lose a little so-called freedom, true. But what is freedom but a much overworked word. What is toiling for the rulers but a more subtle way of toiling for the underdog. And what is life but a slow death, no matter where you look at it from.

So given the latest development, mañana I would give Mel a call and ask him to give his ex-prez a call, and the Prez's secretary would give me a call, and then I would not long afterward call on the prez and deeply dazzle him by my wardrobe, sincerity, experience, devotion to duty, and overall willingness to be a part, a humble part, of a sincerely great, public-spirited organization.

Having finally made the decision, I immediately felt lousy, so much so that I forgot to set my alarm and was late getting into the office the following morning. And by being late, I got there after the mail had already arrived, and decided to open it before calling Mel. Prevarication, I think it's called. And in the mail, along with a tempting offer from a company selling Shetland ponies ("New to California! How your kiddies would love one!") was a surprising epistle that changed everything.

The epistle was in an official LAPD envelope and addressed correctly to me in handwriting I recognized as Tony's. On the back he had scrawled, "This came for you." He hadn't also scrawled "SWAK." Inside the first envelope was a second one, brown, stained, with Mexican stamps. It was addressed to me care of my brother care of the Los Angeles Police Department, Los Angeles, California, U.S.A.

I put on my specs and read:

> Dear Running Deer,
> August sometime. Not much paper so I'll keep it short & sweet. Hope this gets to you. Remembered your bro. was an L.A. cop and hoped still was. I'm in high sec. prison Febrero Segundo 50 miles west Mérida, Mex. Done 2, 4 more years to do and will never make it. Buddy, I need out. Dysentery, malaria, infected hand. God wouldn't recognize me. NOT here for dope, murder, anything heavy. Gov't can't help. Get me out, buddy, somehow, or I'll die in this hole. Money no object. For Christ's sake, please.
> Gray Wolf, known here as John Brown.

Were you ever a kid? Did you ever build a treehouse or maybe just a shack in the woods with your best friend? And did you ever nick your fingertips and press them together and, using your secret Indian names, bond yourselves together in blood?

Old Running Deer did once. With my best friend Billy, Billy Baker, aka Gray Wolf.

I read the epistle a second time, then a third, then looked, I suppose somewhat blankly, out of the window for a spell.

Davenport, Iowa. Way back in the long ago. Lux Radio Theater. Camay. Modess Because. Quick, Kato. Jell-O, folks. Mortimer, how can you be so stupid?

The Daniels (us) lived at 114 Elm, the Bakers in an almost identical house on Oak, number 113, one street over. It was a house I knew almost as well as my own, as our backyards not only adjoined each other but had over the years practically merged into one, a process hastened by the tail end of a summer storm that flattened the wooden fence we shared in common and that no one had ever bothered to replace.

Billy, nicknamed Sabu for some long-forgot reason—perhaps his size (short) or his coloring (olive, from an Italian grandmother)—had been my closest friend for as far back as I could remember, except when we fell out about something serious like the Dodgers vs. the despicable Yankees; or why Terri MacPherson, age nine, had sent him a Valentine's card but had sent me some highly realistic fake caca in a small jewelry box, gift wrapped; or how come Billy would never let me fire even one shot from his Red Ryder BB rifle. We sat beside each other in grade school and in high school and even lined up beside each other on the left side of the line (he was end) for the mighty Packer High Panthers. We once got disciplined together by the principal for vulgar behavior: when our cheerleaders begged the spectators to give them a "P" during a game, we stood up and pretended to have one. I liked football. It let me bully smaller kids legally. Billy hated it, but remember I'm taking about days so long ago that everyone who wasn't a girl or in a wheelchair had to turn out for the team, even sissies, even fat kids with funny shoes and glasses.

Oh, dear. Billy Baker. Billy was smart. He could do fractions. He knew where Czechoslovakia was. He could even spell it. He read books that weren't on the official reading list, and I'm not talking about *Snow White and the Seven Dwarfs Gang-bang* or *God's Little Acre*—we all read those. Strangely enough, I became something of a reader myself, later. Orphans may daydream a lot, but so do people in the clink, whatever type of clink it may be, and is not reading a type of daydreaming too, Evonne, my precious?

Well. Billy's pop owned and ran a small trucking business and was also a useful all-round handyman, and when Mr. Baker and my pop found us kids wanted to put up some sort of a clubhouse using the wood from the blown-over fence, they decided to draw up the plans for us and took to sitting out back in one or the other's garden drinking lemonade that we knew was spiked but we weren't supposed to, filling page after page with highly detailed plans until me and Billy finally built the thing ourselves without plans, and for all I know it's still there. It was, of course, in that shack that Running Deer and Gray Wolf swore brotherhood until the last smoke signal rose and the last tale had been told.

Sabu and I used to work for his pop weekends and summertimes, me as slave labor doing chores like toting two thousand bathroom scales from the warehouse along a plank into one of the trucks, him on the road with his older brother, Ed, learning the true trucker creed—which stops had the greasiest foods, the biggest tits, and the worst music.

Different as we were, we shared one common dream (two, if you count getting Marge Freeman's trainer bra off): getting out of town and staying out. Don't get me wrong. I love Davenport and I always will. I go back every chance I get, like every centennial of the town's founding.

Somehow it came to pass that we both in our own ways did manage to get out of town, although in my case I didn't have a lot of choice. I was sent down south to a farm for bad boys outside Springfield, while Billy miraculously made it to state college. Hell, in those days it was a big deal even to finish high school without getting thrown out or knocked up. And Billy got through college too, graduating in something like bus. admin., and then he went to a couple of places I forget and then to New York, while I went to a couple of places I'd like to forget and then, finally, out to the West Coast.

We kept in touch for a while and actually contrived to meet once, in Chicago, but the rest was silence, like the Sphinx, I think it was, said. Mom wrote Mrs. Baker once in a while and still exchanged Christmas cards with her, so I guess that's how Billy knew that Tony joined the cops after he came out of the army. Why Billy hadn't written to his mom and asked her to forward the letter to me was another question. Perhaps he didn't want her to know he was in Mexico, let alone serving as rat food in a high-security slammer there.

All of which led, of course, to a further question: could Running Deer, once the strongest and bravest of all the Apache, ignore the cunning, master tracker Gray Wolf's cry for help? Not while the wind still whistled through the sycamores, he couldn't. It would unfortunately mean I would have to postpone calling up Mel, dazzling the prez, losing my soul, signing my life away, and buying a decent suit, but had Running Deer spoke with forked tongue that afternoon in the shack after school? Forget it, redskin brother.

I got out the memo pad again.

On the top I wrote, in capitals, "MEXICO."

Under that I wrote, "1. Diarrhea medicine (large size)." Under that I wrote, "2. Make that 2 bottles." And under that, "3. Call Benny."

I called Benny.

CHAPTER
FOUR

Benny was in.

Although highly displeased to have been rudely awoken at such an ungodly hour (ten-thirty), he agreed, after simmering down, to make it to my office as soon as possible. To pass the time until he came, I first gave LAX—the main Los Angeles airport—a quick call, dropped by Mrs. Morales's for a coffee, then went back to the office and got down from my small shelf of reference books a *Reader's Digest World Atlas* so I could see what it had to say about Mérida. The handsomely bound volume had been a Christmas present from Porcupine Head a couple of years earlier. I had no doubt at all she'd obtained it by some simple fraud; in my day what you did was to use the address of some friend or friend of a friend who was leaving town and whose apartment lease only had a month to go. Then you joined assorted record-of-the-month clubs and book-of-the-month dittos under a phony name, and you collected all the bonuses they gave you for joining, one of which was often the *Reader's Digest World Atlas*, and then you either sold them or gave them to hicks like me for Noël, hoping I didn't know how the scam worked.

Anyway, about Mérida I found out *nada*. It was there on the map of Mexico, of course, down there in the southeast corner in the bend of Yucatán, not that far away from Guatemala and what used to be called British Honduras, but there was no separate entry giving any details. The atlas did say, at the beginning, some rubbish about it was once thought that the world was a flat disk surrounded by a lot of water and Paradise was in the Far East somewhere, which was terribly picturesque and all that but not exactly helpful.

I was in the midst of listing some of the items I very much wanted to know about Mérida when Benny showed up, looking as ever the exact opposite of what he really was. What he looked like was Sonny Tufts' (Sonny Tufts!) kid brother—with his now beardless baby face, round, innocent eyes, and just the hint of a cowlick in his neatly trimmed ginger-brown hair—but behind that angelic exterior lurked a soul of the purest larceny. Not only had Benny never made an honest nickel in his life of guile, hanky-panky, and knavery, but he loathed the very idea. He told me once he'd begun his life of artful dodging at the age of two when he found out how to cheat his sister playing Fish, and he'd never looked back since.

We were pals, for some strange reason, me and Benny the Boy; we were close. As an example of the depth of our friendship, he let a good ten seconds pass before making a crack about my new glasses, and then all he said was, "Bifocals or regulars?"

"Here," I said, tossing him Billy's letter. "Read and inwardly digest."

He read, while I told him a bit about Billy and me and dear old Davenport. Being a gentleman, I left out the part about Marge Freeman's lingerie. When he was done, he handed the letter back to me. Then I remarked casually, "Mérida, Mérida. If I remember correctly, did you not visit that part of the world a couple times last year?"

"Yep," said Benny. "And the year before that."

"I don't believe you ever told me exactly what it was you were doing down there."

"Nope, I never did," said Benny.

There followed a long pause.

"Well, moving right along to greener, more verdant pastures," I said, "tell me this. Have you got a lot on right now, my closemouthed friend?"

He shrugged. "The usual—this, that, and the other. You?"

I shrugged and filled him in on my meeting with J. J.

"I do have something that could be very, very sweet coming up next month," Benny said. "But that's next month."

I was always interested in hearing about Benny's scams, so I asked him, "Like what?"

"We're going to sell this high roller an interest in one of the Dodgers' farm clubs."

"Do you happen to own an interest in one of the Dodgers' farm clubs to sell?"

"Of course not." He scoffed at the notion. "That's what makes it so challenging."

"So you could be available for a little caper?"

"There's a good word for busting someone out of a Mexican jail," he said. "Caper. I like it. What did you call World War Two, a tiff? As for being available, Victor, let me put it this way—when do we start?"

"We've started already," I said. "There's an Aero-México flight number 943 leaving tomorrow at eight-fifty A.M. I made a reservation in your name just in case. To be precise, in one of your names."

"Which one?"

"The one that's in that forged passport of yours."

"Forged?" Benny said indignantly. "Forged?"

"Well, it's not in your name, is it," I said, "unless I've been wrong all these years and you really were baptized Henry Albert Sanderson? What's the big deal, anyway? You've forged everything else in your life of crime."

"That may be true," Benny said, "but not that passport. It is possible to legally have more than one name, you know. Actors do it. Companies do it. Married ladies have a choice

of names. Songwriters, you may like to know, have the right
to register two aliases with whoever it is they register things
with. It's just a question of knowing how to go about it."

"You must tell me sometime," I said.

"I'd be delighted," he said. "If you'll tell me what I do when
I get to Mérida besides drink a lot of good beer."

"This sort of thing," I said, passing him over the lists I'd
been making under the heading "MEXICO." "You are going
to be a busy boy, I will tell you that. There is a lot I need to
know about and fast."

"It's just a passing thought," Benny said, "but why don't
you go?"

"Because I am extremely noticeable," I said, "due to my
amazing build and stunning good looks, while you are not
only extremely unnoticeable by birth and by life-style, but a
master of disguise. Also you speak the lingo fluently, while all
I've got are a few vital phrases like 'Another pitcher of margaritas
please, garçon' and 'Where is the nearest toilet?' Also, I do
not want to be spotted ambling around pretending to be a
tourist from South Bend and then turn up a few days later as,
let us say—who knows?—a U.S. prison inspector on a good-
will tour."

"Tell you one thing," Benny observed, looking over the
lists. "You were right when you said I was going to be a busy
boy. 'Hotels. Car rental. P.O. box—mail drop. Airport and
access. Official American agencies in Mérida—consulate?
trade mission? Department of Agriculture? Immigration? Ac-
cesses to and from Febrero Segundo. Office equipment rental.
Intercom. U.S. bank? What customs formalities crossing border both ways? Passport? ID? Temp secretarial service.' Good-
ness me."

"Wait till you get to page two," I said. "And pictures," I
said, "lots of pictures, pictures of everything you can get, but
obviously we do not want you arrested for taking closeups of
the locks on the prison gates."

"It might help," he said. "Then you'd have someone on the inside."

"We already got someone on the inside," I said, "remember? Two we don't need."

"Just another passing thought," Benny said. "That's the way they'd do it in the movies."

"What I also would like," I said, ignoring his foolishness, "are your opinions—your hunches, shall we say, as you probably won't have a lot of facts to base them on. Is it possible to bust someone out by physically removing them with a helicopter or maybe one of those cherry-pickers Con Edison men use to change light bulbs way up in the air? How about bribery? Has anyone escaped before, and how? My feeling is, if we're going to get it done quickly without a whole army, we'll have to set up some kind of a con, but I could be wrong. It has happened. Maybe a couple of thousand bucks in the right hands will do it all for us. Billy did say money was no object."

"Yes, I did notice that remark," Benny said. He glanced briefly through some of the items on the second page, then tucked the papers away in his wallet. "I better move it. If I'm flying tomorrow, I've got things that must be done first."

"Need some money?" I said.

"Later," he said.

"Then happy landings, amigo," I said.

"*Hasta la vista,*" he said. He gave me his boyish grin, then a wave, and headed for the door.

When he was just about to open it, I said to him, "Benny, are you sure you don't want to think it over? It could get a bit scary down there."

"No sweat," Benny said. "See, I know a guy who already did what we're going to do, and we have to be at least as smart as him."

"Benny," I said. "Come back."

He came back.

"Sit down."

He sat down.

"Tell me about this guy who has already done what we are going to do, will you please? Otherwise I will kill you."

"You mean Big Jeff?" he said. "Of course. Big Jeff is a Cape Cod fisherman. He owns and operates a thirty-five-foot fiberglass craft, which has a 200-horsepower turbo diesel engine. During the season he fishes for cod, going out early in the morning if there isn't too much wind and laying out two or three miles of baited line. In the off season he puts his boat up and heads for warmer climes, and it was in one of those warmer climes that I met him. On Isla Mujeres, to be precise, which is a small island a ferry ride northeast of Cancún, which is a booming resort popular with American college students, about a four-hour drive due east of Mérida. All right so far?"

"All is fine so far," I said. "But I didn't know you knew anything about boats, let alone cod-fishing techniques."

"I don't," he said, "but I do have an excellent memory."

"That I know," I said. "So go on, go on."

"So," Benny said, clasping his hands neatly on one knee, "from January to March more or less, Big Jeff heads for the azure waters of the Caribbean where he has a friend name of Dan Peel, who I also met. Dan fishes for dorado out of Costa Rica, you may like to know, using a floated long line baited with squid."

"Squid, eh?" I said. "Fascinating."

"What is fascinating," Benny observed, "is that we know someone not far from Mérida who not only has a boat, but who knows that whole coast intimately from Costa Rica all the way up to Brownsville, Texas."

"Hmm," I said. "You start to interest me."

"So," said my pal Benny the Boy. "Picture the scene. Big Jeff and I are downing a few in the Rocamar, waiting for Pepe the cook to start up his charcoal fire so we can have a light snack. But Pepe is taking his time about things, so we down a few more, and after a dozen or so snifters of a dark local rum, Big Jeff begins to wax loquacious."

"He's not the only one," I said.

"He takes a faded clipping out of his worn alligator wallet," Benny said, ignoring me, "the headline of which is 'American desperado escapes in bloody gun battle from Guerrero prison,' which, Jeff informs me, is reputed to be the worst in the country outside the notorious clink in Mexico City."

"I wonder if that's where Pedro comes from," I said.

"Pedro who?"

" 'Pedro who?' " I said. "Listen, pal, if you're going to sell one of the Dodgers' farm clubs to some hick, you might at least know who is on their roster, you might at least know who their main man is. Pedro Guerrero."

"To continue," Benny said, "with the main feature and not the latest sporting news, Big Jeff had a pal who got busted for a gram of gold in the province of Guerrero—and I don't mean the gold that glitters, I mean the kind from Acapulco. He says the family coughed up near on fifty grand trying to bribe him out, but the money never got to the right hands or it was too late or the lawyer they used siphoned off too much or whatever—so finally a group of his pals, financed by the folks back home, decided to try and spring him."

"Sounds familiar," I said, "but in our case it seems to be me who's doing all the bloody financing."

"So what they did, according to Big Jeff, and you can believe him or not, was to contact a career marine out of Pendleton who was game for a weekend lark, and so was one of his drinking buddies," Benny said, "for a fee of forty thousand dollars plus expenses, or fifty thousand dollars plus expenses if they didn't get to kill anyone."

"Well, there's a switch for you," I said, "having a no-kill bonus. What is the world coming to?"

"I will tell you another time," Benny said, looking at his watch. "In fact, I believe I will have to tell you the rest of the story another time as well because I got a million things to do. To conclude, all this is one reason I agreed to lend my talented services to this madcap adventure. The second is, as you know, I already have a contact or two down there who might be helpful, aside from Jeff and his pal with the boat."

"Like who?"

He peered around in a paranoid fashion.

"Promise it'll go no further?" he whispered.

"Scouts' honor," I whispered back.

"I do business down there."

"That's no reason to swear me to secrecy," I said. "You do business in a lot of places."

"This one is legit," he whispered.

"No!" I exclaimed.

He nodded sheepishly.

"Totally one hundred percent legit, not a scam anywhere?"

He nodded again.

"What kind of business might it be?"

"Sleeping," he said, getting up to go.

"Aha," I said. "Sleeping. So you are the mystery water-bed king of Yucatán."

"No," he said, "I'm the mystery hammock king of San Diego." And with that Delphic utterance he took his leave.

CHAPTER FIVE

Shaking my head sadly, I watched Benny drive sedately away in his old Ford that he'd parked just outside. I noticed that he had a new bumper sticker: "Please drive carefully, the life you save may be mine." I sighed, and then, right out of nowhere, I had a good idea. It was so good I couldn't believe I'd thought of it. I called Bat Girl—a new name for Sara I'd just dreamt up, as she was bats—and in my most dulcet of tones invited her out to luncheon. Bat Girl was surprised but pleasantly so and agreed to meet me at one-thirty at a steak and lobster joint nearby that I knew she liked. She liked the Nus' Vietnamese restaurant that was right next to me even more, but it was closed. I'd seen a sign in the window that morning reading, "Death in Family. Opens again Wed. 11:00 A.M. Thanking You." Me and the Nus had been friends for years; I liked everything about them except for their beef in hot peppers.

Then I went back to the mail, wondering if it held any other little surprises out of the past, such as a postcard from Marge Freeman saying she'd be passing through L.A. in a few days and wouldn't it be swell if we could get together in some dimly lit piano bar where we could hold hands and talk about the old days. It is perhaps unnecessary to state that there was no such postcard. Someone from Orange County had written me asking what my fee would be for following someone three nights a week; I wrote back and told her. Then I opened an appealing epistle from one Patrick O'Brien (14), who said he was contemplating taking one of those courses, advertised in comics and the cheaper men's magazines, on how to become a detective in the privacy of your own home, and did I, as a working professional, think it would be a suitable start to his career in detection?

Forget it, was what I told him. The only person a course like that could possibly benefit would be the small-time hustler (e.g., Benny at the start of his career) who was peddling his outdated and badly printed leaflets. Then I opened two checks and one bill and chucked the usual handful of junk mail unopened into the wastepaper basket under the desk. I couldn't help noticing the basket was not only full but overflowing, so I took it to the alley out back and emptied it into the big galvanized iron bin next door, managing to dump a substantial amount of gunk onto my neighbor's rabid nuisance of a cat, who had jumped up to see what was going on.

While I was doing so, I spied with my little eye a dirty, white, unmarked panel truck, with two dimly viewed guys in the front seat, slowly drive up the alley toward me. It stopped outside the back door of the emporium next to the Nus' restaurant next to me. The place was owned by the Nus' cousin Mr. Nu, who sold and rented videocassettes and peddled all manner of home entertainment equipment and also things like cordless telephones and Walkmans. Trucks were often drawing up at Mr. Nu's back door, sometimes in the wee small hours of the morning, loading and unloading various merchandise, so I went back to my desk and thought no more about it for a good ten seconds. Then it struck me that if the Nus were closed because of a death in the family, why wouldn't Mr. Nu, their cousin, also be closed? Was he not of the same family? And if he was closed, what was that panel truck doing parked there. It merited a closer look. It also merited me getting out one of my .38 Police Positives from the locked drawer in my desk where it lived when I was in the office. I spun the cylinder to check that it was loaded (it was), waited a minute, then picked up the wastepaper basket again, with my right hand on the bottom and, being a south-paw, my left hand, the one holding the revolver, hidden just inside the top of the bin as if I was holding down a load of rubbish that would otherwise spill out.

Then back out again I went, whistling cheerfully. The truck was still there, its motor idling, but the front seat was empty. Still whistling cheerfully, I began to walk toward the Nus' garbage bin, which was right between me and the truck. Then a man in overalls and baseball cap came out of Mr. Nu's back door lugging a heavy carton, not hurrying, taking his time, not looking at all suspicious. A second man, similarly attired in plain white overalls and cap, came out behind the first carrying two smaller cartons; they loaded them casually into the back of their truck without giving me a glance, then went back inside again.

Ah-ah, I thought.

If I, I thought, saw someone six foot seven and a quarter walking toward me in an alley carrying a wastepaper basket, I'd give him a glance, a deeply searching one.

When the two men—*youths* would be more accurate—emerged the next time, again toting cartons, I was banging my wastepaper basket against the inside of the garbage bin as if I'd just finished emptying it.

"Mr. Nu around, gents?" I called to them. "Need a quick word with him." A deceptively simple question, I thought. They couldn't very well say he wasn't around, because if he wasn't around, what the hell were they doing being around? So if they had any brains at all, they'd have to say he was around, which the taller of them did. Of course that left them with the problem that if he was around, where was he?

"Yeah, he's here," the tall one said. "He's up front. I'll give him a shout. You hang on here, Mick, there's only one more load anyway."

So Mick, or whatever his real name was, hung on, leaning against the side of the truck, looking cool, calm, and collected while his pal disappeared inside once again, then came back out with a last armful, the greedy thing.

"He'll be right out," he called to me. He loaded the last of the cartons, slammed the rear doors shut, locked them, said to Mick, "Let's do it, man," and then they headed, one on each side of the van, for the front doors. Which move I did not care for overmuch, as it meant they were split up. But I had run out of choices by then, so I let the wastepaper basket drop, revealing the revolver, which I stupidly held pointing down at the ground.

"Let's all wait for Mr. Nu together, gents," I said pleasantly. "Let us do that, just to please an old busybody."

"Hey, man, no sweat," the tall one said. "What is this anyway?"

They weren't bad, for amateurs. With no signal between them that I could see, the one on the driver's side, the side away from me, wrenched the door open and jumped in while the tall one pulled out some kind of popgun (a homemade .22, we found out later) and fired three quick shots at me. Luckily for me he was on the move when he fired; he was jumping for the door on his side, and all he did was (again, I found out later) drill two neat holes in the left leg of my second-favorite cords. I assumed the position—a half crouch, feet planted firmly apart, left hand holding the weapon, the right hand under the wrist of the left hand—and caught the kid in his upper right shoulder just before he got all the way into the cab. The one in the driver's seat revved the motor, and I thought he was going to try to make a run for it, but he left it too long. I put the next two shots into the windshield, shooting high on purpose; he cut the motor and that was that.

Mrs. Morales popped out her back door about then to see

what all the commotion was about. I asked her to please call the cops and an ambulance pronto and to keep everyone else inside, all of which she did without going into hysterics or asking any foolish questions. The cops arrived surprisingly quickly. Too late to be of any help, of course, but still quickly, closely followed by an ambulance and then two more cop cars.

I told my story for the first time, but far from the last, to a sergeant from one of the squad cars who seemed only mildly interested, but when he started slipping in the occasional trick question, I realized his uninterested manner was just part of his technique. The ambulance took off with the wounded youth. Two of the squad cars left. One of the remaining cops tried Mr. Nu's back door, but it had locked automatically and hadn't been forced; the boys must have gotten hold of some legitimate keys somehow.

I told my story again in my office, this time for a lieutenant, and produced my firearms license and investigator's permit without being asked. The only lie I told was I said I'd pegged the tall one from just inside my premises, from the doorway. As bizarre as it may seem, I could legally have a weapon at the office or at home or in my car, but not about my person out in the brave, cruel new world. The lieutenant didn't believe me, but he let it pass, given the satisfactory outcome of it all. I made a date with him to go down to the station and make a formal statement; then we went back outside. A cop sealed the back doors of the van and drove it off to the police pound; in all the excitement no one had remembered to get the keys from the driver, who had automatically pocketed them, so someone had to radio in the van's model and year, and finally someone else showed up with a spare set. I wondered vaguely how much of Mr. Nu's merchandise would be left when the van's contents were finally released to him. I wondered how hurt the man I'd shot was. A lot, I hoped. I do not get a thrill out of shooting people, but I get far less of one being shot at. And then, of course, there is the expense: the kind of bullets I use, copper points, cost roughly eighteen bucks for fifty, which works out at about thirty-six cents each (plus tax). I wondered vaguely how late I would be for lunch with Sara.

I locked up and then, ears still ringing and adrenaline still pumping, strolled the few blocks to Sam's Turf 'n' Surf, and found out. Sara was already there, walking impatiently up and down the sidewalk in front.

"You're twenty-two minutes late," she informed me coldly. "Here. My latest report." She held out a sheet of paper. I took it and stuffed it in a back pocket, then calmed her down by telling her why I was twenty-two minutes late and letting her poke her finger through the holes in my slacks. When we were finally settled into a booth across from the charcoal grill and after I'd complimented her on the luggage strap she was wearing as a necklace, I said to her, "Sara, I've got a big favor to ask."

"So ask," she said, handing me a menu. "Better put your glasses on, Prof, the print's kinda fine." In fact, the menu was written in huge letters.

"Maybe I don't have any right to ask," I said, "but I don't know who else to turn to." I bit my lip and looked away.

"Well come on, Prof, out with it." She waved one hand, the one without the glove, wildly in the air to try and get the waitress's attention.

"Better we eat first," I said. "Perhaps I'll feel better with some nourishment in me."

So we ate—me, a reasonable rib steak; her, grilled lobster tails with melted butter—then I got out the violins again. I told her about Billy, about us being kids together and growing up together and what his present predicament was and how I felt that I had to try and help him somehow.

"Natch," she said, wiping most of the butter off her chin with her gloved hand.

"I'm going to need all the help I can get," I said, making a sizable dent in my second bottle of beer. "Benny leaves tonight for a preliminary look around. I figure on going down there in a few days, and I'd like you to come with me. I'll need a skilled assistant there aside from Benny."

"Terrific," she said, giving my arm a couple of friendly punches. "Ready when you are, Prof. You'll have to square it with Mom, though, but she won't be any problem."

"I'll tell you what will be," I said. "You know what the Mexicans are like about punks."

"Yeah," she said proudly. "They hate us, like everyone else, 'cause they're afraid of us."

"Not only that," I said. "They are so blind and intolerant they won't even let you into their country looking like you do. Do you know there have been a lot of cases reported in the papers lately where they've arrested Mexican punks and forcibly shaved their heads and made them put on proper clothes? It's medieval, if you ask me." I shook my head sadly.

"You said it," she said. "What a bunch."

"I absolutely agree," I said fervently. "But here's what it comes down to, Sara. I need your help. But for once you can't help me looking like you do, because I need your help south of the border and south of the border they will not let you go looking like you look. Also, looking like you look can't help me in the first place because for reasons that I will reveal later"—when I've thought of them, I thought—"you'll have to pose as a nice, pretty, conventional American girl, like a secretary type or, say, an airline hostess."

"Yecch," Sara said loudly.

"I know, dear," I said sympathetically, patting the cleaner of her two hands, although there wasn't a lot in it. "So the sacrifice I am asking you to make for me, for Billy, is to pretend you're normal for a while."

She gave me a look, so I hastily went on.

"Now come on, Sara, you know what I mean. What the

world thinks of as normal. Hair that's all one color and that doesn't stick up a foot. A dress. Heels. Nylons that aren't riddled with holes. A purse instead of a horse's feed bag. Ah, hell, it's too much to ask, maybe we'd better forget it. To hell with Billy, let him rot. I haven't seen him for twenty years anyway."

"Yeah, to hell with Billy," she said absently, noisily slurping the last of the melted ice from the bottom of her Coke glass. "How long did you say it would be for?"

"A couple of days, a week, I don't know exactly."

I counted out some money for the bill, leaving a generous sixty-cent tip. "But forget it, babe, it's too much to ask. I can probably get someone else. Benny's got a sister someplace."

"Why do you call Willing Boy Willing Boy?" she then asked out of the blue. "He does have a real name."

"I know," I said. "He told me once. Gorgeous George. What's he got to do with the price of apples?"

"Oh, nothing," she said, reddening slightly.

But nothing was what I was not a detective for, and it did not take me long to deduce that (a) young Sara was smitten with Willing Boy and (b) he must have made some passing reference to her bizarre appearance—as in, Why? I almost felt sorry for the airhead, since it seemed that she was getting pressure put on her from both the men in her life, but then I remembered Evonne's theory and realized that Sara was only getting what she secretly wanted, so what was there to be sorry about?

When we were out on the sidewalk in front of Sam's, I made one more pitch, an unhittable spitball that dropped at least a foot.

"Sara," I said somberly, "I know you. I know you would never change or even bend your principles for anything, let alone a man, whoever that man may be. I figured, though, that there was an outside chance that if some bigger principle was involved—call it what you will, justice, friendship, loyalty—

well, I guess I was wrong. Don't feel bad. I'll send you a card and let you know how it all turns out." I gave her ungloved hand a sincere shake and turned to go.

"Know what?" she said. "You're so obvious it's pathetic. You're so full of it it's seeping out through your enlarged pores."

"Sara!" I said. "Language!"

"You didn't have to go through that whole hammy number. What do you think I would have done if you had just said simply, 'I need your help, pal. Go away and come back in two hours looking like Doris Day in *Pillow Talk*?'"

"You would have come back in two hours looking like Doris Day," I said. "But it wouldn't have been nearly so much fun."

CHAPTER
SIX

After lunch I kept my appointment at the East Valley Station and made a formal statement about the morning's attempted robbery. I must say things have really speeded up in places like police stations since the introduction of computer technology; making the deposition, having it typed up, and signing all three copies only took me the whole afternoon. Then I fought my way through the rush hour traffic to Tony's, picked up Mom, reentered the demolition derby, and drove us back to my place. She was in a good mood; Feeb came up to say hello and have a gossip and invite us both downstairs for supper. I pleaded a (nonexistent) former engagement. Feeb mentioned she was cooking her famous clam rissole, never one of my favorites.

As Evonne was busy doing something with one of her girl friends that evening—she'd told me but I'd forgotten what; I think it had something to do with clay—that left me on my own. After watching the boob tube for a while, I donned a clean Hawaiian shirt, made a man-from-Mars face at myself in the mirror, brushed my hair gingerly so as not to dislodge, let alone uproot, any more of my thinning tresses, and betook myself out for a stroll and a bite and mayhap a brandy and ginger or two and certainly a rumination or two. God knows I had plenty to ruminate about.

After a plate of corned beef 'n' cabbage and a wedge of cheesecake at an indifferent local deli, I made my way to one of my favorite spots for ruminating—the rear table at Dave's Corner Bar, the one facing the pool table and next to the pinball machine. I noticed a new sign on the wall behind the bar: "In God we trust. But if you're not the head of MGM, it's cash on the line." While I was reaching for my wallet to pay for the first drink, I found Prickle Head's report. I reproduce it here, as it will tell you far more about her than any poor words of mine could.

> *Tues.   Sept. 22.   5.45 P.M.*
> *CONFIDENTIAL REPORT No 14.*
> *From Agent S. S. to V. D. (Ha-ha)*
>
> *My poetic musings interrupted by el Cheapo on le*
>   *phone;*
> *Surprised he didn't call collect.*
> *Later, chez lui, après mucho grumble & moan,*
> *He revealed to me my latest delect-*
> *Able assignment—roller skating for measly bucks*
> *From A to B—I said it sucks.*
> *But what's a girl to do?*
> *This babe needs new shoes too.*

Does she ever, I thought. And how about new everything else?

> *When Willing Boy gave me the eye*
> *To heat him up I flashed some thigh—*
> *From whence comes this wierd sexual power over*
>   *men?*
> *V. D. leant me his $5.00 Timex, and then*
> *Off we all went on our A to B chore*
> *That could have been done by a simpleton, more*

Or less. Mostly less. Then—hang on to your wig,
We trekked from A to B again—can you dig?
Is this any life for a spirit like mine,
Is this the fodder on which my thirsty soul must
*   dine?*
Didst Katherine Mansfield skate through the
*   grime . . .*

There was more, but enough's enough, especially after corned beef 'n' cabbage. "From whence comes this wierd sexual power over men." She had about as much sexual power over men as Ma Kettle. What a twerp. And in rhyme, suddenly. What happened to the flowing free verse of yesteryear? I must have a serious talk with her someday, like in the next century, about the passé-ness and déjà vu–ness of rhyming couplets that weren't even couplets.

But pondering on Sara's lamentable limitations as a poetess was not what I was ensconced in Dave's Corner Bar for. I was there to ponder over such trifles as how to spring Billy from an unknown Mexican can, what to do with him (and the rest of us) afterward, what to do with Mom while I was away, and what to say to the Silvettis, Sara's parents.

Somewhere between the third and the fourth brandy and ginger ale, I began to get a useful idea or two. Carla, Dave's latest bar girl, a stacked redhead if ever I've seen one (and I have seen one, more than one—further details on request), kindly provided me with a pen and a handful of cocktail napkins to make notes on. All the napkins had illustrated jokes on them; the one I started with depicted an attendant in an insane asylum remarking to another attendant, "There's a lady on the phone wants to know have we had any female patients escape recently." "How come?" says the other attendant. "Because," the first says, "she says someone just ran off with her husband."

The problem was, of course, that there was only so much,

or rather so little, I could do from where I was, not having
any idea of what we'd be up against down in the Yucatán,
land of contrasts, where the old nudges the new, etc. So after
covering some three or four napkins with mostly undecipherable scribbles, I gave up and applied myself to a more immediate challenge: beating the pantaloons off Bill the Butcher at
Eight Ball. And I would have too, if he hadn't distracted me
in the third game when we were one game all; as I was lining
up my shot, he took a swig of his Coors, gargled noisily with
it, and I scratched off the black.

So I took myself over to the Two-Two-Two for a nightcap
and then, like a good boy, went home, looked in on Mom,
downed a glass of buttermilk, and curled up in bed with a
good book, just the kind I liked, a detective story in which
the private op was older than me but still got the girl.

. . .

Bits and pieces were what the next couple of days were.
Bits and pieces were what a lot of my days were, since many
of my jobs were little more than errands involving one trip
somewhere or keeping an eye on someone or something for
a few hours. Someday I planned on penning a short but pithy
essay on bits and pieces.

On Wednesday, for example, I started off by phoning Lt. L.
Carstairs, whom Sneezy had told me had been the arresting
officer the last time Peter "Goose" Berry had been picked up
for being naughty. But the lady cop on the switchboard down
at South Station told me Lt. Carstairs was off sick for a week,
and I didn't want to bother him at home, even if he was there
and not off being sick shooting craps in Reno. Which meant
the case of the beleaguered basketball player would remain
in limbo for a while longer.

Then I had a visit from the Nu clan, all of them—the Nus
from next door with their grown-up kids, Johnny and Linda,

and the diminutive Mr. Nu from next door to them. Mr. Nu was just back from the local police station, where he'd heard the whole story, and he'd come by to thank me for my efforts on his behalf, which he did with great politeness and not a little dignity. The Nus graciously invited me and any other guests I might care to bring to eat with them that evening. I accepted for myself and Evonne politely, with considerable dignity of my own. Mr. Nu pressed a large package on me as an additional thank you; when all had left, I opened it and discovered not what I was secretly fearing, a selection of the latest in adult videos, but a gorgeous brand-new matrix printer to go with my Apple II, something I'd long wanted so badly that although I might not have killed for one, I certainly would have severely wounded for one, as I had done, come to think about it.

I got my computer out of the safe and was fiddling around trying to hook up the printer when Benny called from darkest Yucatán.

"*¡Amigo!*" he said. "*¿Cómo estás?*"

"OK, OK," I said. "How about you?"

"*Muy bien, compadre,*" he said. "I'm at the San Carlos, on the top floor near the pool, room 333. Got it?"

I said I had it.

"Just reporting in," he said. "I'll call later with all the news."

"Attaboy, Benny," I said. "Soon as you can. And, Benny, at the risk of pulverizing your feelings, when you do phone with the real McCoy, be careful you don't go through too many strange switchboards."

"That's why I'm calling later," Benny said. "*Buenos días, amigo.*"

"The same to you with bells on," I said.

He hung up. So did I. The phone rang again immediately. It was my nearest and dearest, my favorite blonde in the whole wide world and then some.

"Don't be a smart aleck" was the first thing she said.

"I haven't said a word," I said.

"No, but you will," she said. "So don't."

"Evonne, my little cherry cheesecake," I said, "what are you talking about?"

"You'll find out," she said. I heard a click in my ear, the click that the phone makes when someone hangs up on you.

I shrugged. Ah, the ladies, I mused, not for the first time, and then went back to fiddling with the printer. I had just gotten to the stage where according to the instructions everything was connected properly and there was power everywhere and I had entered all the right instructions but the thing still wouldn't work, when I had to pack everything away and lock up and drive downtown to the courtrooms on top of the old County Sheriff Building and give evidence in a fraud case I'd worked on for Mel the Swell six months ago. What happened was, this sucker bought a small piece of real estate out in the canyon, part of a whole development, on which he was planning to build his dream house, but he found out accidentally almost immediately afterward to his shock, to say nothing of his horror, that the company he purchased the land from did have legitimate title to it, all right, but it did not have planning permission to build dream houses or any other kind.

So what Mel had needed was someone else to go through the whole procedure again, but this time checking that the vendors, in their sales talk, did indeed fraudulently promise the right to build, which, as it turned out, they did, to me, the next sucker in line. It was slightly tricky, as the timing had to be right. The vendors, a smooth husband and wife team—or so they claimed—the David Harrisons, were undoubtedly going to take off for Rio at some time with all the deposit money they could collect. However, we did not want them to do so with either the money I forked over or Mel's client's $14,500. But the Harrisons weren't about to fork over the deed of ownership to me until I'd forked over a lot of money to them. Finally, we worked it out so Mr. Harrison got picked up ten seconds after he'd cleared my (Mel's) check at the Bank of America on Sunset and Fountain, and that was that.

The David Harrisons were being finally arraigned, which means they were coming up in front of one judge, no jury, where evidence would be put forward for said judge to decide whether to take it further, i.e., put the sneaky creeps on trial for grand theft.

Which is exactly what happened after I put forward my evidence in my customary courtroom manner, low-keyed but decisive, as did Mel's client and as did Mel, who had all the relevant documents, or rather lack of them, from City Planning. Mrs. Harrison was well-spoken and so seemingly contrite that I almost but not quite hated to do it to her. Mr. Harrison was so much the What Makes Sammy Run, California Mark II, type—open-necked shirt, gold medallions and chains nestling in curly chest hair not even gray yet, blow-dried locks, pebbled moccasins, silver Navaho belt buckle—that I adored doing it to him. It all did take a while; we were down at County over three hours, and my part of the proceedings took a mere six minutes, but what the hell, there were plenty of attractive visuals. Just for starters, there were innumerable bored cops in rumpled suits waiting their turns and going over their lies under their breath, and then there were the antics of the legal professionals as they plea-bargained and car-name-dropped—always fascinating to the discriminating beholder. Their wardrobes alone are a trip.

When we finally emerged into what passes for sunlight in that part of the world, Mel took me for a late lunch at an Oriental ricery he knew in the nearby Little Tokyo, which was just north of him, more or less. Japanese restaurants always make me slightly nervous. It isn't the raw fish; I'm always afraid they might ask me to take my shoes off on the way in.

Back at the office I bit-and-pieced away the rest of the afternoon. I billed Mel for my time in court and the traveling time involved, plus mileage. I finished up an estimate for a security system for one of Elroy's apartment units. My computer let me know my pal John D., owner and prop. of the Valley Bowl, was late with his monthly contribution to the Daniel Exchequer, so I wrote him a dignified, polite reminder: "Pay or you die, punk. You have been warned. The Black Hand." I addressed and stamped envelopes for all the above and popped them into the mailbox on the corner. I sat on a wooden bench for ten minutes with Mr. Amoyan, looking at girls. I disassembled, cleaned, oiled, and then assembled again both Police Positives. I tinkered with the printer but still couldn't get it to work, so I asked Mr. Nu to have a look and he got it going in two seconds.

"You like?" He grinned at me on his way out.

"I love," I said, marveling at the way a line of dots under another line of dots under another line of dots suddenly became clear dark letters—and with serifs, even. (For those of you lacking my classical background, serifs are those little decorative flourishes at the top and bottom of letters, especially capitals, which make them look classy.) I was still marveling when Evonne drove up, parked right outside, and came in. She was not alone. Following her was Doris Day Jr.

CHAPTER SEVEN

Doris Day Jr. was wearing a simple white short-sleeved dress, cinched at the waist by a wide black belt. Doris Day Jr. was also wearing holeless light-gray pantyhose with a little row of diamond-shaped decorations running up the rear seams, or where the seams would have been if pantyhose had seams. Simple, medium-heeled black pumps. Doris Day Jr.'s hair no longer stood straight up like a lot of candles on a birthday cake; it was arranged in a soft page boy, like Evonne's, who had obviously taken Doris to her own hairdresser. The color of hair was no longer screaming yellow, but blond, like Evonne's. Around Doris Day Jr.'s skinny neck was not a luggage strap or a man's tie or a pajama sash but a single-strand necklace of small pieces of blue glass, the same blue as the barrette in her hair. Doris Day Jr. was wearing just a hint of lipstick—not black, not Day-Glo orange, not lime green, not blue on the top and white on the bottom, but a light frosted pink. As a matching accessory, Doris carried a small dark-gray shoulder bag, not a World War II map case or a tin lunchbox, or an old clarinet case or a cardboard Tide soap flakes box dangling from a length of red wool.

I rose to my feet.

"Evonne!" I said. "My precious!" I moved out from behind the desk and gave her an affectionate buss on one cheek. "And who is this with you, your dear little cousin from Terre Haute come to visit the big city?"

"I warned you," Evonne said. "Be nice."

"Nice?" I exclaimed. "Who wouldn't be nice when two such visions of loveliness appear out of nowhere?" I turned to Sara. "And what is your name, my dear? Will you be staying in town long?"

"Oh, shut up, Prof," said Doris Day Jr. "What piece of junk is this?" she said, referring to my new printer. "Your latest toy?"

"Don't touch that!" I said. "I've just got it working. It was a very costly thank-you present from Mr. Nu, if you must know."

"What was Mr. Nu thanking you for?" Evonne asked.

"Oh, nothing much," I said modestly. "Doris Day Jr. here didn't tell you while she was getting her ringlets back-combed at Sassoon's?"

"I never gossip, man," Doris said, scowling up at her bangs. "You know that."

"Come on, big shot, give," Evonne said. I gave, as briefly as possible. Evonne went from being worried to being disgusted to being angry.

When she finally simmered down, I said, "If you're still being seen in public with a violent roughneck like me, we're invited for a thank-you feast next door tonight sometime."

"Me too?" said the twerp immediately.

"Of course," I said warmly. "And listen, Doris, I didn't mean to ride you. I think you look terrific and thanks for doing it."

"Get stuffed, Prof," she had the nerve to say. "I like you better when you're being your real self, a grumpy, miserly old fart."

"Attagirl, Doris," I said. "I'm glad to see you've only changed externally."

We made a rough date for later, and the ladies exited, leaving me to get on with my chores. I hoped Willing Boy liked the Doris Day look. I wished Benny would call; I was getting impatient with just putting in the time.

By four-thirty or so I'd had enough and was clearing up my desk when I did get a call, but it wasn't Benny, it was Mrs. Silvetti, Doris's adoptive Mom. I'd met her and her hubby, Max, a couple of times, once at the Silvetti apartment, east of me off Woodman Avenue, and then at Lubinski, Lubinski & Levi's (Family Jewelers For Over Twenty Years) reopening party. The missus was a pleasant, short lady in her middle forties, I guess, although guessing people's ages isn't the easiest game in Tinsel Town, Cal. It turned out Mrs. Silvetti had called to thank me.

"I don't know how you did it," she said. "I almost fell through the floor when Sara came in a while ago."

"Me too," I said. "But it was nothing much. I somehow came up with the idea that Sara was tiring slightly of her number and, given the right encouragement, might drop it. Nothing, really."

"Max'll just curl up and die," she said. "Max will take one look at her, fall on the floor, kick his little legs in the air, and shout, 'God be praised.' "

"It might be better," I suggested, "not to make a big thing about it, to underplay it, like I did. Say something casual like, 'You look nice, dear. Done your hair differently?' "

Mrs. Silvetti laughed. "Differently," she said. "Differently!"

I took the opportunity to ask her how she felt about Sara's going down to Mexico with me and my friend Benjamin for a few days on a completely safe, routine investigation.

"Of what?" she of course wanted to know.

"Eh, penal conditions," I said, not entirely mendaciously. "I need someone to help with the paperwork, and I naturally thought of Sara, as she's bright and she types and she can spell everything except *weird*. Naturally she would be properly, indeed, generously recompensed, and needless to say, all her expenses covered."

"Well, it might be good for the child to get away for a while," Mrs. Silvetti said. "Max and I are always saying our pet needs some excitement in her life."

If you only knew, I thought. If Max ever found the copies of all Doris's silly reports she once told me she was keeping for possible publication when she became famous, he'd not only fall on the floor and kick his little legs up in the air, he'd have an instant coronary occlusion. Anyway, that took care of one of my problems. Now all that remained were a jailbreak, a country break, and that dear old mother o' mine.

As it happened, what to do with Mom while I was off capering in southern climes was resolved five minutes after I arrived home that early evening. What I was planning on doing was what I always did when the need arose—ask Tony and Gaye to take her, and then I would keep her whatever extra days were involved when my turn came around again. My niece and nephew didn't mind, they liked their old gran, but my brother and sister-in-law, especially Tony, always made me pay for the favor somehow. I put it down merely to a younger brother's jealously, but I could be mistaken, I suppose.

Anyway, when I told Mom it looked like I'd be going away for a few days, she said, "That's nice, dear, so am I. Where are you going?"

"To Mexico," I said. "But down south this time, not where I went with Evonne last year. Where are you going, to Feeb's sister again, the one who lives in that mobile home outside San Diego that you thought was so cute?"

"Maybe," Mom said with a little smile.

Maybe? What did that mean? I knew what "maybe" meant when I said it; it meant forget it, not a chance, except when I said I was maybe going out for a drink, in which case it meant I was going out for a drink unless large lumps of sky fell on my head and prevented me. But what did "maybe" mean issuing from the sweet lips of Mummikins?

"Want to eat Vietnamese with me and the girls tonight?" I asked her then.

"No, thank you, Vic," she said, bending over suddenly and picking up some lint from the carpet. She did a lot of lint picking, and most of the time I couldn't see any lint. I kept forgetting to ask her doc if it was another symptom of what she had. "I'm cooking Feeb something. I forget what, but I thought I might, so I left the cookbook open to the right page to remind me."

"That makes sense," I called out from my room where I was donning a clean shirt, a slightly garish but nonetheless striking Hawaiian number featuring many of the same hues Doris's hair had been over the past year.

The phone rang; I jumped for it, but it was Evonne, not Benny. She just wanted to confirm the time we were to meet. I was watching a pretty good thriller on TV with Mom, sipping a weak brandy and ginger and nibbling from a box of awful cocktail snacks when the phone rang again, and thank God, this time it was Benny the Boy. I asked him to hang on a minute, turned the sound down on the TV, got a pad and felt-tip, told Mom to shush, then picked up the phone again and said, "OK, Benny, shoot."

He shot.

Considering he'd only had one working day down there, he'd done wonders, and I told him so more than once. He'd found a safe phone. He'd found a car and truck rental. He had rooms provisionally reserved for us at his hotel. He had verified precisely what documentation was required for an American citizen to cross the border into Mexico. He had cased the airport. He'd cased the jail and the collection of huts across from it. He'd found two American concerns in town, the consulate and something called the U.S. Cultural Association. He'd located an office equipment rental, also a jobbing printer, also a sign maker. He'd been directed to a restaurant that served good French chow. He'd bought maps of everything we'd possibly need. He'd picked up airline schedules and bus schedules. He described the jail and the surrounding terrain. No one had ever heard of anyone escaping from it although plenty had tried. The rumor was that the one gringo prisoner had been smuggling something, but no one was sure what. The guesses ranged from cocaine to guns to young girls.

I made notes furiously as he talked, and did he ever. When he was finally done, I told him I figured I'd need two working days to get everything together at my end, which would bring us up to Saturday, and that I'd try to book me and Sara on the same flight he'd taken, which would get us into Mérida late that afternoon, so book us into the hotel starting then.

"Under what names?" he said.

"Did you need an ID when you checked in?"

"Nope," he said, " 'cause I paid in cash, in advance."

"Doris," I said. "Doris . . . Jameson, and me, something neutral like, what the hell, John R. Wood."

He said, "Consider it done. Love to everyone," and hung up. I said, "All right!" to myself and hung up.

All right! Now we can move. Hang on, Billy, the A-team is a-comin'.

.   .   .

Plane. Dirigible. Flying carpet. Water wings. Boat. Bus. Car. Dune buggy. Pogo stick. Levitation. Time machine. Skimobile. Rule out the silly ones, but that still left land, sea, or air, which was hardly narrowing down the ways of getting Billy from A to B, wherever B turned out to be.

Guile. Force. Charm. Bribery. Mechanical means. Tunnel. The Indian rope trick. Others. Billy would have to be removed from prison by one of these, which again was hardly narrowing it down.

The next two days, in between making such helpful lists as

the above two, I did, among other things, the following: Thought a lot. Placed a hefty order with Mrs. Martel, owner of M. Martel, Stationer, one street over from my office, for some curiously headed, good bond stationery. Purchased certain items at a celebrity photo service on Sunset. Phoned Sacramento. Visited my oculist. Moved Mom downstairs to Feeb's spare room. Couldn't get a word out of the ladies on what their plans were for the time I was away. Purchased round-trip airline tickets for Doris and myself—tourist class but still *mucho dinero*. What ever happened to steerage? Dropped in on Wade, proud owner of Wade's Pictorial Service out near Burbank Airport, where he ran his one-man business out of his brother's garage. Visited a flag and banner retailer at Beverly and Vine. Visited Mr. Nu. Visited my bank. Visited Fred's to put a couple of bets down with Tim. Ate quickly and slept fitfully. Stayed over Friday night at Evonne's. Had buttermilk pancakes with fake maple syrup for breakfast Saturday morn. Downed three (3) Bloody Marys at the airport bar while Doris, attired in new traveling finery, had two Bloody Marys without the Bloody, or is it without the Mary. Strapped myself into a ludicrously tiny seat in a newly painted torture machine. Let Doris hold my hand as we took off. Hang on, Gray Wolf, Running Deer comes like March chinook.

Whatever that means.

CHAPTER EIGHT

I read an interesting article on the plane in a copy of that day's *Herald-Examiner*, which I borrowed from the guy in front of me when he was done with it. It was all about freezing.

I don't mean what Eskimos do when they take their mukluks off outside or what Margaret Dumont used to do with a haughty look; I mean having yourself well chilled after you're dead, and then stuck into a deep freeze for a couple of hundred years in the hope that when they finally defrost you, the medical profession will be able to cure you of what you died from in the first place.

Obviously, if you died by being run over by a steamroller or crushed by one of those machines that compresses a four-door sedan into a shape roughly the size of a Mexican airline overhead luggage compartment, this scheme holds little promise for you. I had two major misgivings about the whole idea to start with, one being that doctors' fees already being what they were, who could afford them in 200 years? and the other, what if all they could save after the defrosting was my brain, and they put it into the body of a five-foot female punk vegetarian?

Speaking of which—punks, I mean—while I was perusing said article, Doris kept sneaking glances at her new self in the mirror of her equally new compact when she thought I wasn't looking. As if I cared. Once she said to me. "Do you think I have bedroom eyes?"

"More like bathroom," I said.

As for the flight itself, what can I tell you? As a veteran, nay, blasé air traveler—five times already, totaling almost twelve hours up there in the wild blue yonder—I am no longer frightened witless by such traditional airline scare tactics as planes with wings that have movable bits that keep flapping up and down (ours) or the old crosswinds-on-landing routine (at Guadalajara, our first stop). I shrug them off now because I learned from an even more well-traveled friend of mine a brilliant technique for dealing with such minor nuisances. For copyright reasons I am unable to reveal precisely what the technique involves, but did you know that on the bottom of every bottle of Carta Blanca beer, there is a sort of serrated hollow section in the middle that one uses to open the next bottle of Carta Blanca beer?

When we finally deplaned at Guadalajara a mere two *horas* late, I was relieved, although in no way surprised, to discover that Benny's information on what official documentation was required to get into Mexico proved to be correct. The immigration authorities accepted passports, of course, but also either a voter's registration or a birth certificate, neither of which has one's photo on it, and the first one of which I had and had had for some time, in the name of John R. Wood (no thanks to Benny the Boy for once). Doris, amazingly, had a passport, as she had proudly informed me when I broached the subject of ID a couple of days earlier. God only knows why she went to the trouble of getting one because she'd never used it, and it must have been trouble; as a foundling, she didn't even have a father, let alone any proof of birth. Maybe the idea of merely having a passport excited her in some obscure teenage way; maybe she lay in bed at nights listening to Johnny Rotten on her Walkman and popping uppers and scanning her pristine passport, imagining herself in exotic, faraway punk heavens like Liverpool. Who knows about kids?

Anyway, we nipped through both Immigration and Customs speedily and without problems, waited ten minutes slouched in Naugahyde and chrome chairs in the modern-looking terminal, and then one of the stewards in his pretty blue uniform herded all of us who were continuing on to Mérida back on board.

As soon as we were airborne again, we were treated to a tasty snack of chicken and mushroom soup on rice, beside which lay several large chunks of that mother-in-law of vegetables, squash.

"Remind me to ask the chef for the recipe," I remarked in an aside to Doris.

"Remind me to tell you to stop complaining about everything," said she, who had devoured every morsel on her tray including the green marzipan cake-thing with the desiccated coconut on it, as she brushed a few errant crumbs off the skirt of her incredibly expensive innocent-office-girl-on-vacation outfit Evonne had helped her shop for.

"Well, excuse me," I said. Hell, if you can't complain about airline food, what can you complain about? Houston, I thought to myself. In some bland metropolis like Houston, I bet there's a cooking school that all airline catering personnel have to attend where they teach you how to make fresh rolls go stale in seconds and how to glue down the little end bit on those packets of nondairy creamers and salad dressings so passengers have to use their knives to open them and how to pack crackers in cellophane so tightly that you can't open them without crumbling the crackers into microscopic bits. I could go on about those antediluvian, cast-iron wagons the poor stewies have to haul up and down the aisles and which have been brilliantly designed so as to fill up the whole aisle so you can't get by to go to the bathroom until your whole section has been served, but why bother? Who would listen to one plaintive voice emerging from just another face in the milling throng? Above the milling throng, actually, and while I'm at it, how about a section for tall people that you only get to sit in if you're six foot two or over (which happens to be the same height requirement as the Sacramento Tall Club, which I might modestly mention here I was once invited to join)?

About then the captain was kind enough to let us know how many feet in thousands it was straight down to earth. I once flew with Evonne on an airline that actually had a sense of humor, albeit slightly black. The chief steward or whoever it was would say things like, "It looks like Magellan managed to find the airport for once, so welcome to Portland," when we were landing in Las Vegas. Or he'd say, "In case of emergencies, parents of small children should put their own oxygen masks on first and then assist the child with his, but only if he's been good."

Well, time passed, as it loves to do, even at thirty-two thousand feet, and eventually we managed to somehow land safely at Mérida, where long ago the Indian village of Tho once lay, you may be interested in learning. I don't really care one way or the other—Tho what? it is tempting to say—but it seems the least I can do is to insert from time to time a spot of local color and history, gleaned from various tourist brochures and the like. For example, amongst other things, Mérida is famous for Panama hats, which are woven in dark caves where the damp coolness gives the fiber a supple texture. What precisely the darkness and the damp coolness do to the hat makers aside from turning them into blind albinos my brochure did not say.

And speaking of Panama hats, guess who was wearing one, waiting for me and Doris when we finally struggled out of the baggage retrieval section loaded down like Tibetan porters on their way to establish a base camp at the foot of Everest— Señor Benny the Boy himself. I politely introduced him to

Doris in case he hadn't recognized her, and then after fond embraces all round in the Latino style, we loaded up the last year's Chevy Benny had hired and headed demurely eastward into town, which turned out to be no more than ten minutes or so away.

The tremendous charm and appeal of this "Old Mexico" village, I discovered later while idly leafing through the local yellow pages, reside in its picturesque Colonial homes, horse-drawn carriages, beautiful parks, and old marketplaces, which all create the atmosphere of a Mexico almost gone. True, true, all too true, but it also unfortunately gives the sad impression of a people who are not only broke—and I mean on the tortilla line—but from what Benny said, only too likely to remain so. He mentioned to Doris on the drive in that the day before, he'd read in the English-language newspaper printed in Mexico City that the basic daily minimum wage had just been increased to a whopping $3.75 U.S. a day, and it was even being rumored some lucky workers were actually getting that much.

Our hotel, the San Carlos, was in the southwest corner of a small square called Plaza Hidalgo, on the corners of 60th and 49th streets, and it was a proud example of Mexican Colonial, which basically means your tiles, your dark woods and greenery, and your heavy, even darker wooden furniture. I signed in as Sr. John R. Wood, and Doris as Doris Jameson, as per instructions. I left a hundred-buck deposit with the pretty receptionist to obviate the necessity of giving her the number of a credit card as security, which item I did not have, at least not in the name of John R. Wood. There was a real John R. Wood somewhere—at least there was once, be-cause John R. Wood used to play fullback on the mighty Parker High Panthers with me and Billy Baker, aka Gray Wolf, presently aka a name that was all numbers. Then we toiled up two wide flights of stairs to our rooms. We were all on the top floor in a row right next to the tiny pool, rooms 333, 332, and—you guessed it—331.

It was late in the afternoon but it was still hot, so I turned on the overhead fan, unpacked and hung up what had to be hung up to get the creases out, washed up, took some diarrhea medicine preventatively—and there's wishful thinking for you—carefully combed my curls, then rejoined the others out on the tiled patio next to the pool where Benny had already managed to produce six bottles of ice-cold local beer. We were not alone al fresco—there were two elderly ladies in the water doing timid breaststrokes and a young blond couple who, we found out later, were students from Lund in Sveden, so we kept the chatter away from serious topics and generally tried to look and behave like ordinary Yankee tourists, which we did by complaining loudly about the prices, the weather, the exchange rate, the water, the cupidity of the local tradespeople (waiters, taxi drivers, and such like), and the impossibility of finding an edible hamburger anywhere in the country south of the Mexico City McDucks.

One had a good view of Mérida from where we were, even though we were only three floors up. Almost without exception, the whole city was—and needless to say, still is—laid out in a symmetrical grid, and thus it was that all even-numbered streets ran north and south and all odd-numbered ones east and west. All were one way, with every other street running in an opposite direction—all other cities in the world please copy. Looming up one block to the west of us was the enormous Cathedral of San Ildefonso, circa 1598, which made it even older than the pretzels at the Two-Two-Two, but not by much; next to it a brick-red museum; and in front of them the main square, the Jardín de los Compositores. I do find travel broadening—there's so much darn culture in other countries.

After a half-hour or so, when we'd finished up the last of

the beers (me, three and a half out of the six), we moved into Benny's room for a more private conclave. He spread out on one of the two beds the local version of a Rand-McNally (Asorva Ediciones) map of Mérida and its surroundings, as well as a bunch of Polaroids he'd taken, and pointed out to me and Doris the items of particular interest to us, but not before Doris had reminded me I'd better put my specs on, even though she could see I was already fumbling for them.

"If you strain your eyes, they'll only get worse," she said with a solicitude that wasn't even skin-deep. I didn't give her the satisfaction of an answer, naturally. Benny showed us where the road that ran westward to the prison was; he said the clink itself was in a stretch of barren sand and old sisal plantations between the bustling metropolises of Tesip and Molas, combined population roughly thirty, counting the *cucarachas* and scorpions.

"Right there," he said, putting one well-manicured finger on the map, "at the crossroads where the road, if you can call it a road, that goes to the prison starts, are a rundown collection of cafés, a sort of restaurant, old grannies selling tacos and oranges, and kids hustling what they can hustle. Anyway, right there is where I heard something that might be of interest."

"The only thing of interest I want to hear," said Doris, shaking out her new coif in that way women have, "is the supper bell."

Benny, always the gentleman, or a lot more of the time than me, anyway, immediately leapt up, went to the small table in the corner, and came back with a tin of green salty things that might have been dried pumpkin seeds or might not, took a modest handful himself, then passed them on to Doris Jr. By the time the tin got to me, you can imagine how many were left.

"What I heard were the words one old man sitting at the

table next to me right there at the crossroads café said to the other old man he was sitting with," Benny said.

"Fascinating," I said. I made a lightning grab at the pile of pumpkin seeds Doris was holding in one cupped hand, but she was too quick for me for once. "And what was this scintillating dialogue you overheard, something about the Mexican team's chances in the next World Cup?"

"No," said Benny, "it was about the *commandante* of the prison's chances with the delectable young daughter of his wife's new cook."

I arched one eyebrow at Doris, who looked away disgustedly.

"The point being," said Benny, "that this dialogue occurred just after the *commandante*'s car turned out of the prison road and headed off in an easterly direction. And what the *commandante* was doing was being driven to his home for lunch, to be followed by a lengthy siesta—a daily event, I inferred."

"Interesting," I said. "What else have you got for us?"

"A safe phone there," he said, pointing to an intersection on the map a few blocks southwest of our hotel, his pal Jorge's shop, it turned out, about which more later. "American consulate," he said, pointing again, "at the end of Paseo Montejo. The nearest pharmacy. My Panama hat connection."

"That should be useful," I said.

"How about a dope connection," Doris said. "I don't see a picture of that anywhere."

"So, Supremo," Benny said, folding up the map neatly, "what is the master plan to be this time? I presume you have one."

"I presume so too," said Doris, bestirring herself to go over to the control for the overhead fan and turning it to a faster setting. "Otherwise, what are we doing down here in this steam bath."

71

"I do have the beginnings of an idea," I admitted modestly. "The merest modicum. I'll know more anon when I can get a look at the consulate and that other U.S. concern in town that Benny found."

"The U.S. Cultural Association," Benny said. "It's not far from here, we can take a look tonight if you like."

"I like," I said.

"I don't," said Doris. "What the heck has the U.S. Cultural Ass. got to do with anything?"

"Patience, Doris, patience," I said. "Soon all will be revealed. As we can't really get started until tomorrow, except for giving the Cultural Ass. the once-over, I propose that tonight we relax, we stroll, we absorb the charm of Old Mexico, we wine and dine moderately and then betake ourselves early to bed."

"I dunno if I can take all that excitement," said Doris.

We relaxed downstairs in the little outdoor café next to the hotel entrance, although it is not particularly easy to relax when constantly fending off a small but voracious army of hammock vendors, hat peddlers, grubby urchins thrusting cardboard boxes of *caramelos* and Chiclets in your face, to say nothing of ancient females in traditional Mayan costume—loose-fitting white dress with brightly embroidered hem and neckline—who'd stop at the table and hold their hands out politely but insistently. To my surprise, Benny knew several of the hammock sellers by name, and vice versa, and they were constantly greeting each other with energetic handshakes and *abrazos* and floods of Spanish spoken far too rapidly for me to be able to pick up more than the occasional word.

We strolled the one block westward to the cathedral and the main square, passing on the way Benny's Panama hat connection, then a souvenir shop next to it, in the window of which, among various cheap artifacts, was a large sign reading Broken English Spoke Perfectly, also a money changer, where an amiable gent handed over 2,200 pesos for every dollar I handed him. I was rich at last. We strolled around the four sides of the tree-lined and bandstanded square. Then we strolled back to a restaurant across the Plaza Hidalgo from our hotel and leisurely wined and dined at a table set just off the street, where we had a good view of the passing parade.

The passing parade was predominantly Mayan, with touches of Hispano-American, also touches of Teutons, Scandinavians, Yanks, and Canucks, mostly in shorts. The Mayans are short, dark-brown folks with typically wide cheekbones, slightly hooked hooters, and often slightly receding foreheads or chins or both. All trustworthy observers, me included, have remarked on their polite, quiet, one might say poker-faced demeanor, as well as their honesty and industry.

The theory is that they are one of the many Amerind tribes descended from Mongols who way back in the long ago, even before TV dinners, walked from Russia to Alaska when there must have been a bridge or a tunnel there, and then they turned right and kept walking until their vodka unfroze and stayed unfrozen. A Swede called Thor not long ago had another theory, and to prove it, he built a boat out of reeds and matchsticks and sailed it from Peru to Polynesia. But as what he was trying to prove was that it was the mighty and fearless Norsemen who long ago had brought civilization to the Andes and then inspired the poor locals, who only wanted to stay at home and snort a little coke in the evening, to head west across the Pacific in leaky balsa rafts, no one took his theories too seriously, although you had to admire his nerve.

The men in the passing parade were all lithe, damn their insolence, also handsome, but also short, of course. The babies were beautiful and the old folks likewise. One small child who passed wore a T-shirt with Mickey Mouse on it; Benny informed us Mickey was known as "Miguel el ratón" in Mexico. He didn't know what Bugs Bunny was known as. One more thing I noticed while trying to chew a bit of charred gristle euphemistically referred to as "steak prime" on the restaurant menu: only 1 of every 7.4 natives wore glasses.

In the remote possibility anyone is interested, Doris wined and dined on two "sonwich club" and two Pepsi-Colas, while my friend Benjamin slowly but steadily worked his way through innumerable tamales wrapped in banana leaves and then for dessert had the banana part of the bananas, broiled.

As it was still early, just after nine, Benny took us off on another short stroll, along a couple of blocks and up a couple and stopped in front of a four-story office building that housed the U.S. Cultural Ass, as I immediately deduced from a large brass plaque beside the front door that read U.S. Cultural Ass. Under it was another sign, this one reading FEL-MEXCO, Segundo Piso (which means "second floor," though Doris humorously translated it as, "I'll take a leak after you").

We enjoyed, as nightcaps, small Nescafés at the café next to our hotel; then I purchased us copies of one of the local papers, the *Yucatán Novedades*, from yet another one-legged vendor who chanced by, and we all retired to our homes away from home after agreeing to rendezvous back at the café at nine the following morning. Doris, typically, muttered that she hadn't been to bed that early since she was six.

Climb the stairs. Unlock door. Fan on. Shower on. Water hot! Me in shower. Anoint locks with special preparation purporting to combat hair loss. TV on. A lot of people being funny in a hospital in a foreign language. TV off. Climb into bed. Set traveling alarm clock (birthday present from Mom many eons ago). Open *Novedades*. Bruce Lee was starring in *El Gran Jefe* at the Olympia. Richard Chamberlain was Allan Quartermain in *En Busca de la Cuidad Perdida*. The *Los Harlem Globetrotters contra Los Generales de Washington, La Plaza de Toros, Jueves, Viernes, y Sábado. El Famoso Trupo Argentino de Tango hoy al Teatro José Peon de Camara.*

The tango ... now there was a dance. If I could dance at all I'd choose the tango. Someone once said something meaningful about the tango; I know it was Valentino but I cannot remember what it was.... Was it something about a tango being a sad thought that is danced?

Buenas noches, amigos.

CHAPTER NINE

$\mathbb{A}$mbrose Bierce," said Benny.

"I beg your pardon?" said V. Daniel.

"Ambrose Bierce once wrote something to the effect that a consul is a person who can't get a job in the U.S. but who is finally given one by the administration on condition that he leave the country."

"Screamingly amusing," said Doris Jr. around a yawn.

It was the following morning. Benny was in the front seat, me and Doris in the back, of a Mérida taxicab, an ancient Impala that had been decorated with an attractive slice of a thickly napped orange carpet which was spread over and dangling down from the ledge on top of the instrument panel, as featured in a recent issue of the Mexican *Home & Garden*. A small plastic chap in a red Santa outfit, with a long gray beard and green sunglasses, swung merrily from the rearview mirror.

It was nine forty-five A.M. We had breakfasted on toast, marmalade, and Nescafé. (Marmalade in Mexican means "jam," not "marmalade." I don't know what means marmalade.) We had just turned left off 47th onto the main drag, the Paseo Montejo.

The paseo boasted two one-way highways separated by some wilting greenery, and it contained branches of the major banks, cafés, a movie house or two, old mansions, the local offices of Xerox and the like, and the new Consulado de América, which we drove slowly past, eyes agog. It was a low white structure, well fenced, with a pair of guards out front and a couple more around the back. To one side of it was a large private home and on the other a traffic circle. A block or two farther along, the paseo ended at something called the Memorial de la Patria, a stone wall bas-reliefed with various incomprehensible Mayan symbols.

We circled the memorial, then circled the *consulado*, then drove back down the other side of the paseo, then had the driver take us back to the hotel, having seen all we wanted to see, unfortunately.

It is now perhaps time to reveal an inkling of the V. Daniel master plan.

And the inkling is . . . the setting up of an office (as soon as possible, as days are long, amigo, in stir, and nights are even longer) with some sort of quasi-legal or official front for us to work out of, an absolute necessity no matter which of the many variations of the master plan I decided to go with. For reasons that I won't inkle at the moment, I would have preferred the office to be in an edifice next to the *consulado* or across from it—or at least nearby, or over or under—but that now seemed to be impossible because, as just recounted, on one side was a private home, on the other a traffic jam, behind it a small park, across from it a school, and nowhere near did I spy an Office for Rent sign or indeed note any unoccupied buildings. That seemed to leave our old amigo the Cultural Ass., which was obviously not the consulate but did seem to have some sort of official connection with the U.S., if in name only. So after paying off the cab and telling Doris to take a walk for a while or a swim or to visit the hotel hairdresser and have something done to her split ends, Benjamin and I retraced our steps the few blocks to the Cultural Ass. building.

After a few words together regarding procedure and a few more about which lies we would be using and which we wouldn't, and then a handing over from me to him of assorted business cards (courtesy M. Martel, Stationer) up the stairs we went and in we went. The *portero* ("doorman-guardian"), seated at a minuscule desk in the lobby, informed us that the rental agent for the building had an office on the premises; it was down the hall and to the left. I noticed on the board listing the building's occupants that the U.S. Cultural Ass. was on the third *piso*.

The agent turned out to be a diminutive hombre sporting a spotless white *guayabera* and what looked suspiciously like a classic shiner, which he was unsuccessfully attempting to hide behind a huge pair of shades.

We presented ourselves—Sr. Blackman and Sr. Keith. We presented our calling cards; mine read "V. Blackman," followed by a nonexistent address but a real Sacramento phone number, and Benny's read "B. Keith," followed by likewise. The Sacramento phone numbers belonged to an acquaintance of Benjamin's who for a small monthly sum said whatever Benny had instructed him to say to whoever called, so beware of seeking references for anyone over the phone is my advice. The call to Sac I'd placed before (you may recall) was precisely to said friend of Benny's, to cover our backs if need be.

Benny mentioned we would drop off a handful of business cards to him as soon as we had a local phone number, possibly in a day or two. Then the agent presented himself, don Rafael Moreno, at our services. He presented a business card of his own, which declared he was an agent for the leasing of all types of commercial properties; I hoped his card contained a higher percentage of veracity than ours did. Don Rafael wondered in what way he could assist us.

Did he perchance speak English?

Alas, no, he was desolate.

Had he perchance any vacant office space in his imposing building?

By a stroke of good fortune he did have two fine sites surprisingly still unlet.

Did either of them happen to be furnished?

Alas, he was desolate.

Did there happen to be a furnished office in the building whose tenants were away and might consider subletting to us for a short time?

Alas, he was desolate again.

(For purposes of keeping the narrative flow flowing, so to speak, I have dispensed with the laborious task of telling it like it really happened, e.g., Benny to Don Rafael: "Do you perchance speak English?" Benny to me: "I'm asking if he speaks English." Don Rafael to Benny: "Alas, no, I am desolate." Benny to me: "No, he's desolate." Benny to Don Rafael: "Do you perchance have any furnished office space in your imposing building?" Benny to me: "I'm seeing if he's got any vacancies." Don Rafael to Benny: "Alas, I am desolate." Benny to me: "He's still desolate." In other words, all translations have been omitted and will continue to be so. The flowery style is but my feeble attempt to convey the inherent politeness of the Spanish language.)

Was one of those vacancies by any stroke of fortune on the fourth floor, as we desired to have as fine a view as possible of his beautiful city?

One was, as it happened, but perhaps those premises might be too small for a prestigious company like ours. He did have a recently vacated, newly decorated ground-floor front that he could highly recommend.

Benny demurred, saying that unfortunately we were but a modest concern setting up a Mérida branch as a trial, really, and we would have to see whether further expansion could be justified by our volume of business, which of course would depend on many complex factors—the strength of the dollar vs. the peso, the continuing availability of local products at a competitive price, and so on. That Benny—he was so smooth when he got going that even I found myself believing him half the time, and I don't believe the speaking clock half the time.

Might he, Don Rafael, inquire which of the local products we were particularly interested in, as he had many connections in the Yucatán business world and indeed his mother's brother owned a small but flourishing jewelry concern that specialized in inlaid coral and tortoise shell?

"Principally the famous handwoven hammocks of Mérida," said the hammock king of San Diego.

"Ah, what a happy coincidence!" exclaimed Don Rafael. "It was only yesterday that I was speaking with my neighbor's sister about that very subject...."

And so on. You get the picture. And after a trip to the top floor, we got the office. It was ideal for our requirements, having a small room for a receptionist and a second, larger office connected to it. There was an extra door in the larger office that I thought at first might lead to a tiny kitchenette or bathroom, but on examination it led to a set of fire stairs, at the top of which was a small broom cupboard.

Both rooms had been recently repainted, recarpeted, and redraped. I gave Benny the nod, and he got down to details with Don Rafael, like how much down? (a lot); would he require written references? (usually, to be sure, but in our case, as we were obviously upstanding citizens etc.); could the space be rented monthly to begin with? (yes, with a three-month minimum); could we move in immediately? (*sí*, on receipt of the down payment); were there working phone outlets? (*sí*, two); where was the john? (down the hall); and what time did the *portero* go off duty? (nine o'clock).

Downstairs back in Don Rafael's office, Benny inquired if Sr. Moreno was averse to taking cash for the first three months' rental, plus deposit for wear and tear, as our new business checks had not yet unfortunately been printed up at the Banco de Mejico; Sr. Moreno seemed anything but averse. So I counted out a huge wad of pesos—the equivalent of seven hundred dollars American—and tucked the receipt away carefully. Then we followed Don Rafael out to the lobby to be introduced to one Frederico Romano, the *portero*, who would see to the remaining details. Then Don Rafael reluctantly took himself off, pleading urgent business elsewhere. I never did find out who gave him the shiner.

After some opening pleasantries, Sr. Romano dug out of a desk drawer a set of keys for all the office doors and for the downstairs front and back doors. As for deliveries of office furniture and supplies, he informed us there was no service elevator as such. When suitably forewarned, he, Frederico, would remain behind after his usual departure time, and when the last of the tenants had left, he would hang protective matting in the passenger elevator and take the furniture up in it. And on that amicable note we shook hands all round and took our leave.

"That was quick," I said to Benny once we were out on the street again, with me following him as he headed briskly westward on 55th. "I thought it took years to get anything done in this country. And so another prejudice bites the dust."

He spread his hands apart in a gesture signifying that it was nothing. "Now what?"

"I'd like to get a look at the prison," I said, "but it makes more sense, I guess, now that we got an office, to make it look like an office. In warfare, Benny, always secure your base—remember that. Marriage counselors never said a truer word."

"*Sí, Supremo,*" Benny said. "By chance we happen to be going in the precise direction that in five minutes will take us to the furniture rental place I found."

"Some chance," I said. "Too bad we couldn't have scored a place already furnished, it would have saved me a fortune."

We stopped off on the way at a fresh fruit juice stand for some needed refreshment, and to make out our shopping lists. The blushing señorita who took our orders squeezed right there before my appreciative eyes seven jumbo oranges, pouring the results into a container about the size of what soda jerks used to make milkshakes in, for which ambrosia she presented me with a handwritten bill for thirty-two cents. What kind of tip does a man of the world leave on a bill of thirty-two cents? Do people tip at fruit juice stands? Even us experienced globe-trotters occasionally come face to face with a new dilemma. As it happened, I let Benny solve the problem, as I had my trusty memo pad out and was busy with the lists, which Benny then took from me and wrote out again in the local lingo.

The furniture rental was down at 63rd and 62nd, near the market. We had to stop by the money changer again on the way, as I was already almost out of pesos, so suddenly I was rich again. At our destination, we handed over the first list to an underling who ran his eyes down it and then said, *"No hay problema."* What the list said was:

> Desk, large—1.
> Desk, small—2.
> Occasional chairs—4.
> Filing cabinets, locking—4.
> Typewriters, electric—2.
> Wastepaper baskets (if poss.)—2.
> Shredder (if poss.)—1.
> Teletype—1.
> Intercom system linking offices—1.

We trailed the underling out back to the main storeroom and together selected the items we wanted, which the underling duly tagged. Then he and Benny haggled over prices awhile, and I handed over yet another fortune I was pretty

sure I'd never get back. What price friendship, eh? as Kirk
Douglas was reputed to have said once. Then we settled on
a price and a time that night for the delivery, and that took
care of that chore.

Next on the agenda were office supplies. It was one thing
to have an office and another to have some furniture for it,
but the odd shred of paper scattered around and a pencil or
two wouldn't be amiss either. So after a query from us, the
underling continued in his helpful ways by directing us to a
nearby stationer, where, surprisingly, he not only knew no
one but had no relations working. Perhaps he was new in
town.

At the stationer's, we passed over our second list to an
assistant, who began rounding up the stuff: Pencil sharp-
ener—1. Paper, assorted. Pencils and pens, assorted. Globe.
Desktop diaries—3. White-out. Glue. Large corkboard.
Thumbtacks. Rotary file. Cardboard folders. Assorted hardware and junk to dress the set, as Strolling Players put it. As
before, we settled on a price and a time that night for the
delivery. Then Benjamin and I went our separate ways, me to
the sign store and then to the printer, the locations of which
Benny had already marked on my map, while he took himself
back to our new office premises to forewarn Frederico so he
would be on hand when the deliveries arrived, after which
Benny planned on dropping in at the nearest branch of the
Mexican telephone company to rent or lease or buy or do
whatever you had to do down there to snag a couple of
phones. Not that I didn't already have a pretty good idea.

And what did I do at the sign store? I ordered three signs,
if that's what those wooden things are that sit on desks and
tell you what people's names and sometimes their company
positions are. Then I ordered a discreet sign for the door. At a
small, backstreet printer I placed an order for various business
cards and equally various headed notepapers, a large order,
unfortunately, as I thought it might look a mite suspicious if,

as a new businessman just setting up in town, which I was purporting to be, I ordered only four of each item. ("Various business cards" . . . "various headed notepapers" . . . the suspense mounts. . .)

We all joined forces later back at the hotel, where Sara condescended to join us for a late lunch in the dining room on the ground floor around to the right of the check-in area. While I tried to find something that looked edible on the menu, Benny filled her in on what we had been up to so far that day.

"Flowers," she said, looking over the lists we'd made, absolutely determined to find something we'd left out. "On my desk, as I presume I'm going to be the secretary, not that anyone's told me yet."

So I told her. I also gave her and Benny an inkle of why we needed an office and what said office should roughly look like when fully furnished and decorated. I also let slip the intriguing hint that the office had to have the capability of being transformed rapidly into a different office.

"Ah so," said she.

"Ah so indeed," said he.

"A coffee cup," said she. "And a few, you know, personal touches. Don't you guys know anything about secretaries?"

"Are you kidding?" I said. "I've only got one crazy in love with me. But OK, if you want it that way. Benny, take a list. In secretary's desk, upper left drawer: cookie package with one cookie left. Nail polish remover. Nail polish. Fake nails and glue to cover up broken nails. Nail file. Copy of *Screen Gems*. Copy of *Hollywood Enquirer*. Copy of *Valley Studs*, or whatever the name of Jackie Collins' latest foray into literature is."

"Ha-ha," said Doris. "I don't think."

"Top right drawer," I continued. "Set of ruined nylons. Box of Kleenex. Box of Whitman's Sampler chocolates, with only the Turkish Delight ones left. Nineteen eighty-two diary.

Walkman with Barry Manilow tapes. Well-thumbed copy of
The Beverly Hills Grapefruit Diet. Six empty lipstick contain-
ers. Empty birth control pill thing. Hair spray for difficult hair.
Cocktail stirrer from Top o' the Mark. Furry animal. Another
furry animal. Broken key chain."

"Check," said Benny, pretending to write it all down.

"I thought we were here to eat, not to listen to you trying
to be funny," said Doris.

"Funny?" I said in a surprised tone. "I wasn't trying to be
funny, Doris. I was just trying to give your desk that personal
touch you mentioned."

"Sure, sure," said Doris. "How about giving your desk the
personal touch, Prof? Take a list, Benny. Hair guck. More hair
guck. Spare glasses. Unopened box of rubbers, small size."

"No need to get that personal," I said. "Anyway, all men
know it's the technique that counts, not the size."

"No woman does," said the twerp unkindly and obviously
inaccurately. "Well-thumbed copy of Fiona Richmond's latest
foray into literature. Diary from nineteen forty-four. Well-
thumbed copy of *The Drinking Man's Diet.* Empty bottle of
Four Roses. Toy airplane. Jungle Woman comic."

I winced, then looked around for the garçon.

"Roast chicken," I said. "What can they do to that?"

.　.　.

Caruso once said, "When in Rome, do as the Romans do—
honk your horn a lot." So being in Mexico, I took a siesta after
lunch while Doris went shopping and Benny caught some
rays by the poolette. We met up again just at six, and I took
Doris off to the sign store and the printer to pick up my wares
while Benny the Boy went back to the telephone company
to try bribing someone else.

What the others did with themselves after their outings I
do not know, but what I did was lie on my bed in my undies

reading a Dick Francis and waiting for the next attack of the
Aztec two-step. All of which brought the time up to nine
o'clock, which is when we presented ourselves again at the
desk of a certain *portero*, me carrying a suitcase, Doris a
shopping bag, and Benny the Wonder Boy two—count 'em,
two—telephones, for which he had paid not one centavo
over the official price.

Shortly thereafter Freddy hung some dirty mats up in the
elevator. Shortly thereafter that, a ramshackle vehicle with
wooden sides, containing our new used furniture, pulled up
outside. A brief discussion then ensued between Benny and
the truck driver and his accomplice, who, I assumed, were
angling for a hefty tip, having discovered that all the furniture
couldn't just be dumped on the sidewalk but actually had to
be carried up a whole flight of stairs and lugged all the way
through the lobby to the elevator, then unloaded from the
elevator and transported down an endless corridor to our
office—but was I wrong again. No soiled pesos changed
hands, and yet another prejudice took the count, leaving me
a mere hundred or so. Changing is hard enough but changing
for the better is murder. When the kid from the stationer
arrived in his battered panel truck, he too refused everything
but a handshake.

Freddy took his leave about ten, after loaning us his toolbox
for the night, and we began the task of getting the offices into
shape. Using one of Freddy's screwdrivers, and not without a
curse or two, I tried to attach the appropriate sign on the
outside of the front door. U.S.C.A., it stated simply.

"What's that supposed to mean?" said Doris, who was trying
unsuccessfully to peer over my shoulder.

"It's not supposed to mean anything," I said patiently. "It
does mean something. Either the United States Cultural Association, which we are not, or United Supply, Commodities, &
Appliances, which we are. Perhaps you would care to peruse
one of our business cards." I handed her over one that was

still damp. "You can keep it, I've got another four hundred and ninety-nine. Now go write an ode or something, will you? Or fill up your drawers, or go pester Benny—what's he doing, anyway?"

"He's trying to hang that corkboard," she said. "He might be done in a couple of days. God, you guys make the Three Stooges look good with their hands."

After I'd finally fought the second screw all the way in, I unlocked my suitcase and took out of it a small American flag on a stand, which I set on my desk next to the wooden sign that read "V. Blackman, Director" and right in front of my new, fake marble pen holder. Then I got out a large rolled-up map of the world, which Doris kindly tacked up on the corkboard and then studded haphazardly with pushpins of various colors. Then I unpacked a framed photo of a touching family scene: a proud father holding in his arms a mewling babe while his adoring wife and small blond daughter beamed up at him, as did likewise a collie puppy. Thanks to Wade, of Wade's Pictorial Service, and his handy airbrush, scissors, and glue pot, the father looked remarkably like one V. (for Victor) Daniel.

"Mega gross," said Doris as I was trying the framed horror in various positions on my desktop.

"I think it looks rather sweet and touching," I said.

It was about eleven when we figured we had done all we could do for one day. The furniture was in place, also the (unconnected) telex, the phones plugged in and working. Benny had somehow hooked up the intercom between the two rooms, and all our desks had the appropriate signs on them (Benny's read "B. Keith, Assistant Director"; Doris's, "D. Day, Inquiries") plus a scattering of diaries, rotary files, pencil sharpeners, and the like. Doris had unpacked her shopping bag, which contained of course a small bouquet of flowers, a vase for same, a paperback by someone called Germaine Greer, probably one of those regency romances, also a large coffee cup with a picture of a cat drinking milk on it. I was surprised she didn't pull out a picture of Willing Boy too, talking about personal touches.

And we had, also slightly damp, correctly headed company stationery in the drawers of all our desks, and the top drawer of one of the green filing cabinets was impressively stuffed with cardboard folders, which were themselves impressively stuffed with blank paper. Doris applied a few finishing touches here and there: she crumpled up some scraps of paper and chucked them into the wastepaper baskets; she tangled up her telephone line to make it look used; she creased up the covers of the new telephone books that Benny had scored along with the phones—and so on.

We were taking a last look around to admire our handiwork when Benny said, "Samples. We should have samples around in case we get a visit from Don Rafael. Or his neighbor's sister."

"Damn," I said.

"A desk lamp for me," Doris said. "Otherwise it looks pretty good."

"It sure does, gang," I said, making sure the suitcase I was going to leave behind was locked. "It looks like we're in business."

"I thought that was the plan," said Doris.

"Speaking of which," Benny said, "what is the plan for mañana?"

"Mañana," I said, "after picking up some samples, I figured you and me'd go straight to jail, without stopping to collect anything else."

"What about your wits?" said Doris.

"Those we might need," I said.

"Rotsa ruck, Melvin," said Doris.

CHAPTER
TEN

The hammock you have just purchased was handwoven in the State of Yucatán, in southern Mexico. The hammock is a very important part of Yucatán life. 99% of the population in the State of Yucatán owns and uses the hammock. 87% of them have been born, sleep, and probably will die in a hammock. For 53% of the Yucatán people, the hammock is the only piece of furniture in the house, being used as a chair in the day and a bed at night."

"And who penned this foray into literature?" I inquired, holding up the tag I was reading.

"I did," Benny called down.

There was more: "The hammock consists of two parts: the Body (or Bed), and the Connecting Ends (or Arms). They are woven on a vertical loom consisting of two posts planted in the ground and two horizontal pieces of wood connecting them at top and bottom. It takes 19 hours to make the smallest hammock, giving you an idea of the work that is required to weave a hammock."

"Shakespeare it ain't," I said. "And I suppose you made up the figures too."

"There you're wrong," he said. "I translated them from something Jorge wrote."

It was the following morning after a late breakfast, and

Benny and I were at his friend Jorge Bazu's hammock emporium down on 56th and I was learning far more about hammocks than I cared to. Doris had toddled off to the office to hold the fort and maintain our presence there and also, in between writing in the diary she was keeping, to do such chores as dropping off in Don Rafael's office a handful of our new business cards, with our new telephone number neatly written in. She was also to man—or is it woman?—the phone in case he called, and also to tell Freddy or Don Rafael, if either stopped by to see how we were settling in, that the bosses were out on a purchasing expedition, which, as it turned out, is exactly what we were doing.

Or rather what Benny was doing. Benny was up a ladder selecting hammocks from the shelves full of them that ran all down one side of Jorge's long, narrow shop. The shelves on the other side of the store held skeins of cotton string out of which the hammocks were woven. When Benny found a hammock he liked, he tossed it down to Jorge's number two son, Carlos, who stacked it along with all the others, which were piling up five-deep on the counter.

In twenty minutes Benny had selected 205, mostly the larger sizes, the 10s and 12s. When I asked him out of idle curiosity what his criterion for selection was—was it mayhap their color?—he said no, it was closeness of weave, as in Persian carpets. I must say I thoroughly enjoyed the sight of Benny teetering atop a rickety ladder—and for a strictly legitimate cause. It was surely a once-in-a-lifetime spectacle, like me eating in that Ethiopian restaurant out on Sunset.

How the weavers of the fool things ever made a nickel, God only knows. They bought the string and the polyester end bits from Jorge to begin with, then sold the finished products back to him—after, you will recall, some nineteen hours' labor on each—and guys like Benny bought the hammocks off Jorge for ridiculously low prices, say from $5.50 U.S. for a single up to maybe $9.50 for a family size. After

Jorge took his profit out of both ends of the transaction, that left, say, on the average five bucks for the weaver, for all those hours, which works out to such a pathetic hourly wage I won't even bother to work it out even if I could. Benjamin later told me he had a deal with a hardware chain operating out of San Diego that took roughly five thousand a year, depending on availability, but Benny had to prepack them and put into each a copy of his literature and pay for the air freight and insurance and broker's commission—so all he made out of the whole deal was a goodly number of thousands of dollars, for which he had to visit Mérida once in a while (expenses deductible) and spend a half-hour up a ladder. Who wouldn't do likewise, I'm sure? Of course, Benny did have that dreadful struggle with his larcenous conscience all the while.

After settling accounts with Jorge, arranging for the packaging and the transportation of two hundred of the hammocks to the air freight office in Jorge's old truck, we shook hands all round, departed, went back to our hotel, deposited our five sample hammocks, changed clothes, then made our way around to the back of the hotel, where Benny's car was parked. Suitably attired and even more suitably credentialed, off we went to jail.

We had just passed the airport turnoff west of Mérida and were continuing on westward when I asked Benny how in the world he'd ever stumbled on the lowly hammock as a way to make a buck.

"Carlos, who you met, has an older brother," he said. "Paco. He's not in the store much anymore. He was into pearls when I met him—what?—six, seven years ago, on the Isla Mujeres. I probably met him through Big Jeff, who knew everyone in town, especially everyone who was into things like pearls or silver or coral or running booze or, I blush to say, D-O-P-E. So I put up the capital, and what Paco did was buy ten thousand dollars' worth of pearls from one of his connections, then we walked them across the Tex-Mex border to Brownsville, well strapped up, and a few days later sold them to another of his connections for twenty-two five. Next time down I met Paco's pop, Jorge, and the rest is history."

"So is that," I remarked, pointing to the remains of what once must have been a fabulous mansion set back off the main road but was now a total ruin. "Jesus, there's another one," I said a few minutes later. "What were they doing out here anyway, shooting a remake of *Gone With the Wind*?"

"Sisal," said Benny. "All those things that are cactuses to you, they used to make rope from. As in hemp. There were fortunes being made around here, and then guess what?"

"The dreaded sisal weevil?" I guessed.

"Nylon rope," he said, "got invented, putting most of those guys out of work." He waved at two peons who were standing patiently at a crossroads waiting for their lift. They were dressed in the typical laborer's get-up of loose white pants, white shirt, straw hat, sandals made from old rubber tires, with machetes strung by a cord around their necks. One of them waved back without putting too much energy into it.

"I once ran across a guy," I said, "you know the kind of guy I mean, the kind that never takes baths but instead rubs himself all over with a special dry mud from Nepal. Well, this guy invented and sold a machine that extracted the juice from things like welcome mats and bits of traditional, non-nylon rope, which as you just mentioned are made of hemp, which as you didn't mention is a close relative of the pot plant. So what the guy was saying was you could get high from drinking your old welcome mat. I never tried it myself, although it is true to say I have downed many an exotic tipple in my travels."

"Me neither," said Benny, who was beginning to perspire slightly because it was hot and he was attired, as I was, in a lightweight conservative suit, white shirt, and tie. "I once chewed up and swallowed 120 morning glory seeds, Celestial Pink, I believe they were. Boy, did I get high. Boy, did I get sick first."

We drove on for a while through the flat and monotonous terrain. An occasional slatted truck with a load of *campesinos* in the back passed us and once or twice a dusty car. Occasionally we glimpsed some unhappy-looking *campesinos* at work in what was left of the maguey cactus fields. Once we saw what was left of an armadillo someone had run over. A few minutes after that I had my first sight of the clink called the Second of February, which some might find a slightly bizarre name for a clink—me included, at first—but then again, how does one name a prison? Usually after its location, I suppose, as in Dartmoor, which is in Dartmoor, on a moor by the River Dart, or Devil's Island or the Jacksonville Pen, but why not at least endeavor to be more creative and give prisons designer names like Dun-Rovin' or Bide-A-Wee or, if you want to use a date, how about Father's Day or maybe April Fools? What's in a name, anyway? Wouldst not a rose smell as sweet if it wouldst be called instead limburger cheese? Not to me it wouldnst.

I was nervous is what I was, which is why my mind, usually so precisely focused, was chattering away in so aimless a fashion. I had been nervous for the last few days and trying, with a notable lack of success, to hide the fact behind those two old standbys—thinly disguised insults and forced humor. True, I did have a plan of sorts, but there were a lot of details still to be worked out and who knew if it would work anyway and we were a long way from home and time was going by and Billy was still marking the days off on a cell wall and one mistake from his would-be heroic rescuers and we'd be doing the same.

And if we did get him out, then what? My loyal, doughty assistants, being more or less of a normal height—i.e., short—

might be able, suitably camouflaged, to pass undetected in a crowd of Méridans, but where and how could a Goliath hide in a land of Toulouse-Lautrecs?

I became even more nervous the closer we got to Febrero Segundo, and when I got that first glimpse of it, I achieved a lifetime personal best.

We'd just topped a small rise in the road, and there it was ahead of us and off to our left at the end of a few hundred yards of dirt road. Benny pulled over and pulled up. About all we could see from our viewpoint were the walls, which were bad enough—twenty feet high, we estimated, laid out in a large rectangle with turrets at the corners and another above the huge front door and yet another one in the center of the rear wall opposite the entrance. Around the walls for two hundred yards or so in all directions, the scrub and maguey had been burned to give the guards a clear field of fire. A Mexican flag hung limply above the front turret. We could see that all the turrets were manned and the tops of the walls were being patrolled as well.

I looked at Benny the Boy.

Benny the Boy looked at me.

"A piece of cake," he said, snapping his fingers. I had to laugh.

Then he said, "If you don't mind me asking, Victor, what is it we hope to achieve today?"

"You got me there, pal." I sighed. "All right. We would like a look around. I thought it might be a good idea for us to have our look around when the big boss isn't in, which could give us an excuse to go back another time and see him, which would give us a second look around. I'd also like to see how Billy is and let him know we're on the case and to warn him to go along with whatever it is we come up with. But hell, I don't know if we can bluff our way in to see him. In a lot of jails only immediate family and legally interested parties get

to visit, and God knows what the system is down here. Maybe
at least we can get some kind of word in to the poor stiff."

"No problem there," said Benny. "If I can't find out what
the visiting policy is any other way, I'll just call them up and
ask."

"In that case," I said, "wagons roll, preferably to the nearest
bar with a phone."

So we rolled to the nearest bar—a nameless, tin-roofed café
in that small, untidy cluster of enterprises at the crossroads
that Benny had mentioned—parked, and sat at a tin table
outside that told us to drink Corona beer, not that I had to
be told. The rotund owner came smartly out from behind his
homemade tin bar to take our orders; being on duty, more or
less, we had to settle for Pepsi-Colas. When he came back
with them, he inquired if we were by any chance visiting the
prison up the road.

We were, Benny told him.

Not, the owner hoped, to visit some unfortunate friend
or—and it pained one to even contemplate it—some relative?

"Luckily, no," said Benny. "A small business matter was all.
But merely out of idle curiosity, is it a difficult matter getting
in to visit a dear one?" He winked at me and said in an
undertone, "I think we just saved us a phone call."

With his customary adroitness Benny elicited the following
interesting information over the next five minutes: there were
at present some six hundred men and twelve women in Febrero Segundo; normal visiting hours were from two till four
weekdays, all day Saturday, and Sunday afternoon; permission
for nonfamily to visit seemed to depend on the whim of *el
commandante*; and visitors were permitted to take in food,
clean clothes, and soap and the like but naturally no alcohol,
drugs, or provocative reading material.

"I should hope not," said Benny, affecting to be deeply
shocked.

As all this was going on, I was observing four off-duty guards, with their jackets off, making their way up the dirt road from the prison toward us. They crossed the main road without looking both ways and went into the even more dilapidated cantina next to ours. A minute later four others left the cantina and headed without excessive speed back to the prison.

"Must be lunchtime," said my friend. "Not a bad idea." He ordered a plate of delicacies from the owner, who bustled off to consult his cookbook.

A few moments later Benny was liberally sprinkling hot sauce on the third of whatever it was he was eating. "Chili today, but hot tamale," he said. At that moment a Jeep left the prison and headed toward us; as the driver wheeled into the main road with a flourish, I noticed the vehicle was brand-new and sparkling clean. A man in a neat gray uniform complete with cap sat in the backseat looking through a report of some kind.

"¿El commandante?" Benny asked the owner.

"Himself."

"Does he ever stop here for lunch?"

The owner laughed. "Not him," he said, "he prefers his tacos served by a pretty maid."

"No offense intended," Benny said, "but who doesn't?"

The owner showed us his gold inlays again.

I sprung for the repast and refreshments, we got back into the boiling hot Chevy, this time me in the backseat, and we drove up the dirt road to Febrero Segundo. As we got closer, we saw the dirty white concrete block walls were even higher than we'd guessed.

"There's a wall not built to scale," Benny said.

"What's come over you, kid?" I said. "That's two awful puns in five minutes."

"You're not the only one who's nervous," he said.

"I didn't know it showed."

The front entrance was a massive wooden door with a curved top, above which the turret loomed for another twenty feet or so. We stopped at the door, and Benny tooted the horn. A guard looked down at us from the turret and then turned away again.

"Why did you do that?" I asked him. "There doesn't seem to be all that much traffic around."

"That sign there told me to," he said, pointing with a thumb.

"Oh," I said. "Pardon ma mouf."

After a minute an elderly guard in a gray uniform unbuttoned at the neck peeked out through a grille in the door, then swung the main gate open for us. In we went, slowly, into a sort of tunnel. The gate swung shut behind us. Up the tunnel in front of us was a second gate, this one made of iron bars, through which we could see a bare space with a soccer goal. The first guard disappeared into a small room on our left. After another moment, a second, younger man emerged, the butt of what looked like an antitank gun showing in his unbuttoned holster; he came over to us and asked us politely to please state our business.

I handed him my card. It read, simply but elegantly: V. Blackman. U.S. Dept. of the Interior.

Benny handed him his, which read, simply but elegantly: B. Keith. U.S. Dept. of the Interior.

The guard looked them over, on both sides, then returned them to us. Then he asked Benny to pardon his ignorance, but what exactly was the business of the U.S. Department of the Interior?

Benny kindly relayed the question to me, so I said smoothly, "Our business is concerned with the internal security of the nation."

The guard thought that one over and then, out of boredom or—who knows?—genuine curiosity, inquired precisely what was our interest with Febrero Segundo, which was surely of little or no threat to the internal security of the

United States of America, as far as he knew. Of course, he had not seen the twelve o'clock news on television—perhaps a small war had broken out between the two?

And then it dawned on me what his motive was: he was being funny was what he was being. But enough was enough, so I gave him a chilly look and said we were there to have a brief word with his *commandante*, if such a thing could be arranged.

Naturally it could, but alas his commanding officer was away from the prison and would not be back until roughly five o'clock.

We were desolate, but did not the commanding officer leave someone else in charge when he left the prison, and could we not have a brief word with him instead?

Naturally he did and of course we could, he would arrange it immediately. The guard saluted us and went back into his office. Benny began whistling under his breath. I began sweating under mine. A few more minutes passed in slow motion, or was it hours? Finally the guard returned, saluted us again, handed us a temporary pass, told us to drive straight ahead to *el parking*, then signaled to someone out of sight at the far gate, which promptly slid open.

Onward, ever onward into the depths of the slammer drove the two gringos, through the second gate and into the prison proper, or at least the prison yard, which was hard-packed sand on which had been roughly chalked out a soccer field and also what looked like a volleyball court and also an area abutting one of the outer walls that must have been for some kind of *pelota*, or handball. No grass grew in the prison yard of Febrero Segundo and no rose budded either and no butterflies circled in the oppressive noonday heat.

Straight ahead indeed took us to *el parking*; we pulled up beside a dusty Ford that was neatly parked beside another spanking new Jeep which was neatly parked beside an old but spotless Dodge two-ton. Beside the truck sat that type of enclosed van that is called a Black Maria in some parts of the globe and which is used for transporting groups of prisoners, and beside that an ordinary sedan that had been adapted to transport just one or perhaps two prisoners. There was a thick glass partition between its front and back seats, and the handles to the back doors had been removed; I assumed it took a special key to open them.

The parking lot was directly in front of the administration offices, on one side of which was what looked like a workshop and on the other the kitchens and then a long line of cells. I could tell they were cells because they all had tiny barred windows cleverly positioned so far off the ground that no one but Spiderman could look out. All was quiet in Febrero Segundo; not a creature was stirring except for us and a lizard or two and the guards, so I guessed that the inmates were having a siesta after their mouth-watering luncheon.

After we'd parked and taken a discreet gander around, Benny got out, opened the door for me, his better, then went up to a bell that was set in the wall beside the wooden door labeled Administración, and pushed it. A few more moments, or decades, passed. Yet another grille opened. A face peered out. We peered back. The face said something. Benny held up our pass. The face disappeared. The door opened. We entered.

We found ourselves in a small reception area that contained a desk on one side and a barred and fenced-in passageway on the other, with a long counter in front of it, presumably where visitors and their unprovocative goods were searched. The guard who let us in unlocked a second door behind his desk and bade us follow him. We did, into a second office where three male secretaries or guards or office workers were listlessly pecking away at old-fashioned upright typewriters while a fourth, one of those we'd just seen leaving the beanery next to ours, manned the equally antiquated telephone switchboard, the kind where you have to manually connect the caller with who he's calling by sticking a metal-tipped cord into the right socket. Next to him was another door on which there was also a sign: Lt. Joaquín Esparza, Sub-Commandante, it read.

Our guide knocked twice, smartly. A voice called out, "Enter." We entered. The guard saluted, then left us to the whims and charms of Lt. Esparza, a most handsome gent with a thin, bronzed face and neatly combed black hair. He was obviously of Hispanic rather than Mayan descent, as was usually, if not invariably, the case with those in positions of authority in that neck of the woods.

The lieutenant flashed us a welcoming smile, smoothed his dapper mustache with one well-manicured finger, gestured us to seats, saying, *"Momento, por favor,"* jiggled his telephone receiver until he got a response from the operator, asked for the kitchens, and when he got through, said, "Twenty minutes," from all of which I deduced without too much difficulty that the prison chef had twenty minutes to prepare that day's special.

After he'd hung up, Benny, assuming a subservient manner, introduced me as a high official in the U.S. government and himself as my lowly translator and handed over our Dept. of the Interior calling cards—seeing which, the lieutenant arched his finely drawn eyebrows and asked how he could be of assistance.

I told him (with Benny translating, of course and as usual). What I told him was we would be eternally grateful if he could arrange for us to briefly visit one of his prisoners, a certain Sr. John Brown.

"Ah yes, Sr. Brown," said the lieutenant, heavily stressing the name. "Serving six years for smuggling, as I recall."

"So I believe," Benny said. "Tsk-tsk."

And what was our connection with Sr. Brown? Was one of us perhaps related to him?

I thought of saying yes, then I thought of the lieutenant's next line, "Prove it," which I couldn't, so I had to say no.

Then perhaps we had some legal interest in the prisoner. Perhaps we had been hired to represent him in some way?

I thought of saying yes, then I thought of the lieutenant's next line, "Prove it," so I said no.

Then perhaps we were connected with some international body like the Red Cross, whose representatives were under certain circumstances allowed access to prisoners?

I thought of saying yes, but I said no, mentally kicking myself for not having thought of it first.

"In that case," said the lieutenant, with a charming smile and spreading his hands apart ruefully, "much as I would like to help and much as I value the close and continuing friendship between our two peoples, regretfully, rules are rules. As government employees yourselves, you understand only too well...."

"Only too well," I said, summoning up a smile not nearly as charming as his. "We had but a question or two to ask him, an unofficial survey, really...."

"You might approach the *commandante* on his return," Lt. Esparza said with a notable lack of enthusiasm, "but I am afraid he is a man who is a slave to regulations even more so than I, especially when prisoners of some importance are involved."

Then Benny surprised me by asking me politely if I would mind leaving him alone with the lieutenant for a moment. I took the hint and, after saying *gracias* and good-bye to Lt. Joaquín Esparza, took my leave. A minute later Benny joined me back in the outer office and gave me the barest hint of a wink.

"What's up?" I whispered to him out of the corner of my big mouth.

"You'll see," he whispered back. After another minute the

guard who had originally escorted us to the lieutenant's office came in from the reception area and once again bade us follow him.

We did, out back into the reception room, where he patted us down quickly but efficiently, opened up and closely examined the contents of a box of *caramelos* I'd bought from some kid and brought along just in case, and then bade us follow him again.

We followed him again, through two doors, each of which he unlocked and then carefully locked again behind us.

"Do you *habla* English, señor?" I asked him at one stage.

"Poco," he said, shaking his head. "My son is studying it at school, sometimes I help him." Just in case he spoke a bit more than *poco*, I thought I'd better pay attention to what I said to Benny and Billy in his hearing; it has been my experience that when a lieutenant—indeed, any officer, in any army—wears nail polish, albeit transparent, he is capable of any trickery.

At the entrance to the cell block a guard in a tiny barred cubicle had a brief word with our guard, asked him something, got told something, handed over a set of keys, then pressed a master control behind him. The metal door in front of us slid back into a recess in the wall long enough for us to go through it, and then closed again behind us. A cheap transistor was playing somewhere, otherwise all was quiet. We followed our guide down a long, cement-floored corridor lined with cell doors that had closable Judas windows in them at eye level and floor level, then up a flight of concrete stairs, and back down a corridor identical to the first one, except the numbers crudely painted on the doors were different. Our feet seemed to make a lot of noise on the bare floor. As for the smell, well it wasn't so bad, just about twice as bad as what you get in a tannery or paper mill or slaughterhouse. Hang on, Billy.

Our escort stopped at the last door on the left, peeked

through the slit, said, "Only ten minutes," then unlocked the door and swung it open, and there, asleep on his back on a sort of cement shelf that jutted out from the wall, was my blood brother Gray Wolf, or what was left of him.

While Benny and the guard watched from outside the cell, I went over to Billy, which took about two steps, and looked down at him in what light there was that streamed in from the small, high-set window. Luckily my face was hidden from the guard, and he couldn't see how shocked I was.

All Billy's hair was gone and there were scabby patches on his scalp. From the look of his sunken cheeks, he'd probably lost some teeth too.

His color was a whitish yellow. It looked like he was easily down under a hundred pounds. His head was pillowed on his bandaged hand; at least the bandage looked new and clean. He was dressed in oversized gray cotton pants and a gray cotton shirt. His dirty feet were bare; there was a pair of rubber sandals under his "bed." I kept my face hidden from the guard and gave Billy a gentle shake by one shoulder.

"Mr. Brown. Mr. Brown. Wake up, please."

He made a noise of complaint, rolled over toward me, and opened his eyes. When they focused on me and began to widen, I said quickly and loudly, "You don't know me of course, Mr. Brown. My name is Blackman, my associate over there by the door is Keith, we're from the U.S. Department of the Interior, and we have a few questions to put to you. It won't take a minute, I assure you, and then you can go back to sleep."

Billy struggled to an upright position and rubbed his face with the hand that still had all its fingers. For a moment he was too nonplussed to do anything but blink a few times, but then he nodded and managed to get out, "Sure, anything."

"In case our escort does have the command of languages he denied having, we will keep this short and businesslike." I officiously took out my memo pad and a pen.

"Health." I gave him a cursory glance; he gave me the beginnings of a small, a very small smile. "Satisfactory. Conditions of incarceration." I gave the four-foot by eight-foot shithole a cursory look, and a cursory look was all it took—all there was to see was the ledge, one blanket, on which Billy was now sitting, a plastic bucket with no lid, a spare shirt hung up on a splinter of wood wedged into a crack in the wall, the crack in the wall, and my old Parker High Panther teammate. "Satisfactory." I made another tick on the memo pad.

"Washing facilities?"

"Cold shower once a week, regular," he said in a sort of a husky croak.

"Exercise facilities?" He gave me another small tightening of the lips.

"Too much chlorine in the pool," he said, almost too low for me to hear.

"Cuisine?"

"Beans and rice," he said in his eerie croak. "On Sundays, rice and beans."

"Excellent," I said, ticking off another imaginary entry. "I've always found Mexican cooking delicious, myself. Oh. Here. Compliments of the U.S. government." I took out the candies, made an inquiring gesture to the guard, who nodded that it was all right, and gave them to Billy. He opened his mouth and pointed at where his teeth used to be. "Ah," I said, making another note. "Slight problem with cavities. Well, you can still suck, I hope." I handed over the caramels. Billy took them with his good hand, looked at the box, then looked away and started to cry.

"There, there, sir," I said, patting him comfortingly on the back. "Nothing lasts forever, you know. One of these fine days you will be a free man again. Just remember our old Boy Scout motto: Be *mucho* prepared."

Billy, his back still to me, nodded vigorously several times.

There didn't seem to be anything else to say, so I gave his back one more pat and we left him there, retracing our footsteps all the way back to *el parking* and thanking everyone we met en route. Then Benny drove us back through the entrance tunnel, where he had to get out and open the trunk to show it wasn't crammed with escaping prisoners, and we were out of Febrero Segundo and on our way back to Mérida for a swim and a shower and a beer and a meal and the passing parade and sheets and TV and a lot of other items that were still but a dream or a memory to the occupant of Febrero Segundo's cell 199, the last one on the left on the first floor of A wing.

After a minute I asked Benny if he would mind stopping for a bit on the top of the same hill where we had pulled over on the way to the prison; he said he didn't mind at all. So he pulled over, and we both got out, took a few deep breaths, and looked back at the jail.

"I didn't even recognize him at first," I said. "I knew it was going to be him, but I thought for a minute they'd made a mistake."

"I know," said Benny.

"Benny, we have to do something—and fast."

"We will, we will," my friend said. "There is always a way."

"Yeah, sure," I said. "And while we're talking about ways, how the hell did you get us in to see him?"

Benny rubbed his thumb and fingers together in that universal gesture that means payola, baksheesh, bribery, *la mordida*—in other words, money changing hands.

"No!" I said.

"*Sí,*" he said. "I'm not sure if the lieutenant and all those guards and clerks are in the regular army or a separate prison service, like in some countries, but there is no way they can be getting rich."

"That's for sure," I said. "Did you see where they went for lunch?"

"So I tactfully got you out of the way," Benny said, stretching mightily, "as such behavior might be considered unseemly coming from a man in your exalted position, slipped him a C-note, probably a month's salary, and suddenly all doors were opened."

"I'm glad someone in this country takes bribes," I said. "I was seriously beginning to worry."

CHAPTER ELEVEN

I climbed back into the car, in the front seat beside Benny this time, and we continued on into town pretty much in silence. I don't know how Benjamin passed the time, perhaps trying to recall all the various aliases he'd used during his disgraceful existence or the location of all his bank accounts, but what V. (for Victor) Daniel was doing was thinking, and I'd seen enough during our visit to Febrero Segundo to provide me with reasons aplenty for thinking. Maybe the Two Stooges plus Bat Girl really could spring Billy relatively quickly and relatively bloodlessly—and in particular bloodlessly when it came to our own precious vital fluids.

Benny and I did converse enough on the drive back to agree on a couple of items, one being that there now seemed to be little purpose in involving the prison *commandante* if we didn't absolutely have to, since we already had a certain lady-killing lieutenant on the hook and on the take. We also agreed on what our (but mostly Benny's) next move should be, one that could only be done the following day, if at all. So that meant one more *noche* in old Mérida before we moved on to the move after our next move—call it our second move, if you like—heading south and trying to track down Big Jeff and his pal Cap'n Dan.

That eve the three of us ate at the French restaurant Benny

had mentioned a few days back; and while I was daintily slurping down the first course, potage St. Germain (soup made out of yesterday's leftover vegetables), I let Doris in on where we were going next day and told her as much as I knew about Big Jeff and his successful jailbreak. While I was finishing off the last of my sole amandine (fish with nuts), Benny fell into conversation with a loud-voiced, florid Canadian gent from Winnipeg who was seated with his little woman at the next table. He was attired in an eye-catching all-madras outfit; she in a plastic traveling trouser suit. It soon appeared that he had had a most successful day souvenir shopping and had managed with his bargaining skills to browbeat some hapless hammock vendor down from sixty bucks to forty-five bucks per hammock. Benny, being a kindly sort, congratulated him warmly and didn't bother mentioning that at his pal Jorge's the price to one and all would have been about ten bucks each. After supper Benny had a surprise for us—he took us to a steam bath he'd discovered on his last trip.

The baths were at the Colón, a stately old hotel right around the corner from the bistro, whither we proceeded smartly. In we went, and Benny requested a half an hour please and handed over some pesos and ordered some drinks and got handed in return three large and fluffy towels right out of a soap powder commercial, and we followed an ancient bellboy down a corridor to *baño* number two, which he unlocked for us. He led the way into a tiled room that had slatted wooden benches on two sides and then withdrew gracefully. We all turned our backs politely on one another, undressed, and then wrapped our anatomies in towels. When I turned around, I exclaimed, "Doris! All your hair's fallen off!"

"It was a wig, stupid," she said, rubbing one hand over her almost bald dome. "Francis, my stylist, dig, at Sassoon's, said I'd completely totaled my hair with all that shit I've been putting on it, so it had to come off."

"Francis said that, did he?" I said. "Hmm. But I love the Yul Brynner look, it's so you. It's true it might be considered a soupçon passé, but don't worry, it'll grow out in a year or two."

"That's more than I can say about yours," she said.

"Oh, come on, you two," said Benny. "Walk this way."

"If I could walk that way, I'd save a fortune on talcum powder," Doris said. Sometimes the kid surprised me.

We followed him into the steam part of the steam baths, a small room that was off the front room and also tiled, and also with two wooden benches. Benny turned the handle on the bottom of the steam pipe and an awful lot of very hot steam is what we were immediately in the midst of, trying to breathe. And after a few minutes of steam came the dream— a gorgeous pool next door, done in three levels, into which fresh greeny-blue water was gushing.

Every inch of the room and the pool was covered with decorative tiles—birds, flowers, greenery, butterflies—it was mind-boggling. I tried not to think of poor Billy and his once-a-week cold shower.

"Just one thing, Sara," I said sternly, gingerly testing the water with one big toe. "And I mean this sincerely—no splashing."

"Of course not," she scoffed. "What do you think I am, a kid?"

How long do you think it took from the time I finished enunciating the word *splashing* for the first freezing tidal wave, sent my way courtesy of the queen of the twerps, to drench me and my towel completely? Well, the speed of H_2O may not be quite as rapid as the speed of light, but it isn't far behind either.

So we larked about and drank our drinks, which had mysteriously appeared on a tray inside the front door, and got steamed up again and then cold again, and a good time was had by all.

Afterward, much refreshed, we took our customary coffees at the café in front of our hotel, positively glowing with good health and clean pores. Then I let Benny beat me in two games of chess up in his room, played on his midget magnetic traveling set; then I let Montezuma take his excruciating revenge one more time; then Mrs. Daniel's little boy went byebyes. I hated that stupid pathetic set of Benny's, it was so small that even with glasses on, you could hardly tell which men were which. I was just about to invent the world's most innovative chess move since the Queen's Gambit when the sandman took me far, far away.

The following morning, not too early as mornings can go sometimes, like on farms, in hospitals, and in prisons, we had our breakfast coffees in the hotel dining room for a change, dawdled around a bit, did a bit of shopping and this and that, and almost went for a ride on one of the brightly painted horse-drawn hansom cabs that cruise the avenues looking for unwary tourists, and then we all dropped by the office to say *buenos días* to the *portero*, drop off the hammocks, return his toolbox, and at least try to look like a going concern. I checked out the phones and the intercom; they all worked. Doris checked out the toilet down the hall and reported it worked.

At noon Benny took himself off in the car on his errand. I gave Doris one of the postcards I'd purchased earlier, and told her to be a good girl and drop a line to her folks and I would be a good boy and write my mom. Doris obliged, but with a somewhat faraway look on her face. She put her pen down abruptly.

"What's the plural of *metamorphosis*?" she said.

"I don't even know what the singular is," I said. " 'So, Mom, having wonderful time, wish you were her—' "

"Isn't this office in one of its metamorphosisms supposed to look like the Cultural Ass.?"

"Obviously," I said patiently.

"Well, it doesn't," she said.

"How would you know?" I said, looking around. "It looks OK to me."

"Because I poked my head in the one downstairs when I was going to the bathroom," she said.

"Oh," I said.

"I mean, I figured it made sense," she said. "What's the sense of calling yourself a Cultural Ass. if you don't look like one?"

"There's so many answers to that," I said, "that I won't even begin to start. Also, it so happens," I said, picking up my desk diary and waving it at her, "it so happens that there is an entry in this diary for ten minutes from now and that entry says— I quote—'Check out C. A. noonish.'" I put the diary in my top desk drawer and locked the drawer just in case Doris was petty enough to disbelieve me and tried to take a look before I had time to write the entry in.

"You big fibber," she said.

"So what did you say when you poked your head in?" I asked her. "I hope you didn't ruin our whole setup by saying, 'Hello, we're the fake Cultural Ass. on the top floor. How're ya doin' down here?"

She grimaced in pretended agony.

"'We'll see you in a jiff' is what I said," she said.

"Well, what's keeping us?" I said. We locked up and took the elevator down one flight. I had to admit it did make sense to drop by our neighbor and rival, not only for Doris's reason, which was good enough on its own, but also to make ourselves known so they wouldn't call the cops if they saw us prowling around. On the way down I put on my specs to make myself look even more cultural than usual.

They didn't seem to be up to all that much downstairs, frankly. They weren't even a "they"; they were one middle-aged American lady with a face suntanned to the exact orangy-brown color of an NBA basketball, dressed in all-Mexican finery including leather sandals and embroidered peasant blouse and sitting behind a desk whose top was cluttered with travel brochures, rolled-up posters, piles of hand-printed handouts for local events, and the like. She introduced herself as Ethel Sayers and pronounced herself delighted to see us and wasn't the weather wonderful again! I said it was and introduced ourselves as Mr. Blackman and Miss Day and pronounced us the new upstairs tenants. Ethel was thrilled to have fellow Americans in the building. And wasn't she looking forward to getting to know us real well! The permanent foreign community in Mérida was quite small, actually, and it was always delighted to wheel out the welcome wagon for additions to its little group.

Doris and I smiled and tried to look like welcome additions, despite the odds against. After responding politely and mainly untruthfully to a spate of questions—such as, did we play bridge? were we interested in Scottish dancing? were we perchance amateur painters or pottery throwers or aficionados of the Mexican style of horseback riding? and so on—we finally managed to take our leave, clutching in our fevered palms stacks of leaflets outlining the activities of the association and how it came to be set up in the first place, along with assorted posters advertising upcoming art events in Mérida, which we promised to display *chez nous* prominently.

As to the origins of the U.S. Cultural Ass. (cutting a long story down to almost nothing compared to the original), some fifteen years ago the doyenne of the southern Yucatán foreign community, one Martha M. Moberg (of the well-known Austin, Texas, Mobergs) had died and left a small trust fund to promote American cultural activities in Mérida and environs—exhibitions of expatriate art, pottery, sculpture, weaving, jewelry, batiks and God knows what else, recitals, poetry readings, and the screening of American film classics (every second Friday).

"What are you doing a week from Friday?" I asked Doris as

we waited outside in the hall for the elevator. "I see they're
going to screen that famous American film classic *The Nutty
Professor*, with sandwiches afterward."

"Spare me," Doris muttered.

We delivered our goodies upstairs to our office and scattered some of them on Doris's desk and pinned up a few more
on the walls of Doris's office, but none in the inner office. I
was thinking of telling her that it did make the place look a
lot more cultural, all right, but it was so obvious that there
wasn't any point in saying anything.

A while later we closed up shop. I went back to the hotel
to wait impatiently for Benny to get back, and Doris went to
sit by the pool and bring her diary up to date and maybe
scribble off a mash note to Willing Boy.

I was in the bathroom checking to see how my tan was
coming along when Benny knocked on my hotel room door;
that would have been about two o'clock. I let him in, sat
down on one of the twin beds, folded my arms, closed my
eyes like Nero Wolfe, and said, like the great man himself,
"Report please, Archie."

He reported.

"Satisfactory," I said when he had finished. "How much?"

He told me.

I winced down to my anklets but said, "Satisfactory," again.
"You all packed?"

"Yep."

I checked my watch. "Then let us do it, amigo. The tickets
should be waiting for us at the airport. I stopped at the travel
agency in the lobby and the guy phoned for me. Oh, I also
booked you and Doris on a boat trip up Piranha River in a
leaky pirogue to watch crocodiles mate."

I knocked on Doris's door and collected her. To give her
credit, she, like me, had only a small overnight bag as luggage,
which made sense, as we planned to be away only overnight,
but making sense about luggage is, alas, not always a woman's

strong point. Me, I could go halfway around the globe with a mere couple of steamer trunks and the odd matched set of hand luggage. And enough mad money for emergencies tucked down inside my jockey shorts to make me look like I was auditioning for *l'Après-midi d'un faune.*

We picked up Benny downstairs, where he was unsuccessfully trying to impress the beautiful señorita at the front desk with his fluent Spanish, then piled into the first cab in line in front of the hotel. Benny settled on a price with the driver, and off we went back to the airport.

Shortly thereafter we were thousands of feet up in the air again, with nothing but some obscure and highly unlikely law of aerodynamics holding us up there. Two beers and a pack of stale, peppery peanuts later, and we were beginning our approach into Cancún airport. The landing strip was surrounded by lush, green, dank tropical jungle that was teeming—you could tell that just by looking at it—although what precisely it was teeming with I neither knew nor particularly wanted to.

As soon as we emerged from the airport building, Benny snagged us one of a row of new Volkswagen minibuses that seemed to have the airport monopoly, and for eleven dollars U.S. *each*, the bandit driving it agreed to conduct us just north of Cancún to Puerto Juarez, where the passenger ferry to Isla Mujeres departed. Our route took us directly through Cancún, so we never saw the resort area on Cancún Island, which the Mexican government had bought or expropriated back in the sixties and then proceeded to fill with rows of hotels and condominiums and villas and time-sharing developments and marimba players and drinks served in hollowed-out pineapples.

On the way into town we first passed a long row of billboards advertising things like local realtors and local booze; then we hung a left and drove down Cancún's main drag, which looked like Main Street anywhere you find a lot of

Americans on holiday; then we passed through one of the native *barrios,* which looked liked anywhere a lot of poor Mexicans live who are not on holiday.

We arrived at the Puerto just in time to catch the five-thirty sailing of the Cancún–Isla Mujeres ferryboat. As Isla Mujeres means "Island of Women," I was quite looking forward to the sea voyage (especially the end of it), which took place on a most picturesque, rickety, noisy old wooden two-decker ferry, newly painted in blue and white with red trim. The crossing took some forty-five pleasant minutes, during some of which I amusingly pretended to be getting seasick, as it was getting a little rough out there, and during some more of which Benny told us what few snippets, as he modestly put it, he had been able to pick up about our destination, though, as usual, the snippets turned out to be a lot more than snippets, at least as I understand the word. I do not know where Benny got all his information; the only books I ever saw him read were biographies or autobiographies of famous bank robbers, con men, horse breeders, light-fingered Harrys, great train robbers, and other members of that murky underworld fraternity like Republicans, aluminum door salesmen, and animal psychologists. I did once see in his apartment a copy of the maestro Capablanca's slim treatise on chess opening moves, but I figured that he'd just left it lying around to try to frighten me.

About five miles long and a mile wide, Benny informed us, the island did unfortunately not get its name because it was crammed with tropical beauties with lustrous black hair and wearing nothing above the waist but a hibiscus behind one ear; it got its name because the Spaniard who first landed there circa 1500 spotted large statues of Mayan goddesses on the coastal headlands. Now not even their ruins remain.

The island was nice and laid back and funky and cheap not so long ago, he said, as the playful evening breeze toyed with my curls and the captain cut back the engine for our docking, but after we'd landed and were strolling through the main business section toward the Hotel Rocamar, where Benny usually stayed, it became apparent that the *isla* was moving upmarket and fast. The cobblestoned streets were lined with schlock shops and souvenir shops and T-shirt emporiums and boutiques, and there was even a pizzeria with a small veranda outside, where Doris and I gratefully and thirstily plumped ourselves while Benny disappeared inside to have a word with the management.

What he wanted a word about was Big Jeff. When, on the high seas, I'd voiced my fears about what we would do if Big Jeff wasn't on the island but still up north playing Ahab with the great white cod, Benny'd told me not to worry. Big Jeff was almost certainly around because the last time Benny'd seen him he'd just bought a half interest in the island's one pizzeria (in front of which me and Doris were sitting waiting for a garçon), and he'd also bought a house down near Garrafón, in the southern part of the island, where the coral reef and good scuba diving were. Anyway, Benny figured we could track down Cap'n Dan without Big Jeff if we had to but that it might take a while.

Benny returned at the same time the waitress showed up; after she'd shuffled off to get our refreshments, Benny told us he had found out that Big Jeff (a) was on the island, (b) would be in later that night, and that (c) we could probably catch him earlier during happy hour downing a few at his customary table up at the Hotel Rocamar.

The Rocamar turned out to be full, although it was supposed to be off season, so we moseyed a couple of hundred yards along to the Caribe and were soon installed in three spacious rooms on the first floor overlooking the pool. And soon after that, as there was still an hour of sun and it was still hot, although we were into late afternoon by then, we installed ourselves on the small sandy beach in front of the hotel, accompanied by an ample supply of beer from the snack bar, and watched the rollers finish their long journey across the Caribbean Sea with a gentle lapping over our out-stretched limbs. Doris, I couldn't help noticing, was wearing a new beach ensemble (paid for by guess who), and a new sun hat that had First Mate written on it.

A blessedly tranquil half an hour passed.

I tried not to feel too guilty too often about my being there by the briny and Billy being there in the brig—that way lay madness. I was doing all I could as fast as I could do it, but still . . .

"The last time I was on a beach like this I was with Evonne," I offered finally, breaking the long silence. "The waves were rolling in over our legs like they are now, and I gave her a big smooch just like Burt Lancaster did to What's-her-name in whatever that movie was."

"I wouldn't know what you're talking about even if I knew," Doris said, rousing herself sufficiently to sprinkle a handful of sand on my muscular torso.

"*The Naked and the Dead,* stupe," I said. "By John Jones."

"*From Here to Eternity,*" Benny said from beside us without opening his eyes. "By James Jones."

"Yeah, right," I said. "Anyway, it was all about the last days in Hawaii before the Japs attacked on Sunday, December 7, 1941."

"You probably remember it well," she said, flipping a bro-ken seashell so it landed right on my you know what. Luckily it only weighed a pound or two. I looked around for some-thing damp and nasty to tuck down inside her bikini bottoms, but there was nothing within reach.

After another long pause Doris said, "I like Evonne."

"Me too," I said.

"Me three," Benny said.

"You gonna marry her?"

"None of your business," I said.

"That's what normal people do," she said. "They get it on,

and then if they like getting it on and want to go on getting it on, they get married."

"Thank you, Emily Post," I said, turning over to let some of the scars on my back get some sun.

There was another, welcome, pause. Then Doris said, "Well?"

"Well what?"

"Well, are you gonna get married?"

"Hell, how would I know?" I said. "Anyway, she hasn't even asked me yet."

"So what are you afraid of?"

"Me?" I scoffed. "That's a good one, Doris—me afraid. I've only been afraid twice in my life, once was when the dentist said, 'Open, please,' and the second time was when he whistled and then asked me if I knew a good gum surgeon."

"That's not what she says," she said.

"That's not what who says?" Benny said sleepily.

"Evonne," Doris said.

"Ah," Benny said.

"Evonne says every time superdick here gets even close to having to talk about marriage, he changes the subject so quickly his mind stays dizzy for a week."

"My pet said that, did she?" I said. "That's rather well put. A total lie, but well put."

There was another pause, which I filled by emptying my second beer. It was broken by Miss Nuisance of the Decade saying "Well?" yet again.

"Well, shut up for a change," I said, losing my legendary control for perhaps the third time in my life. "Well, what do you want from me anyway? Well, why don't you take a long walk somewhere cool, like straight out into shark headquarters out there until that silly hat you're wearing, which I paid for by the way, floats, so don't lose it."

"Which philosopher was it who opined that for the thinking

man, life is a comedy, but for the feeling, a tragedy?" said Benny.

"I neither know nor care," I said. "The only philosophy I have ever held was one which I learnt as a boy at my father's knee: to wit, everyone else's philosophy is full of shit. Now come on, the snack bar is a-calling with its old siren song. I'll get another beer or two and buy you two something especially revolting to snack on."

We picked up our leftovers and departed. Then they snacked and I drank. Then we trooped upstairs, showered and changed, met down by the pool again, and then headed off back up the hill to the Rocamar and, fingers crossed, Big Jeff. On the way we passed several open-sided, thatch-roofed cantinas in which merry tourists were busily taking advantage of half-price happy hour booze.

There was but one customer sitting in the small outdoors patio bar at the Rocamar, but he sure looked like a Big Jeff to me. He was tall—not as tall as me, naturally, but well up there in the stratosphere—with a full black beard and drooping pirate's mustache; fancy Stetson with a hatband of Mexican silver dollars pulled down over his eyes; high-heeled, hand-tooled boots up on an adjoining stool; buckskin cowboy shirt; and a gold belt buckle featuring a pair of steer's horns almost as big as a real longhorn's. He was smoking a twisted cheroot and sipping from a tall glass of what turned out to be dark rum, soda water, and a dash of lime juice. In case there was any lingering doubt, the words *Big Jeff* were embroidered in rope lettering over his shirt pocket.

And, sure enough, just as Benny had recounted, behind the small bamboo-topped bar, Pepe the cook was fanning his charcoal fire with a sheet of cardboard trying to get it started.

Big Jeff peered through the darkness as we drew near the lighted patio, and as soon as he spotted Benny, he shouted "Amigo!" leapt up, and engulfed Benny in a huge embrace.

Benny extricated himself finally and introduced me and Sara, by our right names for once. Jeff gave us both hearty embraces and loud kisses on each cheek.

"Pepe!" he bellowed to the diminutive cook, who must have been all of five feet away. "Refreshments pronto!"

"Ahora mismo," said Pepe, meaning "instantly."

"Sooner than *mismo*, you heathen dog!"

Big Jeff sank back into his seat, the worn leather of which groaned audibly under the impact. He waved us into seats opposite him. Pepe materialized beside us, tray in hand and broad grin on thin mug, obviously well used to and completely unfazed by Big Jeff's decibel count. Sara announced she wanted something with tequila in it, 'cause she hadn't had any yet and after all we were in Mexico, weren't we? So I naturally suggested a margarita, the traditional and most genteel of the tequila libations. And about the only drinkable one.

"Never!" Big Jeff shouted to the heavens. "Pepe, bring her an *añejo con sangrita* and make it fast and make it a double."

"Beer for me," I said meekly.

"Añejo for me too," Benny said foolheartedly.

"So what's *añejo con* whatever-it-is when it's at home, Tiny?" Doris asked Jeff, helping herself to one of Jeff's stogies from the pack on the table.

"*Añejo* is aged tequila, darlin', aged as in old, and it is the color of amber that has been rubbed for weeks on a virgin's thigh, not that pale white vomit they made yesterday afternoon and put into cocktails, especially margaritas, for the gringos," he said, polishing off the last of his drink with one long swallow. "¡Pepe!¡*Otro*! And *sangrita* is what you wash it down with, a harmless concoction made from orange juice and chilis."

"I don't see him drinking it," I muttered sotto voce to Benny.

"And if you think that's bad, and it ain't," said Big Jeff, lighting Doris's five-cent special with an old Zippo that had a flame a foot high, "try the local hangover cure some morning—tripe soup." I thought that all in all, I'd prefer the hangover.

Jeff didn't have all that much time before he had to put in his nightly appearance back at his pizza joint, so after Pepe had delivered our various poisons and we had all taken a sip, Benny got right down to it.

"Jeff, do you recall that time you had that small problem up in Guerrero?"

Jeff smiled in fond remembrance, stroking his mustache.

"I believe I might be able to summon up most of the details," he admitted, "if I stretch my failing memory."

"The reason I ask," said Benny, "is because we got the same problem down here." Benny quietly gave him the broad outlines; Big Jeff's flamboyant manner disappeared completely as he listened.

"It doesn't take a great brain to figure out you're down here lookin' for Dan," he said when Benny'd finished.

"Is he around?" I asked.

"He could be," Jeff said doubtfully. "Although I ain't seen him for a couple of weeks, and when he's around, I usually see him. You can always take a run down there tomorrow and find out."

"Where's there?" Sara wanted to know.

"He keeps his boat near Puerto Morelos, that's like a half-hour drive south of Cancún."

"Couldn't we phone?" Benny asked.

"Nope," Jeff said. "Better you take like the nine o'clock ferry tomorrow morning and then hop a cab. Even better if I go with you."

"Thank you," I said. "I appreciate it."

Big Jeff gave me a close look, then sat back and waved one beringed mitt expansively. "We just gotta hope ol' Dan ain't got nothin' on right now."

"You said it," I said. "Otherwise, I don't know what the hell we're going to do. I think we can spring my friend from the can OK, but then our real problems start. If you don't mind me asking, how did you manage it? Benny started telling me about it but he only got as far as when you signed up those two marines out of Pendleton."

Jeff put away half his new drink, wiped his beard, winked at Doris, and said, "We had a pilot in the organizing committee who owned a four-seater Cessna—the two ten, I think it was—and someone else in the committee got a-hold of three of those Israeli submachine guns somehow—"

"Uzis," I said. "They are called Uzis."

"Whatever," said Big Jeff, frowning at the interruption. "Probably out of some Texan's glove compartment. So after me and the kid's pop reconnoitered the whole deal around the prison and in Acapulco—just another couple of tourists; we said we were lookin' to buy some real estate in those parts—we got out of the way and left it to the marines, like they say.

"The plan we came up with mostly depended on the kid, Willy, or a lot of it anyway, and he was only a kid, I think he was like just nineteen, it all depended on him getting so sick that they would have to move him to the hospital in Acapulco where they had operating facilities and all that. But that meant sick, darlin', as in deathly ill, not simply coming down with the sniffles from a summer cold or maybe getting a spot of collar rash."

We all smiled at that. He did have a certain style, ol' Jeff.

"So," he said, uncrossing his long legs and then laboriously crossing them again the other way around, "one way to make yourself sick, a doc told us—and it makes me sick just to think about it—is, pardon the vulgarity, darlin', to actually eat shit, and I don't mean take a little abuse from the mother-in-law over your drinking problem, I mean eat shit. Which, somehow, Willy managed to do."

"Probably a welcome break from Mexican prison food," I remarked, always seeking the *mot juste*.

Jeff ignored me.

"So Willy gets sick. The leathernecks, using a one and a half ton they'd rented in San Diego and driven down in, hijack the ambulance taking Willy to the hospital in a narrow back street by cutting it off suddenly. One marine sprays the engine and rad of the ambulance from the front so it won't be going anywhere, while the other one shoots out the lock on the back door, then shoots off the chain attaching Willy to his bed, which is also attached to another poor sick mother and *his* bed. This second guy takes one look at the ferocious madman with a face painted in black, red, and green stripes who is shooting bullets everywhere and screaming and hollering, and he promptly passes out."

"Holy cow, who wouldn't?" said Doris.

"Holy cow is right, darlin'," said Jeff, pinching her cheek in a friendly fashion. "So. They grab Willy, and all pile in the truck and take off for out of town where the Cessna is waiting, warmed up, in the middle of a field somewhere. They climb aboard, chuck a grenade at the truck—because why leave a useful thing like that behind for the greaseballs?—their term, not mine, darlin'—and after one stop for refueling somewhere along the line—where, they never told me—they made it back to a ranch outside San Diego. And that's all she wrote.

"Well, almost all," said Big Jeff. "I had a card from Willy the other day saying hello, and he's now living in a cave near El Paso with a girl, her two kids, four cats, two dogs, eight, at last count, rabbits, a burro named Jane Fonda, and a hand loom."

For once no *mot juste* came to me.

CHAPTER
TWELVE

By the time I did finally come up with *le mot juste*, Jeff, having devoured everything on Pepe's snack platter except the design, was long gone, and Sara, after three of those *añejo* doubles, was well on her way. I must confess that I too, after eight or so Mexican beers, which are somewhere between half and twice as strong as ours, was beginning to feel the first hint of that old familiar glow back behind the peepers.

After our pleasant interlude on the Rocamar's patio, we strolled down the hill toward the center of things, pausing briefly to watch two of the local basketball teams in action at one end of the large town square. In another corner hordes of kids who should have been long in bed by our stuffy standards were disporting themselves at a row of tabletop soccer games. As we were wandering by, Benny and I somehow got challenged into a game by this urchin who must have been all of seven and who had one arm immobilized in a full plaster cast that was covered with the usual scribblings penned by his pals. Benny and I protested vigorously that it would be too cruel even to contemplate such a mismatch, but to make the cheeky little devil happy, we finally inserted our five pesos in the slot that released the ten balls, and a small but noisy crowd of ragamuffins began to gather around us. Me and Ben agreed in a whisper to take it easy on the poor kid, because after all, we didn't want to completely humiliate him in front of his gang, so we'd let him score a goal or two accidentally on purpose.

I guess we took it a little too easy because he beat us in the first game 8–2. Then Benny and I withdrew slightly for a strategy conference; what we decided was to prohibit the little hustler from using his broken arm to help. See, although he of course couldn't grip any of the handles with his broken arm, the cheater was using it to nudge a row of men over from time to time. Having straightened that out, we really bore down during the rematch, the final score of which was 9–1, and the one goal we did score he scored on himself trying a flashy back pass.

"Well, you can't win 'em all," Doris said unnecessarily as we slunk ignominiously away into the night in the general direction of the pizzeria. "Some guys can't even come close."

"Win, lose," I said witheringly. "Is that all you can think about? Is that how you see life, an eternal contest between weak and strong, hunter and hunted, the fleet and the lame, the predator and the victim? You disappoint me, Doris, you really do."

She grinned and hopped up a hopscotch layout some kid had chalked on the cement path. I was so glad to see the twerp happy for once that, what the hell, I hopped up it too. So did Benny, behind me.

The pizzas were surprisingly good at Jeff's, not so the vino, an overchilled, overfruity California burgundy type. When we were replete and had decided when and where to meet the following morning, Benny and Sara traipsed off to a disco recommended by Jeff that was down near the dock, and V. Daniel wended—or is it wove?—his lonely way through the balmy tropical evening to the Hotel Caribe, subtitled The Pearl of the Caribbean, and lights out.

.   .   .

The ferry chugged its way clear of the end of the dock and shifted into high. It was crowded, but we all had managed to find seats up on the second deck, near the stern, which is a politer way of saying rear. Off on our left was a long line of assorted crafts in assorted stages of disrepair, ranging from a slight list to visibly sinking before our eyes. Big Jeff informed us they had all been confiscated by the Mexican navy, with the help of the U.S. Coast Guard, for running contraband up the Yucatán Channel. He also mentioned that the most luxurious of the sailing craft so confiscated were kept sea-shape to be used by various government officials on which to entertain their lady friends. I scoffed at the very idea.

After disembarking at Puerto Juarez, Jeff made a deal with a cabby he knew who was unloading some passengers for the boat's return trip. He hopped in front with the driver leaving Benny, me, and Sara to squeeze in the back, and off we went. Both Sara and Benny were looking a little worse for wear that A.M., I was not unpleased to observe; served them right, dancing to all hours. Maybe we could make a quick pit stop on the way for some tripe consommé. Big Jeff was bright eyed and bushy tailed and as full of energy as a five-year-old at bedtime. He was dressed that sunny morning in long khaki shorts, a safari shirt, and a battered straw hat with one side curled all the way up. Doris was in yet another new outfit, I was pained to see, although come to ponder upon it, any price was worth the forking over that got her out of her punk phase when, if she ever donned one article of clothing that didn't have at least one jagged hole in it, it was by mistake. I was trying to get used to a new pair of prescription sunglasses I was wearing for only the second time, but otherwise was feeling fit.

Past the airport turnoff we went, and into the teeming jungle we sped, south, ever southward. Some twenty minutes later the cabby took a left and headed back in toward the coast and Puerto Morelos. The once sleepy fishing village was undergoing a building boom at that time, and probably still is, and probably always will be, so it did not present a particularly attractive vista to the discerning eye, even if said eye hadn't been plagued with grit, cement flakes, and brick dust thrown up by all the construction.

I thought we'd head directly to the port area because that is where one generally finds boats parked, but no, Jeff directed the driver to the new and exclusive-looking Ceiba Hotel, which was out a dirt road on the northern side of town, where we pulled up under the welcoming shade of a canopy of palm fronds. Jeff hopped out, said he'd be right back, and took off down a sandy path toward a thatched hut that had a large sign in front of it: Diving Shop. He disappeared inside. All of us except the driver got out to stretch and walk around a bit. Jeff returned a few minutes later accompanied by a short, muscular Mexican in a skimpy yellow bathing suit; when he drew closer, I noticed his legs were even more scarred than mine. Jeff introduced him to us as Alfredo, and we shook hands all round. He said something to Benny I didn't catch, and Benny said something to him I didn't catch. Then Big Jeff said something to Alfredo that I didn't catch either, but Benny did because he said something to Alfredo again. Just to get into the act, I then said something to Doris.

Whatever it was all about it worked because as soon as we were all back in the car Jeff said to me over one shoulder, "He'll meet us," and then told the driver to head back into town please.

"Is he always this hard to meet?" I said.

"Yep," Jeff said.

"I wonder why," I said. "Fear of crowds mayhap?"

"Probably fear of fuzz," Sara said.

"Perhaps he's merely a man who values his privacy," Benny said. "Much like you, Vic."

"Oh really?" I said, surprised. I didn't know I valued my privacy all that much, maybe ten bucks' worth, but that's all.

Jeff kept his silence on the subject, but he rattled on about everything else under the sun, including girls, boats, Costa Rica, and how to avoid the runs in hot climates. Wash your hands a lot is what he said. His monologue continued until the cabby deposited us at the port. Jeff asked him if he could find something to do for an hour or so, then he could take us back to Cancún. The driver said there was not the slightest problem and see you later. He took off one way, we took off the other, down to the narrow beach, where I washed my hands thoroughly, and then out a wooden pier past a few old-timers and some kids who were fishing. At the far end some enterprising local had erected a bamboo hut out of which he sold drinks and last week's tortillas and rented fishing rods; he also had a couple of leaky-looking rowboats for hire.

So we sat on a bench on the seaward side of the hut and waited. The crescent-shaped port area looked busy, at least to a landlubber's eyes. Two commercial vessels of a fairly good size were unloading at the pier next to ours, and sail-boats were doing what sailboats do, and down at the public beach a handsome stripling was giving a windsurfing lesson to a plump lady who'd had too much sun the day before. Every once in a while a motor boat pulling a water-skier arced across the bay in front of us. Jeff pointed out a fiberglass-hulled boat off to our left that he said was something like his, only on his the cabin was farther aft and that his wasn't a stern-dragger.

"Nor is Sara's," I said.

Time passed.

More time passed.

Finally I said, "Jeff, being hard to meet is one thing, but this is ridiculous. Are you sure he's coming, or should I just forget about him and work on my tan?"

"Relaxez-vous," said Jeff. "He's comin'." So I immediately relaxé'd and got up to buy soda pops all round, spying, as I did so, someone who looked suspiciously like Alfredo flimsily disguised as a fisherman, back near the beginning of the pier. I regained my seat on the bench beside Benny without saying anything.

A few minutes after that, one of those boats that look like they are made out of rubber tires, and probably are, with an engine stuck on the back (or stern), and which had been meandering lazily back and forth in the bay changed directions and began heading straight for us, but not before I'd detected or thought I'd detected sunlight reflecting from some brightly polished surface such as the lenses of a pair of highly powered navy binoculars. I suppose it could have been from a sardine tin.

The boat pulled up smartly at the foot of the pier right below us; the pilot cut the motor, lashed his craft securely to one of the wooden supports, then speedily climbed the few rungs of a small ladder I hadn't noticed, doffed the worn captain's cap that was the only other garment he was wearing aside from a bleached-out set of once-blue denim cutoffs, took a beautiful conical seashell out of a pocket, and presented it to Sara with a mock bow.

"Foah the ladah," he said. "A *Conus delessertii*, moah commonly known as Sozon's cone." (My attempt to try and reproduce his "honey-chile" accent stops here.)

"Muchas gracias," said Sara.

"Cap'n Dan, I presume," I said.

"The one and only," he said, with a brief but wide grin of whiter than white teeth. "Howdy, Jeff." Jeff gave him one of his rib-crushing embraces.

"V. (for Victor) Daniel," I said. "My associates B. (for Benny) and S. (for Sara)." We took a minute to size each other up. What I saw was a man pretty much Jeff's physical opposite, as Dan was short, wiry, and almost completely hairless except for a quarter of an inch of blond crewcut. His eyes were small and blue; his ears tucked in neatly close to his head. He was sunburned almost black except for the tattooed bits—mermaids on each upper arm, and crossed anchors and skull and crossbones below. And, not least, strap hinges tattooed on the inside of both arms right where they bent. I made a mental note to remind myself to ask him who his tattoo artist was. Wouldn't Evonne be surprised when she got her first sight of them as I disrobed to slip into something more comfortable. I might get the back of my knees done as well.

And what he saw was six feet seven and a quarter inches of male splendor, albeit studded with the occasional scar, burnt patch, bullet-wound pucker, dent, and old stitch mark, which, like a beautiful woman's one small birthmark on an otherwise flawless face, merely served as an alluring—nay, intriguing—contrast to the overall perfection. At least that's what he would have seen had I, like him, been vain enough to walk around in a pair of shorts little bigger than a weightlifter's *cache-sexe*.

"Jeffrey, a word, please," Dan said when we'd finished eyeballing each other. They strode out of earshot, then Dan came back and Jeff went off on a little amble down the pier. Dan squatted down on his heels in front of us but in profile—so he could keep one eye out to sea, I guessed.

"So what's on your mind, Victor?"

"A sea cruise," I said, "is what is sort of on my mind. A healthy sea cruise."

"Where to?"

"Anywhere but here," I said.

"Here being Mexico, I take it," Dan said.

"You take it right." I said.

"Brown pelican," he said as a large, foolish-looking bird flapped by us and gave us the once-over. "Well. Anywhere but south presents problems. Considerable problems. If you follow the coast all the way up Mexico to, like, Matamoros, planning to walk across to Brownsville, first of all it takes forever and second of all you've got continual hassles from both the Mexicans and the U.S. Coast Guard."

"Yeah," I said. "Big Jeff mentioned something on that subject."

"And it is a long run, too, to Miami or Key West," he said, "unless you hop off somewhere like the Dry Tortugas, where something really fast is waiting for you. I doubt you particularly want to go to Cuba, and both the Caymans and Jamaica have their problems, or to put it another way, I have in the past had my problems with both of them."

"For shame," I said.

"So," he said. "That leaves south, meaning that way." He gestured off to our right with one thumb.

"And what's there?" Benny asked.

"Belize is what's there," Cap'n Dan said. "Frigate bird," he said, pointing up at a long-winged, forked-tailed feathered friend who was trying to steal a fish dinner right out of the mouth of a gull. "Largest wing span in proportion to body weight of all species."

"Why doesn't it catch its own fish?" Sara asked. "Too lazy?"

Dan grinned at her. "Not waterproof enough," he said. "If it gets too wet it sinks."

She gave him a disbelieving look. She wasn't the only one.

"Belize," I said. "Speak to me of Belize."

"Once British Honduras, now independent," he said. "Bounded on the north by dear old Méjico, the west by Guatemala, the east by the ocean, and the south by the never-was-British Honduras."

"Hmm," I said. "Let me ask you this, Cap'n Dan. Would it be possible for one to slip into Belize quietly some eve without having to be bothered with all those utterly tiresome customs and immigration formalities?"

"More than possible," Dan said. "Extremely probable." He stopped for a moment when the cantina owner emerged from his hut to chuck a bowl of scraps into the water. "One has several choices, one has. One could simply take a bus or drive down to Chetumal, last town on the Mex side, and look around for an Indian guide there to take you up the river until you can ford it. If this 'one' you keep referring to is more than one—"

"Four, actually," I said.

"Ah," he said. "Then one of you crosses legally into Belize, if that's possible, and picks up a guide there where it is both easier and safer, they tell me. Once in Belize, there's a bus that goes to the capital, and from there you can even hop the mail boat as far as Livingstone in Guatemala, if you're crazy enough."

"I don't know if I'm crazy about fording that river," I said. "I suppose that means the whole *African Queen* number, with leeches and barracudas and eels and they're the good news. I don't know if Sara could take it."

"What a sissy," said Sara.

"Or," Dan said, shifting his weight slightly, "you find some amiable seadog with a suitable boat and he drops you off on the Island of Belize, where you wait for the morning ferry to take you to the mainland, where you pick up a cab that takes you to the airport, where there are things called planes, which take you anywhere in the world."

"Speak to me of this island," I said, "where one might have to spend a night."

"He wants to know if there are any leeches there," Sara said. "Or electric eels in the bidet just waitin' to ring his bells."

"Really, Sara," I said. "Vulgarity is always unbecoming in the fair sex. Or unfair sex, as someone, not I, once quipped."

"I guess you got to watch your back there like anywhere," Dan said, "but most of the time it's so laid back it's half-asleep.

I remember once though, pulling in to the little dock there and everyone in sight was hopping around and speeding away like in some old movie being projected too fast. Finally one of them tells me what happened was a container of coke got washed up and the whole island had been tooting it for days. So the village elders get together to try and figure out what to do, which isn't easy because they're all out of their skulls too. They decide to collect all the rest of the coke, or what they can, and then send a trusted representative to the mainland with it to flog it and split the money and they'll all be rich. So off goes the trusty representative with a suitcase full of coke, worth on the streets like a quarter of a million, but of course all Belize knows what's been going down by now, so he gets robbed five minutes after leaving the ferry."

"Oh, terrific," I said. "Sounds like my sort of real estate. Anyway. To regress slightly. You mentioned that what would also be required would be some amiable seadog with a suitable boat. Would you describe yourself as amiable, Cap'n?"

"The very picture of, sometimes," he said.

"It would be too much I suppose to expect that boat you own to be suitable, I guess," I said.

"Oh, I don't know, . . ." he said, as if he was thinking it over. "She is a staunch old lady come to think about it, seventy-six foot long, Texas built, glass hull, eight seventy-one Detroit diesel main, double electronics, paper recorder, Raytheon loran, sleeps six at a pinch, she might be up to it."

"Is she parked out there by any chance?" I asked, indicating the bay.

"Golly, no," Dan said, looking innocent. "Someone might scratch a fender or something out there, it's so crowded. I've got my own parking place, or moorage, as we like to put it, right over there." He made a gesture up the coast that took in about fifty square miles of tarantula territory.

"Makes sense," I said, nodding, "if boat hops are anything like car hops."

Dan grinned again, then said, "Well, citizens, this is all very enjoyable and all that—I like sitting in the sun and yarning as much as the next sailor—but maybe it's time we got down to it, *comprende?*"

I said I comprendoed. I told him what we were up to as briefly as possible. When I was done, he had a few questions, quite a few, which didn't surprise me all that much.

"When are you springing him?"

It was then Wednesday. I said, "All being well, Friday afternoon."

"How?"

I shrugged. "Where there is a will, there is a way."

"Then what?" Dan said. "How are you going to get him and you all down here?"

Oops, I thought. Actually I thought something a lot worse than oops. I hadn't even considered that part of it, I'd been so busy being clever about the rest.

"Don't worry, we got that in the bag," Benny said unexpectedly.

"Of course we do, Dan," I said, recovering with customary adroitness. "It was one of the first things we took care of."

"All right," said Dan. "I'll take your word that you can get him out and get you all down here sometime Friday evening, even though every *federale* south of Nuevo Laredo will be looking under every cactus for you. What traces will you leave behind? What kind of a trail? Are your backs covered at all? It's not going to do you any good if you do get to, say, Belize and then onto a plane if your names are waiting on a list in every port of entry in the States."

"Ah," I said. "I'm glad you asked that, Dan. There will be no names on no lists, at least not our real ones because we didn't use real ones in Mérida or when we first crossed the border. So no comeback there. As for a trail, I thought about that too. I suppose it's remotely conceivable, if they wanted to go to the trouble, that they could find one of mine or

Benny's or Sara's fingerprints, despite the cleanup we'll do before we leave and also despite the care Benny and I took— because we talked about it before—in places like Febrero Segundo and our hotel rooms. I mean, we did go to cafés and took taxis and steam baths and all, so it is possible. Sara's no problem because she told me she's never had her prints taken. Mine obviously are on file as a registered private detective and an ex–soldier boy and an ex–couple of other things I won't mention right now, so are Benny's. Say they got a print. Let's even admit they might have sufficient liaison with the appropriate law enforcement agencies back home too. Let's even admit they have the technology to link up their computers with U.S. ones and eventually get an ID on us. Señor, we'd be long home by then, and the Mexican authorities would have a hell of a job trying to extradite us bona fide American citizens back down here for anything less than wholesale manslaughter, and even then they'd have problems.

"Also," I said, "we have a little surprise up our commodious sleeves that should take the heat off us, if there is any, immediately and put it somewhere else that I assure you is guaranteed heatproof."

"We hope," said Dan. He took a small penknife out of his pocket and began to trim off a jagged splinter he'd found on the pier by his bare feet. "All right," he said again. "Let's say you can get him out and can get down here and you are clean when you get here. And let us say you and me make a deal and we sail away into the setting sun, and let us further say I get you to Belize Island and you catch the morning ferry and then a taxi to the airport. Let us say all that. You all got passports?"

Sara looked offended. "Only for years," she said.

"Me too," said Benny. "Several, if needs be."

"Well ..." I began. They all looked at me as if I was the Thing from Outer Space.

"I don't believe it," Doris said, shaking her (actually my)

wig. "Mastermind here hasn't even got a simple, ordinary, everyday item like a plain old passport."

"Oh, shut up," I said. "How was I going to know I'd need one?"

"You could have figured it out without booking too much computer time," she said. "I mean it was obvious from the start we couldn't go back to the States directly from Mexico."

"Oh, it was, was it?" I said. "And what about Billy? Where's his passport supposed to be? I know it's not under his mattress because he hasn't even got a mattress."

"Calm down," said Dan, without looking up from his whittling. "Where there's a will. Are any of you wanted right now in the States, for anything serious, I mean?"

"My mother probably seriously wants me," I said. "But that's it as far as I know."

"Bear with me," he said. "And none of you is on any FBI list prohibiting you from reentering the States for serious offenses in the past?"

We all shook our heads, even Benny.

"No sweat, then," said Dan. "You hit the U.S. consulate in Belize as soon as it opens—as I remember, it opens for a couple of hours Saturday mornings. You tell them you got mugged in a bar Friday night and lost some money and all your ID and you naturally didn't want to go to the cops because your money and IDs were long gone anyway and you couldn't pick out the two muggers if they were in a two-man lineup, and besides, there was no way you all wanted to hang around Belize for a couple of weeks while the cops got nowhere, and besides, your mother is sick and you've got to get back for business reasons and you get the picture."

We all agreed we got the picture.

"What they do in cases like yours is make one check by telex to the FBI to see that you're clean as far as they are concerned, and that is usually it," Dan said. "I hope so for your sake. We do not want them checking to see if you all had passports issued to you at some time, passports that were still valid, meaning you had entered Belize legally."

"No, we certainly do not," I said.

"And we do not want them phoning your home addresses to check that people with the names you give them actually live at those addresses but are presently on holiday in Mexico because who knows if Billy even has an address after all this time and if he gives his parents', who knows what they'll say if some government type phones them up and asks them, 'Oh, by the way, where's your son these days?' "

I shuddered at the thought.

"Let us be optimistic," Dan said. "Let's hope they are busy or hungry or lazy or hung over and just get the usual clearance. Then what they do is issue you temporary traveling papers good for one one-way ticket back to the land of the free. If you're broke, which they do not like, they will finally, reluctantly lend you the fare to the nearest point of entry in the U.S., if you are unable or won't wire home to someone for money yourself. So better is, what you say is luckily you had just enough fare money or one credit card stashed away down one sock. *¿Comprende?*"

I not only said I comprendoed but that I was grateful for all the survival tips, deeply grateful at that. I only hoped he knew what the hell he was talking about. Then I asked him the 64-million-peso question: how much?

He finished up his good housekeeping chore and put his knife away again.

"Without going into all the details," he said, proceeding like all good salesmen to go into enough of them, "in our favor is that no one smuggles anything from here to there, it's always the other way round, so it's rare to get stopped, and if we do get stopped, we're not smuggling anything anyway, we're just gringos out for a sail. Also all our sailing in Mexican waters will be done at night. And if the *federales* are together for once and the navy has been warned to look out for dangerous types like you because your backstop hasn't worked, then first of all, they have to catch us in the middle of the night, and by the time they do, the easily identifiable ones, Victor and Billy, will be safely hidden away under the bulkheads, where they could look for a month without finding you, and Benny and Sara won't look like Benny and Sara anymore, and anyway if they do hear about you and find us and board us and find the stowaways, we'll just pay the buggers off, won't we?"

I nodded confidently.

"On the other hand," Dan said, ticking the points off one by one on the fingers of his other hand, "there are such expenses as diesel fuel, oil, my deck hand—"

"If you mean Alfredo the invisible," I said, "he's back there trying to find someone to bait his hook for him."

"My deck hand, whoever he may be," Dan went on smoothly, "food and water, and this and that, and remember, if we do get caught, I can always plead innocence. What captain asks to see his passenger's papers before a little cruise down the coast?"

"You won't look so innocent if they find us hiding in the bulwarks, wherever they are," I said.

"There is that," he admitted. "And it's bulkheads. At the least they'll confiscate my boat, and insurance companies are notoriously unwilling to pay out if your boat has been confiscated with just cause."

"I bet," said Sara.

"So all in all," said Dan, furrowing his brow in deep thought, as if he hadn't already worked out the price per passenger per nautical mile per hour afloat and per stale sandwich eaten. "So, all in all . . ." And he named a sum that had more zeros in it than Tokyo airport during World War II.

"How would you like that paid?" I said. "Gold bullion do?"

"Dollars, traveler's, certified check, even pounds," he said. "I don't care. Half when you board, please, half on arrival."

I looked over at Benny, who gave a noncommittal shrug.

"You're a big help," I said. "OK, Cap'n, you got a deal." We shook hands briefly. "Sara, got three grand you can lend me till a week from Friday?"

"Sure, in pesos," she said.

All that remained was for Dan and me to agree on where and when. He told me where—if we took the dirt road that goes to the Ceiba but continued north instead of turning off to the hotel, in about fifteen minutes we'd get to another turnoff, which we wouldn't take either, but we would take the next one and bear left when we got a chance, and it would take us to the estuary of a small river that was just big enough for Dan to back his boat into, bulkheads and all. Then he told me when—midnight on Friday. He asked us for a phone number in Mérida where he could get in touch with us or get a message from us Thursday or Friday morning to confirm. Benny gave him Jorge's.

"Anything else?" Dan said, effortlessly getting to his feet with nary a creak from his leg bones.

No one could think of anything else, so we made our farewells and were just turning to leave when he said, "Oh, there is one thing. There's a chance something may come up and I may not be able to make it."

That time I located the *mot juste* with no trouble at all.

CHAPTER THIRTEEN

A s far as I know, only one," Big Jeff said, lighting up one of his stogies with his flamethrower.

We were in the cab driving back to Cancún.

In light of the severe shock to my system, already wobbly, delivered a few minutes previously by Cap'n Dan, I was putting a few searching questions to Jeff about his erstwhile shipmate. The way we had left things with Dan was like this— if whatever the hell it was that was more important even than saving my life did come up, he'd try to keep our rendezvous seven nights later at the same time or, failing that, seven midnights after that. And that was the best we could get out of him.

So what I was quizzing Jeff about were such trifling matters as, was Dan reliable? If he didn't show, would it be because of something truly world shattering or merely some picayune get-out, like his dog had the mumps or his horoscope in that day's *Puerto Morelos Gazette* said avoid sea trips? Jeff assured me his old pal was reliability itself. What about his barnacle-hulled, bulkheaded, double electronic (whatever that meant) clunker of a boat we didn't even get to see? Extremely dependable but a mite slow, said Jeff, max speed about twelve knots. I wondered aloud how many boats Dan had already run on the reefs or scuppered or floundered, which is when Jeff said, "Only one."

"Oh, is that all?" I said with exaggerated relief. "That's like dying only once. I suppose all hands were lost, except him."

"Nope," said Jeff calmly, puffing away. "Ever heard of Morro Bay?"

"Nope," I said.

"I have," Sara piped up from beside the other side of Benny. "It's in California somewhere."

"Correct, darlin'," said Jeff. "You get real heavy surf in the harbor mouth there, sixteen-foot waves easy. You also get about three deaths a year up there from boats capsizing, so Dan did good just walkin' away from it."

"More like dog-paddling away," I said, beginning to quiet down slightly. "Probably collecting seashells as he swam. Oh, look, everyone," I said, pointing, "a *Bananias treus*, you can recognize it by those bunches of green, banana-shaped things hanging all over it."

Jeff chortled, then said, "It's up to you of course, darlin', but I doubt you'll do better than Dan Peel, not that you have a lot of choice this late in the game."

"There is that," said Benny from the seat beside me.

"Right on," said the twerp.

"You, I'll get to later, Benny," I said.

I got to him on the airplane on the afternoon flight back to Mérida from Cancún, as soon as I'd opened my eyes again after takeoff and had visited the bathroomette to wash my hands.

"Benjamin," I said. "Excuse me ever so for disturbing you," I said. "I can see that you are busy looking out the porthole at those fascinating white fluffy objects, but I was wondering, if you didn't mind terribly, letting me in on how we are going to get ourselves from Mérida down to Dan's mud scow. Or if that's too much to ask, perhaps you might drop me a wee hint. Maybe we could make some kind of guessing game out of it to while away the hours."

He grinned across the aisle at me.

"OK," he said. "I'll give you a hint. How does Jorge transport my hammocks to the shipper?"

I thought back.

"In his old truck," I said.

"Voilà," he said. "I already had a word with him about it just in case. Who's going to look for us under a pile of hammocks in that old wreck of his?"

"No one, I hope," I said. "I also hope we can breathe under all that close-weave."

"At least Benny came up with a way to get to the boat, which is a lot more than you did," Guess Who offered unnecessarily from the seat adjoining mine.

"The delegation of insignificant details to trusted hirelings is surely *the* key to successful leadership," I reminded her, smiling at her fondly. "Do you really imagine Caesar spent his time worrying over trifles like whether his elephants were getting enough vitamin C in their diets? Of course not. His mind was on other, larger matters."

"It's the first I've heard that the Romans used elephants," Benny said. "I always thought it was the other guys."

"Well, Benny, even you don't know everything," I said. "And besides, it's been a closely kept family secret for ages."

Even the twerp was amused at that one, although she rolled her eyes heavenward in mock disbelief.

After we'd landed at Mérida, we caught a cab to the hotel, where we all changed into apparel more suitable for the business types we were supposed to be—me and Benny in suits; a skirt and blouse for Doris—and then we walked the few blocks to our office building. We said *hola* to Fred, who was reading a tattered old Mexican wrestling magazine, as we passed his desk, caught the elevator, opened up the office, and then me and Benny went into conference in the inner room, while Doris plopped herself down at her desk and started bringing her diary up to date, which literary work I seriously doubted would ever rival Pepys'.

I began the conference by asking Benny what the time was. He looked at his watch and announced it was a quarter after four.

"Do you think lunchtime is over now up at Febrero Segundo?"

"I should think so," he said. He went over and opened one of the windows to air the place out a bit.

"OK," I said. "Here is what we are going to do, or rather what you are going to do while I sit back and admire your prowess." I got out the local phone book and after several red herrings finally found a number for Febrero Segundo under "Governmental Services—Provincial." Then I switched on the intercom connecting the offices and asked Doris to please join us if she could bear to tear herself away from her purple prose for a minute or two. I jotted a few words down on the slip of paper with the jail's phone number on it, then explained to Benny the gist of what he should say to Lt. Esparza and what we wanted from him.

When Doris slouched in, I handed her the piece of paper, which she looked at with a mild show of interest.

"Doris," I said. "Would you get a Lt. Joaquín Esparza on the phone at that number, my little chickadee? What you say is written underneath: *'Lt. Joaquín Esparza, por favor, Sr. Keith aquí,'* which means, "Mr. Keith here." Then when you get him, you say, *'Momento, por favor,'* and Benny'll take over. *¿Comprende?*"

She tossed her phony curls, turned, and went back out to her desk to use the phone there. Benny picked up the one on my desk.

"Anytime, Doris dear," I called out.

She dialed. She said to whoever answered, *"Lt. Joaquín Esparza, por favor."* There was a pause. Then Doris called out, "What's he saying?"

Benny called back to her, "He's saying he's out of his office at the moment."

"Even better," I said. "Benny, leave a message asking him to call back, like we said."

Benny nodded.

"Thank you, Miss Day, that'll be all," he said into the phone. "I'll take over." Then he asked whoever it was on the other end to kindly ask the lieutenant on his return to call Mr. Keith, whom he met briefly the day before, at the United States Cultural Association, spelling out the difficult bits. Then he said, "Thank you," and hung up.

Doris came back in immediately. "You really are a bunch of totally dim bulbs," she said scathingly. "Why didn't you leave him our office number?"

"Oh, damn!" I said. "Benny, how could you be so thick? God almighty, you've ruined everything."

Benny looked suitably crestfallen.

"If he looks up the number in the book, as he probably will," Doris steamed on, "that Ethel downstairs will probably invite him to *The Nutty Professor.* I don't believe you guys sometimes."

"Doris," I said. "Would you do me a small favor, please? Pretty please?"

"I doubt it," she said, wandering around the room looking for something to break or throw or spill.

"When the phone rings, as it will shortly do, answer it by saying sweetly, 'U.S.C.A., good afternoon'—or *'buenas tardes,'* if you so desire."

She directed a suspicious look at me.

"OK, big shot," she said, marching over to my desk and glaring down at me. "What's goin' down?"

"Why nothing, darlin'," I said, trying to look as innocent as

Benny always does. "Can't a busy executive expect a call?
Now simmer down and trust your elders and wisers and
go back and scribble some more in that searing, scorching
diary of yours, the book that tells it like it never was, the tome
that plumbs new depths of raw, naked emotion but is also
a sensitive and moving tale of a tender young bud's first
flowering under the gentle twin caresses of sun and spring
rains—"

Just as I was getting into my stride, the phone rang. All of
us jumped out of our skins. Doris ran to her desk; she and
Benny picked up their phones at the same time.

"U.S.C.A.," she trilled. *"Buenas tardes."* Then she said, *"Momento, por favor,"* pressed the talk switch on her intercom,
and said loudly into it, without covering the telephone receiver with one hand so the lieutenant could hear, "Mr. Keith,
Lt. Esparza on line one."

Line one, I thought. What next. That's the trouble with
working with amateurs, they always want to ad lib.

"Thank you, Miss Day," Benny said. Doris hung up, then
propped her skinny frame in the open doorway to listen.

"Lieutenant, thank you for calling back so promptly," he
said. "You may recall meeting myself and Mr. Blackman yesterday."

The lieutenant said something I couldn't hear, but he was
obviously admitting that he did indeed recall.

"I am telephoning for Mr. Blackman, of course, on a matter
of some considerable gravity," Benny went on pompously,
"to the United States of America. There may also be a not
inconsiderable sum of money involved." Here Benny dropped
me a quick wink; there was a brief pause while the subcommandant said something else.

"Well, sir, therein lies the problem," Benny said. "As it is a
matter of some confidentiality as well as some importance, I
am reluctant to go into details on an open phone line. I'm
sure you can appreciate that."

Another brief pause.

"We could indeed," said Benny. "But I am not sure it would be wise for Mr. Blackman particularly or for myself to be seen on your premises too often—we do make a rather noticeable couple, I'm afraid." Here Benny gave a mild chuckle. There was another brief pause.

Then he said, "Exactly. What I, therefore, propose is this, if it meets with your approval, naturally. Perhaps you could drop by here at our offices on Calle sixty-three—at your convenience, of course, but we would prefer the meet to take place tomorrow if at all possible. Naturally we would cover any expenses that might be incurred by you and your driver"—another little wink—"or if you prefer, we would be delighted to send a car for you."

There followed another pause, not so brief this time. Benny told me later, when he was translating the conversation for me and Doris, that under all the politeness what the lieutenant said was to the effect that World War III couldn't prevent him from paying us a visit and that tomorrow would be fine by him but it would have to be either before or after the commandant's siesta, since as second in command, he was forbidden to leave the jail for any reason but a dire emergency while the Big Boppa was off duty, so how did noon mañana grab us?

"Excellently," Benny said. "Tomorrow at twelve would be ideal for us. In your own vehicle, as you wish. By the way, we're at Four-nine-nine Calle Sixty-three, between Fifty-eighth and Fifty-sixth. *Hasta mañana*, then, and many thanks from Mr. Blackman, myself, and the government of the United States."

He hung up and turned to me with a self-satisfied expression, and quite rightly.

"How was that, amigo?"

"Sensational," I said, patting him on the dome. "As usual.

And I loved your ad libs about 'a not inconsiderable sum of money' and 'any expenses that might be incurred.' Then I added magnanimously, "Doris, 'line one,' good thinking, my pet."

"So now you got your lieutenant comin' tomorrow," said Doris from the doorway. "Then what?"

"Then what?" I exclaimed. "Wait till you cast your orbs on him, then what. Your false eyelashes will be fluttering like a hummingbird's wings, only faster. You'll have to insert a few asbestos pages in that diary of yours is then what."

"Ethel," said Doris. "She's got to be in it somehow. You got to Ethel, but I don't see how. Or when."

"Simple, child," I said smugly. "You must try and keep up more with the latest technology, as I strive to do. Why, I daily pore over communications manuals and electronic textbooks."

"Sometimes twice daily," agreed Benny solemnly.

"There exists," I said, "a device. A gizmo. A hookup. Call it a connector, which is a simple tool that might best be described as a cradle for two telephones. What you do is lay one phone one way and the other the other way, as close together as possible, so the speaking end of one is talking into the listening end of the other. Ethel, say, gets a call from a certain lieutenant, say. She immediately rings me up on her second phone. She puts the two receivers in their little cradles and there we are, me and the Louie, chatting away merrily to each other."

Doris looked disappointed.

"Oh, is that all?" she said. "Although when you set it up with Ethel beats me."

"I never said I did set anything up with Ethel," I said. "Did you hear me say anything like that, Benjamin?"

"Not in so many words," Benny said.

"I merely said it could have been done that way," I said,

getting to my flat feet. "Now, anyone hungry? I must admit to feeling a bit peckish. I don't know why, but that iguana fricassee I had on the plane didn't fill me up."

"Those six beers you had might've," Doris muttered.

So we locked up, we departed, we elevatored, we said adiós to Fred, we strolled to a café, we snacked, we drank moderately, and then Benny and I, hoping to give the locals a thrill, went off to search for a pool hall whose location he vaguely remembered, while Doris went back to the hotel and the pool without a hall. In fact, it was so small it was almost a pool without a pool.

We found the pool hall eventually, a large, windowless abode open to the street, with a good twenty battered and cigarette-burned tables in it, most of them in use. The cost per table was forty-five cents an hour. All the youths seemed to be playing Chicago, a bizarre variant of pool wherein, to start the game, half the balls are lined up with gaps between them against one long cushion and the other half along the other, with one ball, the four, I think, against the middle of the cushion at the far end. I soon got the hang of it, though, and whipped poor Benny two games out of four and then thrashed a wall-eyed, drunken local who tried to hustle me one game out of five, at fifty cents a game. I'm not one for making excuses, but you try shooting decent pool on felt that's been repaired with Johnson's Band-Aids. It also had channels in it you could have sailed shrimp boats in.

On the way back to the hotel I bought us ice cream cones; next to the ice cream stand was a busy laundromat, and Benny remarked, "Those things kept me alive for six months once."

"What things?" I tasted my strawberry cone, which was fair.

"Washing machines," he said, licking his double chocolate.

"How did washing machines help you stay alive?" I reflected. "Maybe it was cold and you slept in a dryer. I saw a TV program once where a guy showed how you could cook all these things in an automatic dishwasher."

"Must have made the macaroni soggy," Benny said. "What I did was borrow this official collector's key for an hour—cost me a hundred bucks and another fifty to get the key copied. It was one of those complicated brass cylindrical ones, and what it did was open all Bendix machines cash boxes. I'd put on a white cap and white jacket and hit the laundromats about noon, because the real collectors do it last thing at night. I never took enough out of any one machine so anyone would notice a few quarters less, but I heard now they got a sealed counter in them like juke boxes so the operator can tell how many times each song is played or each machine is used, but I don't know for sure, I just heard it."

When we arrived back at the hotel it was, by happy coincidence, apéritif time, so we sat in the café out front and apéritifed, me on a cold, cold Corona and Benny on a gin and tonic with a squirt of fresh lime juice in it. After a while he said, "What kind of shape are we in for tomorrow?"

"Pretty good," I said. "We got a few things to do but they won't take long."

"We better fill Sara in," he said, "somewhere along the line."

"Yeah, I guess," I said, waving off a kid about a foot high who was trying to sell me a packet of Cheez-its.

"She's something else, she is," he said. "She'll go anywhere, she'll do anything, she's got all the guts in the world, and she's bright."

"She's coming along," I said. "I've always prided myself on my ability to see the hidden potential in people, and was hers ever hidden."

"She looks kind of cute, too, in her new duds."

"Really?" I said. "Can't say I've noticed. And they're *my* new duds, if you want to get technical."

We sat there for a few minutes eyeing the passersby—the endless stream of vendors, the energetic tourists, the long and the short and the even shorter. Pretty Mayan girls with their white-shirted escorts were starting to form a line at the

Rex movie house just off to our left, where something called *Escape from Cuba* was playing.

"Maybe we ought to see that," I said to my friend. "It might give us some ideas."

"We're cool," said Benny. "Not to worry."

"You may be cool," I said, "but I am impatient, *amigo mío*, I tell you that. I am ready for action. Action is ready for me. It's all been very pleasant, traveling around hither and yon, taking in the sights, listening to grizzled sea dogs spin their tales, and seeing you in a steam bath is something I will long remember, but enough is enough. I am ready for action. I crave it. I must have it. I thirst for it, I dream of it. I am also worried, Benjamin. I haven't slept a wink since last night except for a bit on the plane. I am deeply worried."

"About what particularly?" Benjamin gingerly patted the top of the head of a limping mutt that was scrounging under our table.

"About everything particularly," I said. "As if we didn't have enough to worry about before, now we got that damn bird watcher to worry about too."

Benny thought it over for a moment. Then he snapped his fingers.

"I got it," he said. "Have another beer."

I acquiesced. Was it not Leonardo who once remarked that the simplest solutions are often the most elegant?

CHAPTER FOURTEEN

We drove to the office early, or comparatively early, the following A.M. While I'd told Benny that the few things we had to do before the entrance of Lt. Esparza wouldn't take long, they still involved a couple of hours of toil and trouble.

So after opening up, I unlocked my suitcase, we distributed several more props about the premises, and I dumped the suitcase out back. Then, while I dictated a couple of letters to Doris, Benny made a quick shopping run for some last-minute items. When he came back, while Sara was typing up the letters, we devised our scenario for the forthcoming drama, ran over it three or four times to fix the details in our busy little brains, then ran over it with Sara when she was finished with the typing; after that, I tore up and burned in an ashtray on the window ledge the scrap of paper on which I'd made notes.

At eleven-thirty, all was prepared and we were as ready as we'd ever be. I was surprisingly calm, considering the pressure on me, considering that I had the leading role, after all; but my supporting cast evinced plenty of first-night nerves, despite their gallant attempts to hide them.

At eleven forty-five I was sitting in our rented Chevy about a half block down the street from the office building, waiting for the curtain to go up, hoping it wouldn't be a balloon instead.

At five to twelve, whatever it was going to turn out to be went up.

One of Febrero Segundo's immaculate new Jeeps turned down out of 53rd onto our street and drew to a halt just outside 499, i.e., us. I got out of the Chevy in a controlled hurry and timed it so that I drew level with the Jeep just as the driver was opening the back for Lt. Joaquín Esparza, who stepped out nimbly, recognized me, threw me a smart salute, then shook my paw effusively.

"¡Sr. Blackman! ¡Qué gusto!" he said.

"Absolutely," I said. "Shall we *entrar*?"

I gestured toward the front door. He snapped a curt order to the driver, who was standing at attention by the Jeep, then led the way up the steps to the entrance. I drew his attention to the brass plaque beside the door.

"Nosotros," I said modestly, which means "us." Luckily the sign didn't mention what floor the real Cul. Ass. was on. We could have gotten around it somehow, maybe by distracting the lieutenant in the elevator so he couldn't count the floors, but most elevators have floor indicators inside them that light up, so we might have had to claim we were an annex or whatever, but we didn't have to, which was just as well, as it was already complicated enough. A lot too complicated, was the message that occasionally fought its way to my consciousness from that deep inner recess where invidious truth lurks.

It is perhaps apparent that the reason I'd waited outside for the lieutenant was to prevent him from asking Fred (or anyone else he came across) what floor the real Cul. Ass. was on and have him drop in on a mystified Ethel. I also made sure I interposed my not inconsiderable bulk in between him and the notice board that listed the whereabouts of all the building's tenants and which we had to pass to get to the elevator.

I only prayed he wouldn't spot it on the way out or that if he did, he'd merely assume it was a mistake or, like I said, that the Cul. Ass. had more than one office in the building.

After a spot of Alphonse and Gaston when the elevator arrived, in we went and up we went without further conversation. When we entered our office, Doris was (pretending to be) on the phone, a pencil behind one ear and a wad of gum in her mouth, the pencil her idea, the gum mine.

"Certainly," she was saying. "One hundred and fifty posters, no problem. Monday at the latest. Will you send someone to pick them up or do you want us here to arrange delivery? Fine. We'll leave it like that, then. Grassy-ass. Adiós."

She hung up and scribbled a note in her desktop diary.

"That was Mrs. Oliver about the posters for the pottery exhibition," she said.

"Oh, swell," I said. "Lt. Esparza, may I present our Miss Day."

He had been casually checking out the place while Doris finished up on the phone; now he advanced on her, clicked his heels together, took one of her hands reverentially and kissed the air an inch above it.

"*Ay, qué linda,*" he said, holding on to her hand perhaps a second or two longer than strict protocol demanded. But perhaps not—how much do I know about kissing hands?

"Why, hi there, Lieutenant," Doris said coquettishly. And she had the nerve to flutter her false eyelashes at him, but the effect wasn't quite as devastating as she'd hoped because the last thing I'd done before leaving to meet the lieutenant, to make her look more like a secretary, was to present her with a horrible, garish pair of plain-glassed specs I'd bought in L.A., the kind with pink plastic wings sticking out both sides.

"You're just doing this to get even, Prof," she'd said when I'd handed them over to her with a flourish.

"How right you are, Teach," I'd said.

I made a big production of unlocking the inner office door, which caught the lieutenant's attention, as it was supposed to do, then I held it open and gestured him in.

"Any calls?" I asked Doris over my shoulder.

"The big chief called, twice," she said.

"Right," I said, following the lieutenant into the main office, but not before he'd bestowed a last, gleaming smile at *qué linda*, and her likewise at him. I carefully locked the door behind us. Benny, who was tearing a (blank) strip of paper off the (unconnected) telex, crossed to one of the filing cabinets, unlocked a drawer, took out a cardboard file, inserted the message into it, then locked up the drawer again.

"More about Nicaragua," he improvised to me in an aside meant to be overheard. He then greeted our visitor, apologizing for keeping him waiting momentarily, asked him to kindly seat himself, which he did, in one of the spare chairs drawn up in front of my desk, Benny taking the other.

"Keith," I said, putting my glasses on, "would you get me the latest from the file on John Brown, please."

"Certainly, sir," he said. Hopping up again, he went back to the filing cabinet, unlocked a different drawer, took out another folder, extricated two pages from it, locked the drawer again, then came back and deposited the papers gently in front of me—during which time I thumbed on the intercom and told Miss Day to hold all calls except Washington. Miss Day said, "Sure," and popped her gum. During the same time Lt. Esparza was taking a not-so-casual look around.

Among the items of particular interest that he saw were the flag on my desk, of course, the telex machine, of course, the large map of the world, of course, all the office fittings and fixtures, of course, the photo of me and my adoring family, to say nothing of the cur, of course, and also a few new touches we'd added just for lucky old him—a framed, signed (by me, "To my good friend Blackie") photo of J. Edgar Hoover's unmistakable mug, which was sitting on my desk, courtesy Celebrity Photo Service on the Strip (with retouches by Wade's Pictorial); also, from the same source, a framed photograph of Richard M. Nixon apparently shaking hands with Blackie; and from the same team again a framed photo of Gerald Ford on the White House lawn waving at the camera, standing in front of a group of businessmen of some kind, the tallest of which bore a distinct resemblance to L.A.'s tallest and most cuddly private I. And Sara had contributed a framed reproduction of the United States Declaration of Independence, the one with all those signatures on it, which she claimed to have won for being first in her class in American history one year in high school, which I thought was about as likely as her winning the Nobel Prize for poetry one year. But anyway, there it was up on the wall behind my desk.

When I was sure the lieutenant had taken in all the visuals, including an ashtray I'd picked up in a junkstore one time that was made out of a brass shell case, I rustled the papers in front of me importantly and began, with Benny again acting as simultaneous translator.

"We have quite a file on your Mr. Brown," I said, "of which these sheets are but the immediately relevant material. And when I say 'we,' I am not necessarily referring to the United States Cultural Association. I trust that you catch my drift."

He gave a meaningful glance at the picture of Mr. Hoover and said something to the effect that my trust was not altogether misplaced.

I iced the cake by taking out my wallet and flashing my FBI ID at him, a fake, needless to say, which I must confess I'd used more than once before in my shameful career, but it looked real enough with the fingerprint and photo and signature all in the right places.

"Excellent," I said. When I reached forward to pick up the pen from the desk set, I inadvertently let my unbuttoned suit jacket fall open just enough so he could see I was wearing a shoulder holster. "Dear me," I said then. "I am forgetting my manners. We in the organization are not, of course, allowed to have alcoholic beverages on the premises at any time—it was a particular bugbear with our late, lamented chief—but may I offer you a coffee? I could sure use one. It's my one bad habit, my wife says." Here I laughed falsely. We all agreed we could use a coffee. I pressed the intercom and said into it, "Miss Day, please, front and center."

Benny got up and unlocked the door for her, and when she came in, he asked her for coffees all round, please, and why didn't she make herself a cup while she was at it.

"A small kitchenette," Benny said to the lieutenant when Doris had flounced through the door that did not lead to a small kitchenette but to the back stairs. Benny and our guest at the feast made small talk until Doris reappeared with four steaming cups of coffee on a tray alongside a small pitcher of milk and a bowl of sugar cubes, all of which, including the thermos of java, Benny had shopped for earlier. Sometimes my guile appalls me. But not always.

As soon as we had all served ourselves and Doris had vamoosed and Benny had locked the door again, I continued: "Are you at all familiar with the laws of extradition between our two countries, Lieutenant?"

The lieutenant confessed that his knowledge of that complicated subject was minimal at best, which I was pleased to hear, since so was mine.

"I'm not surprised," I said, sitting back and shaking my head. "It can be a highly tortuous affair, and it is sometimes to everyone's benefit to endeavor to simplify procedures." I gave the handsome officer a long, cool, calculating look, as if I was trying to sum him up. Then I said, as if I'd made my mind up, "May I speak with total frankness?"

I may, it turned out. And I could also be assured that whatever I said would go no farther than the four walls of that very office.

"Among men of honor, that is sufficient guarantee," I said

sententiously. "Now. Your Mr. 'Brown.' We know a good deal
about him, including of course his real name." I nodded in
the direction of the filing cabinet. "We know where he went
to school. We know what his grades were. Who his friends
were, and are. We know every address, every phone number,
every car he has had and every job. We know what taxes he
has paid. And we know of some he hasn't."

Benny smiled like a true yes-man.

"We first became aware of his criminal activities in late . . .
'seventy-six, was it, Keith?"

"Right, sir," said Keith.

"When he was part of the crew of a seventy-six-foot
shrimper that capsized in Morro Bay, in upstate California," I
said. I hoped it was upstate. "A so-far confidential amount of
Colombian cocaine was discovered in the wreck, behind the
bulkheads, to be precise, by Coast Guard officials, but as nothing could be proven against the crew and the captain had
disappeared, perhaps drowned, the case, as far as we were
concerned, wound up in the dead file. He came to our attention again in 1979 and this time we managed to convict him
on three counts relating to the trafficking of drugs, the up-
shot of which was that he spent three years in a federal prison
in New Mexico, the state in which he was finally appre-
hended."

My intercom buzzed once.

"Excuse me," I said. I pushed the listen button.

"Washington again," said Doris's voice.

"Oh, good," I said. "I'll take it in there. Keith, I may need
you."

Keith excused us politely, saying we might be a minute or
two, and we went out to Doris's office, closing the door
behind us. She gave us a mouthed "How's it going?" I gave
her the thumbs-up signal and took the phone from her. While
I was chatting to Washington, who certainly wasn't saying
much back, I was hoping that Lt. Esparza, as would only be

human, would check out the papers I'd carelessly left on my desktop, which were what I'd dictated to the Secretary of the Year earlier, both pages of which were typed on FBI-headed notepaper, or facsimile thereof, courtesy of we all know who, and which discussed the intricacies inherent in extradition procedures and outlined several possible ways to streamline the problems. Words that the lieutenant could easily understand whether or not he knew any English—like *Mr. Brown, Febrero Segundo, extradition, policy, cooperation*, and *dollars*—were of course prominent, and in several cases underlined, just in case. I was also hoping that Joaquín mayhap might just decide to press down the listen button on the intercom, so temptingly near his manicured pinkies, because what he would hear would be me saying in as simple English as possible how well things were going and that we had made a superior local connection, one Lt. Joaquín Esparza, *subcommandante*, a hightly intelligent, responsible, patriotic officer, and the very devil with the ladies. (I didn't really say that last bit.)

All right. We'd done all our numbers, laid all our traps, showed all our cards—it was time for the rousing finale. And when I returned to my desk. I noticed the two directives weren't quite lined up the way I'd left them, another hopeful sign.

"Sorry about that," I said. "Now. Where were we?"

"In a federal penitentiary in New Mexico," Benny offered helpfully.

"Thank you, Keith," I said, giving him a look. "The question was rhetorical. In 1983, after a massive undercover operation spanning over five years, which we had code-named Snow Removal, my organization was successful in smashing one of the largest drug distribution setups in the country. As a result of which, Mr. Brown was again arrested, again sent to federal prison, this time in Utica, New York. During a subsequent riot there, which we suspect was organized and financed by East

Coast drug money, he and nine others escaped, killing two guards on the way and one of our agents later in a car chase."

The lieutenant continued to listen intently, swinging one of his highly polished boots from time to time. I don't blame him, I thought it was a real spellbinder myself. When he finally did interrupt me, it was to say that he was still uncertain what his role in the affair might be.

Then he took his cap off, placed it carefully on his lap, and ran one hand over his pristine mane to see that it was still pristine.

"I was just coming to that very point," I said. "There is a way you could be of inestimable help to us, and all it would involve would be a couple of hours of your time and that of a driver and perhaps one other. Lieutenant, we of the organization would very much like to get our hands on Mr. Brown again. He has not only an unfinished prison sentence to serve up at Utica, but we also want him for suspected murder in cold blood of a law enforcement agent as well as inciting to riot, car theft, transporting drugs across state lines, and so on. As far as we are concerned, the most serious is the brutal slaying of one of our men. It had been a tradition since the organization's founding that such cases remain permanently in the active file until the perpetrator has been caught, even if it takes decades."

"We, too, have a similar reputation for avenging the loss of one of our own," the lieutenant said with a small smile. I believed him without any trouble.

"So, here is what I have been leading up to in a somewhat roundabout fashion, I'm afraid," I said, taking off my specs and looking for something to clean them on.

"Allow me," Benny said hastily, taking out his neatly folded breast-pocket hankie and handing it over.

I went on without bothering to thank him: "Binding extradition papers can be served on a U.S. citizen in a foreign country only by handing them to him directly on American soil. The process itself takes only a few minutes." Who knows? It might even be true. "But what American soil does one find in a foreign country? By international treaty, the Treaty of Vienna, actually, in nineteen twenty-four—"

"Eh, 'twenty-six, Chief," Benny said in a servile fashion.

"Thank you, Keith," I said coldly. "By the Treaty of Vienna all embassies are deemed to be an integral and legally constituted part of the country they represent. As is well-known, they are not owned and do not come under the legal jurisdiction of the local country; they have, as do all personnel concerned, diplomatic immunity. This is also true of consulates, naturally, which are sort of a second-class embassy, if I may put it that way, headed by a consular official, not an ambassador. What is not as well known is there are other governmental agencies in foreign countries that are similarly protected; these others include libraries, occasionally a trade mission, sometimes a diplomatic mission, like one to the UN or the UNO, sometimes a military mission, such as a foreign base, and sometimes—" Here I paused expectantly and smiled gently across the desk.

"Sometimes perhaps a cultural association," he obliged.

"Sometimes perhaps a cultural association or club. These can range from elaborate and well-financed operations like those the U.S. and Canada and India and Korea and a host of others maintain in the capital cities of the world, like Paris, down to the more modest level of ours here. What all such U.S. establishments abroad share, including ours, is that the moment you pass through the front door your feet are legally treading on American soil. Are you with me, Lieutenant?"

"I am in the seat beside you, señor," he said. "Correct me if I am wrong, but what you are asking me to do is to briefly visit your offices again, but this time in the company of Mr. Brown."

"When I will read him a prepared statement two paragraphs

long, then hand him one document. And then the day he steps through the front gate at Febrero Segundo, myself or more likely my successor here, as I am due to be rotated to another post next year, will have him on a private plane we have access to, heading for America within an hour, and I can assure you, sir, it will be a long time before he gets to enjoy any more of your delicious Mexican food."

We all smiled at that one, for different reasons no doubt.

Then there occurred a more lengthy pause while Joaquín thought things over, into the middle of which Benny stepped smoothly.

"Did you mention the contingency fund, sir?" he asked me.

"Ah yes," I said. "The contingency fund, which is a fund that is contingent; on my approval, mainly. As a small gesture of gratitude, the United States would want to make some contribution to the overall well-being of your prisoners. The latest information we have from our penal reform studies suggest that such monies be best spent on recreational facilities. What was the sum mentioned, Keith?"

"Five thousand dollars, I believe, sir. That would be roughly . . . er, eleven million pesos."

"That should buy a few Ping-Pong balls, eh, Lieutenant," I said. "And perhaps new nets for the soccer field."

The lieutenant's dark eyes twinkled in merriment.

"It might even run to a table to bounce the balls on," he said, and we all smiled again conspiratorially.

"Did you mention that we can only suggest possible usages for such funds but that their ultimate disposition can only be decided by the appropriate prison authorities?" Benny asked.

"I was just about to, Keith," I said testily. "It seemed obvious to me that in a ticklish matter like this, our interests end when we hand the cash over to, say, the lieutenant. Did you think I was going to ask him for a receipt for some prying journalist to uncover some day? Perhaps you would like us to all have our photos taken at the handing-over ceremony. Perhaps you would like to have a plaque affixed to the Ping-Pong table reading Donated by the Organization."

Benny looked suitably chastened. I wondered if I wasn't overdoing it slightly; it was remotely possible. Joaquín hid his amusement by stroking his dapper lip adornment. I hid my satisfaction by glaring at Benny again. We had Joaquín, no doubt about that; we had one fascinated dandy sitting in front of us already spending his millions.

There remained little more to discuss. Could the lieutenant devise some dire emergency that would allow him (and Billy) to leave the jail briefly while the *commandante* was also away, because one would not like to risk the *commandante*'s ire (or, possibly, his desire to be cut in) by trying to sneak off while he was there and getting caught. A dire emergency could and would be arranged; for that much *dinero* Joaquín could have probably arranged the return of the Great Plague. Could he arrange for Mr. Brown to appear clean and as smart as possible, in civilian clothes and without handcuffs, as we naturally wanted to maintain our Cultural Association cover as much as possible, which would be difficult to do if a manacled skeleton in prison rags showed up in a Black Maria surrounded by a half a dozen armed guards.

Easiest thing in the world, the lieutenant assured us. Clothes would be provided. A closed sedan-type vehicle was available—as I knew, I'd already seen it. And one guard plus himself and his driver would be more than enough.

"I hope so," I said worriedly. "I'd hate to be responsible for a dangerous criminal attempting to escape."

"Dangerous?" Joaquín laughed. "Mr. Brown couldn't run ten meters without stopping twice for a rest and once for an injection of anabolic steroids. And where would he go, anyway? He has no contacts, no money, no forewarning of his visit here, and thus no time to plan anything. I do not believe we have to worry overmuch about any attempted escape, señor."

I looked relieved. We set the meeting for the following afternoon, at three o'clock. We shook hands with great amiability. I pressed on him a pamphlet, one printed in both Spanish and English, describing the origins of our association. He kissed Doris's hand again with considerable style and strutted out, Benny accompanying him to the elevator and then down to the lobby and out to his Jeep just to prevent any encounters with Fred or lingering at the notice board.

As soon as I'd closed the door behind them and their footsteps had died away, I grabbed Doris.

"Doris," I said, "prepare to get those attractive glasses of yours fogged up, because I am going to give you a kiss Yankee style." I looked deep into her eyes, murmured, '*Ay, qué linda,*' bent over, and gave her a good smack.

She made a big production of pretending to go weak at the knees. When she recovered, she said, "What does that mean, anyway?"

"Who knows?" I said airily. "I think it's got something to do with Linda Lovelace, but if it's good enough for ol' smoothie, it's good enough for V. Daniel."

CHAPTER
FIFTEEN

When Benny returned a few minutes later, we celebrated all over again.

"Oh, did we hook him," he said, grabbing Doris and twirling her around. "Did we hook him, Sara, or did we hook him?"

"We hooked him," she said breathlessly, one hand holding on to her peruke. "At least I think we hooked him. From what I could see, we hooked him, but as Doris the dopey secretary, I was out here, wasn't I? while you guys were in there having all the fun."

"Darlin' doubtin' Doris," I said, "hooked isn't the word. Hooked, gaffed, netted, and then strung up by the feet having his picture taken isn't even the word. Look at it from his point of view. One. According to the pamphlet I gave him, the U.S. Cul. Ass. has been in business for fifteen years. Let him check if he wants. Who cares? It's true. Two. As far as he is concerned, we are the U.S. Cul. Ass. We have a plaque out front. We have one on the door. We look like a Cul. Ass."

"No thanks to you," said Doris.

"Doris, if I was in this merely for thanks, I'd be a pretty low type of individual," I said. "Three. We have an address and a phone number, which both check out, and how could they be faked?"

"That bloody Ethel and her awful serape," Doris said. "That's how. I don't care what you say."

"It was a shawl, Doris, not a serape," I said. "And let me give you this to ponder, my sweeting, my shorn angel." I perched on the corner of her desk as she was so wont to do on mine back home. "What kind of front do you think the CIA and the FBI habitually use as covers for their covert operations? Legitimate companies is what they use; no doubt they stole the idea from the Mafia. Travel agencies, language schools, charter airlines, innocuous friendship clubs, and dare I say it? cultural associations. It's no secret, it's no more secret than the fact that anyone attached to an embassy with the title second secretary or cultural attaché is automatically assumed to be in intelligence."

"You don't mean Ethel!" Doris said. "That windbag?"

"Maybe not her," I said, "but what goes on in her back room? It's the easiest thing in the world to set up some phony trust to bankroll an operation. Mrs. Moberg, of the Austin Mobergs. Really. That is why I didn't go near dear garrulous Ethel. All we needed was for me to ask the real FBI to pass on phone calls to a false FBI office right above them. That would be brilliant, that would. Anyway. The fact that we had established ourselves as the real Cul. Ass. is surely beyond any reasonable or unreasonable doubt, will you allow me that?"

"I will," said Benny.

"I will, too, if Benny tells me what *'ay, qué linda'* means," Doris said.

" 'What a beauty,' " said Benny.

"Really?" she smirked.

"As for the FBI side of it, surely we established that as well, beyond all possible doubt—the pictures, the ID I showed him, the shoulder holster I flashed, the Washington phone calls, the files, the papers with FBI heading, the secrecy, the locked doors, our skillful acting ability, even the Department of the Interior calling cards. I mean, what's to doubt?

"What's to doubt is what if he knows the FBI doesn't operate outside the U.S.?" she said. "Why didn't you make us the CIA or something like that?"

"Who's the head of the CIA?" I asked her. "Or for that matter, who ever was?"

She shrugged. "Who knows. Who cares."

"Exactly," I said. "Even if I did have a picture of him, who'd recognize him? Also, since everyone knows the CIA has been doing things inside the U.S. it wasn't supposed to, as it's only supposed to operate outside, what's so impossible about the FBI doing the reverse?"

She shrugged again. "OK, OK, get on with it."

"While we were in there having fun, as you put it," I said, "Benjamin and I, with razor-sharp cunning, managed to achieve several extra bonuses. We planted the fact we have a private plane nearby at our disposal, so maybe they won't come looking for us in leaky *Titanic*s. We hid the fact there is a back way out by having you pretend to make coffee in a nonexistent Mexican kitchenette, so it didn't even dawn on the lieutenant he might have to bring an extra guard along or have his driver cover the back door, which would give us one more problem we don't need. We also have Billy coming in normal clothes, which saves us time and trouble. Also unhandcuffed, ditto. Also in a normal-looking car, not a paddy wagon that might attract the interest of every city cop who passed by. And presuming the driver stays downstairs like he did today, that leaves us with only the lieutenant and one other guard to deal with up here, and we should be able to deal with them quietly and with ruthless efficiency."

"Like beat 'em to death with one of these," Doris said, picking up one of our sample hammocks and swinging it over her head like a war club. Benny immediately picked up another one, and they began to playfully whack each other with them. I smiled tolerantly at their high spirits.

"The part I like," I said, deftly dodging a flailing no. 10 close-weave that the twerp directed my way, "is that either way we win. If by some enormous chance Ethel is up to monkey business, she is not going to so admit to Joaquín unless he produced enormous official pressure, by which time we will be long gone. And if she does finally so admit, what can she do but plead total ignorance, likewise any superiors she might have, because that is what they are—totally ignorant? And if she is really just plain old Ethel from Des Moines putting on shows of macramé plant hangers no one goes to, she'll plead ignorance again because she is still ignorant, or more ignorant, or whatever it is."

"Perhaps, again ignorant," Benny suggested.

"Perhaps," I said. "Either way it's a dead end for the Mexican fuzz. Of course whatever Ethel is or says they won't believe, but by the time they've sorted it all out, if they ever do, I'll be back sitting in a deck chair in Evonne's garden watching appreciatively as she bends over to weed her parsley; Doris'll be back at her typewriter editing extracts of her diary for publication in *Cosmo*; and you, Benny, 'll be back selling used Dodger farm clubs.

"But let us not forget," I warned, "that up till now it's all been, if not fun, Doris, relatively easy. Tomorrow we will have two armed men to overcome somehow and incapacitate somehow, an office to clean up, a getaway to make, a rendezvous with Jorge or one of his innumerable sons to keep, a drive of several hundred kilometers to suffocate through, another rendezvous to make in blackest night in anaconda country, a lot of seasick pills to swallow, and then the hard bit starts."

"I'm glad you reminded me," said Sara sarcastically. "I wanted to go sightseeing tomorrow to the ruins of Chicken Little, or whatever it's called."

"Whatever it may be called, it is not that," I said.

"Chichén Itzá it is called," said Benny. "Famous for its well."

"Jack Benny was even more famous for his," I said. "Now if you two are finished skylarking about, let's go and eat something and talk over what we have to do before three o'clock tomorrow."

On the way out, Fred gave me a wave and called out, *"Buena suerte mañana, señor,"* which even I knew means "Good luck on the morrow, o handsome one." What I didn't know was why he said it.

"Benny, why did he say that?" I said as soon as we were out on the street. "Does he know something we don't know he knows?"

"I had a word with him after I saw the lieutenant off," Benny said. "To cover the lieutenant's presence here I told Frederico he was a buyer for the army and I was trying to sell him hammocks. A lot of hammocks. I also mentioned he was coming back with a couple of his associates tomorrow."

"That was clever, Benjamin," I said. "Well thought and well done. Doris, I think you might deposit that gum somewhere, chewing gum in public is totally gross, Melvin, and nerdish."

Benny took us somewhere. We ate something thin and brownish green. We talked a lot. Then Benny took himself off to arrange things with Jorge while Sara and I went shopping for the assortment of items we'd need the following day— first to a hardware store, then to a clothing store, then to a pharmacy. I must say it was a relief to go into a drugstore and for once not head directly for the diarrhea display. Maybe washing your hands really did help. If Lt. Esparza ever kissed one of mine, I'd wash it in sheep dip. I don't know why, but I've always had this thing against truly handsome men. To the superficial, this might seem like mere jealousy.

That night I dreamed of Evonne. I was kissing her somewhere moist, like in a steam bath. True, she didn't look like my blond bombshell; as a matter of fact, she looked surprisingly like the beautiful, dark-haired, sloe-eyed receptionist at our hotel, but I knew it was really Evonne because my lips, which are without hirsute adornment, unlike some I could mention, are strictly reserved for her.

. . .

Came the dawn, which I was not up to see.

Came nine o'clock, which I was.

Came ten, which found us in the office. Came eleven and, reluctantly, twelve. I took out the rust-pitted cannon Benny had borrowed from Jorge's number three offspring and looked it over with mistrust for the umpteenth time. It was an ancient, made-in-Spain copy of a Colt .45. At least the cylinder still spun like it was supposed to. I had originally hoped that Benny could score us some knockout drops or similar fast-acting soporific that we could dose the coffee with, but it was not to be, which I found slightly peculiar in a country where all minor downers like Libriums were not only available at any pharmacy without prescription but were handed out free as samples by druggists with every purchase of a family-sized tube of Ipana.

It seemed that I was the only one who was impatient. Benny was at his desk engrossed in some chess problem he'd laid out on his portable set, or at least pretending to be, while Doris was at her desk repainting her nails, which I figured was probably just her way of keeping herself from nibbling them down to the quick.

By one o'clock I was so restless I took myself out for a walk around the block. I returned by the back way to check, first of all, that the key Fred had given me for the rear door downstairs worked—it did—and second to check that the stairwell was open all the way up to our floor—it was. It had belatedly occurred to me that perhaps Ethel stored her millions of unwanted posters out there or that Fred had rented the entire staircase between floors one and three to a tribe of gypsies plus a llama or two, which carried the loads that were too heavy for even the women. While on my stroll, I noticed a Yucatán gray pigeon engrossed in its courtship ritual with a rather scraggly-looking female of the species. I also noticed that our Chevy was still parked where Benny had left it that morning—in the nearest legal parking place to the downstairs door—and also that it still had all its wheels as well as all our baggage, which we'd stowed in the trunk after checking out of the hotel.

At two o'clock me and the troops ran over the plan of action one more time, just for something to do. At two-fifteen, just for something else to do, I began climbing the walls. At two-thirty, I said a dirty word loudly.

"Now what have we forgotten?" said Benny.

"Now what has *el supremo bizarro* forgotten, is more like it," Doris said.

"I forgot to have someone posted downstairs like I was posted last time for the same reasons," I said. "Which one of you is the more distracting today, I wonder."

"Her," Benny said immediately.

"Yeah," said Doris, "especially in this sleaze you made me buy yesterday."

"Now, Doris," I said. "You have the perfect figure for a four-inch miniskirt and you know it. With that, ol' smoothie'll probably kiss your hand all the way up to your opposite shoulder. And with any luck, it'll give the guard something to pop his eyeballs at and keep his mind well off his work, which is just where we want it."

"So what am I supposed to do down there while I'm waitin'?" she wanted to know. "Practice my nonexistent Spanish on Freddy?"

"Why don't you lurk in the ladies' room next to the elevator," I said. "That's what I would do—only in my case, of course, I would select the men's room. Then pop out and herd 'em all up here pronto before they get into trouble. Simple."

"Sure, sure," she said. "And what if they're late? Won't Fred start gettin' suspicious if he sees me go in and not come out for twenty minutes?"

"Must you always look on the difficult side of everything, Doris?" I said wearily. "It seems obvious to me that he'd find it a lot more suspicious if he saw a tourist who went by a bathroom and didn't go in for twenty minutes."

"You oughta know," she said. "But OK, you're the boss, although who elected you, I'll never know."

"Benny, got all your stuff ready?"

"Yes, Vic."

"Have I asked you that before, Benny?"

"Yes, Vic."

"I thought I might've," I said.

At ten to three I said to the kid: "Time to get moving, sugarplum. Break a leg—beat it, to you." She beat it.

At three-ten I said, "Maybe they're not coming."

"They're coming," Benny said.

At three-fifteen I said, "I told you they're not coming."

"They're coming," he said.

At three-twenty they came, or at least we heard someone heading our way down the corridor. Benny folded up and pocketed his weeny chess set just before I told him to.

It was them all right, and without any extras. Doris entered first, followed by the lieutenant, who had gallantly held the door open for her, then Gray Wolf in a clean but unpressed white suit far too big for him. He was limping slightly, perhaps from having proper shoes on for the first time in a long time. Billy was followed by a large, uniformed, unsmiling, armed sergeant of the guard, who closed the door behind him and immediately came to attention in front of it.

I went into Doris's office to greet them; Benny remained at his desk frowning down at some paperwork.

"Lieutenant!" I exclaimed. *"¡Qué gusto!"*

He saluted me con brio with panache, and we shook hands warmly.

"And Sr. Brown," I said. "So glad you could make it."

"I managed to find the time," he said in a croak, keeping his eyes submissively downcast. "But I hated to miss basket-weaving class, it's my favorite."

"¡Silencio!" said Joaquín sharply. *"Por allá."* He prodded him vigorously toward my office. Billy stumbled and fell in through the door.

While he was slowly picking himself up again, I said, "Tsk-tsk. You really must take better care of yourself, an ex–Eagle Scout like you." In other words, another reminder to be prepared. He nodded once to let me know he'd got the message.

I threw a *"Cinco minutos"* to the guard over one shoulder and followed Billy and Joaquín, closing the door behind me. Which action, necessary to our plans, I did not think the lieutenant would object to as he was about, he dreamed, to be handed 11 million pesos in used cash, an activity he surely wouldn't want his sergeant to oversee.

When we were all seated—the lieutenant directly facing me, Billy on his right, and Benny over at his desk putting his papers away in a folder—I got out a folder of my own from the top desk drawer, then hit the intercom and asked Doris to please hold all calls except Washington, which was our signal for her to start making some noise. Billy raised his eyes enough for one brief glance at me, then lowered them again.

"You got it, Chief," Doris said and began rattling away on her typewriter as well as commencing to loudly hum one of the Sex Pistol's more tender ditties. I also hoped she was keeping the sergeant's optics well occupied.

I took a breath. I needed one.

"Oh, drat," I said, reaching into the top drawer again as if I was hunting for something. "Keith, you got those two-oh-two forms over there?"

"Right here, sir," he said.

He arose promptly and headed my way with the folder. I picked up the cannon from the drawer, leaned across the desk, and not too gently pressed the working end of the muzzle against Joaquín's bronzed forehead, then half-cocked it with one thumb, all so quickly the startled lieutenant had no time to move anything but his eyebrows, which went up. Billy made a move to help, I told him to get out of the way. I looked into Joaquín's eyes, held one finger of my free hand to my mouth, and went "Sh-sh-sh," which I hoped meant the same thing in *español* as it did in English.

Benny was behind the lieutenant by them. He dropped the folder and slapped across Joaquín's mouth, to say nothing of his mustache, two large pieces of adhesive tape he'd been hiding. Then he taped two more, longer lengths over his eyes. Then he took out lengths of precut, single strand, copper-cored electric cable from one pocket and quickly tied the lieutenant's hands behind his back. It was when he was starting on his legs that the trouble erupted.

Being no fool, the lieutenant had decided that we didn't want to kill him, at least not right then, or why go to all the trouble of trussing him up, so he heaved himself backward and toppled both himself and Benny onto the floor, making a hell of a commotion. Then I heard a scream from the other room and it sure wasn't the sergeant, unless he screamed coloratura soprano. Billy launched himself into the melee on the floor, and he and Benny fought to bring Joaquín, who was lashing out wildly with both booted feet, under control. I briskly moved me and the cannon to the door and was just about to open it when the sergeant came through it from the other side without bothering to open it. I went flying. My glasses went flying. The cannon went flying over behind Benny's desk. I started scrabbling after it, then changed my mind and began scrabbling toward the sergeant, who was desperately trying to claw his cannon out of its holster.

"Look out!" I think I shouted. I know I shouted something clever because Billy looked up, took in the scene, jumped up and threw himself onto the guard's gun hand, which couldn't have done his own bandaged hand much good. By then I was close enough to hook one of my feet behind one of the guard's legs; with my other foot I kicked him on the knee as hard as I could. He screamed and went down. Oh, fine, I thought. One more scream and we'll have the whole street in here. I rolled myself heavily onto the guard, leading with a stiffened forearm to the adam's apple, which took most of the fight out of him, and stayed on him till my brave allies finally got him trussed, bound, gagged, blindfolded, incapacitated, and generally *hors de combat*. We then secured Joaquín's remaining free limbs, after which I stood up and panted for a moment, then found my mercifully undamaged specs and put them back on.

"Those shits," said Billy. He gave them both a hefty kick with his new footware; I can't say I blamed him. Then I thought, Oh, Christ, Doris. I ran the few steps to her office. She was stretched out on the floor beside the desk. A small pool of blood was forming on the carpet under her head.

"Sara!" I knelt down beside her. She was still breathing, but she was out cold. I turned her head gently, took off her wig, and discovered that the blood was seeping from an inch-long gash on the back of her head; it didn't look too bad. Thank God for the stupid wig, which gave her some protection.

I grabbed a handful of tissues from the dainty dispenser on her desk and pressed it tightly to the wound. Her color looked all right and her skin wasn't clammy. I took her pulse and that seemed OK too. There was quite a lot of blood about, but even minor head wounds tend to bleed a lot, I reminded myself.

Benny appeared beside me.

"How is she?"

"I think she's just knocked out," I said. "We'll have to wait and see if there's anything else like a concussion. God knows how it happened. I'll stay with her for a bit, you guys better start packing it up."

I remained there on the floor with her head on my lap. Benny retrieved my suitcase from out back, and he and Billy began cleaning house. After a minute I pillowed Doris's head on my suitcoat and went in to help. We packed up every FBI connection or suggestion thereof—all the photos and mementos and then every bit of paper with writing on it from all three desks, both filing cabinets, and the wastepaper baskets. At one point the sergeant, who was lying in a corner, face to the wall, started stealthily shifting his position; Billy went over and gave him another solid kick. The shifting ceased. The lieutenant, lying in the opposite corner, wisely made no move at all. Perhaps he was twitching his mustache under the tape.

Billy had an idea; he took off their boots to lessen the amount of noise they could make drumming their heels on the floor trying to attract attention. I cut both phone lines to stop the boys using them to call for help if they did get free and to stop them knocking one over and making strange noises into it if they didn't.

With the three of us working at it, we had the whole place clean and tidy in something like five minutes. I took one last look around, made a final check of our prisoners' bonds, then said, "Benny, tell the sarge quietly in one cauliflower ear that one of us is waiting in the front office for a phone call that could take half an hour and that if he moves during that time, the next kick he gets will be in the coconuts, or whatever the expression is down here."

Benny told him.

Then I said, "Benny. Tell the lieutenant quietly in one ear that one of us has to wait in this office for half an hour for a phone call, so no getting clever or else. Tell him too that if we do make it safely to the airstrip, he'll get his money anyhow."

Benny told him. Then me and Benny lugged the lieutenant into Doris's office.

"Fat chance," Billy whispered to me when we came back.

I grinned and gave him a big hug. He held on tight for a moment.

"Thanks, Vic," he said, his voice muffled.

"Ah, hell," I said. "You can do the same for me sometime." I gave him a couple of friendly pats. I figured it wasn't exactly the appropriate time to bring up the delicate subject of, quote, money no object, unquote, so I went back and checked up on Doris instead. She was still out but breathing normally, and her skin tone was still good.

"I'm going to have to carry her," I told Benny, "so you better bring the car as close to the back door as you can. We'll give you a couple of minutes head start."

"I go, amigo," he said.

"Good luck," I said.

He went, taking the suitcase with him.

Billy said, "Vic, whatever happens, I won't forget about all this. I'll make it up to you somehow." He winced and grabbed the wrist of his injured hand. "Jesus, that hurts. But now I can do that old joke for real. You know, the one where a guy in a bar holds up two fingers and a thumb and says, 'What's that?' "

"It's a guy who works in a sawmill ordering five beers," I said. "You lost two fingers?"

"Yeah, working in the jute plant," he said. "On a bandsaw, making wooden crates to pack their bloody rope in."

"That's a drastic way of giving someone the finger," I said. "Apart from the hand, how're you feeling, Billy? Can you make it? We got a lot of traveling to do, starting now."

"I can make it," he said grimly. "I may be feeling shitty but I'm feeling terrific too. So let's go, Injun Joe."

"You go on tiptoe," I said. "They might actually believe one of us stayed behind." I locked the front door, just to make it as difficult as possible for any rescuers, gave the keys to Billy, then picked up Sara as gently as I could. Billy retrieved my jacket and Sara's wig, which we had overlooked. He locked the door that connected the offices so the boys couldn't try rolling together and untying each other, then the back door behind us. Halfway down the stairs Sara gave a little moan. I turned my head to look at her; her face was cradled against my shoulder and she looked about six. Her eyes fluttered, then opened, then peered into mine from a distance of maybe a couple of inches.

"Prof?"

"Right here, darlin'," I whispered. "It's all OK and we're on our way."

"Phew," she said groggily. "Did I go out like a light."

"Did you ever," I said, starting down the last flight, hoping it wasn't Fred's day to take down the garbage or Ethel's day to smuggle up her mestizo lover. "Just hang on tight, ol' Uncle Vic's got you."

"It hurts, Vic," she whimpered. She started to close her eyes again. I blinked once or twice; that stairwell hadn't been dusted for an era.

Just before she dozed off again, I thought I heard her murmur, "Who turned on the waterworks, Prof?"

Waterworks? From me? I was going to tell her that the last time V. Daniel shed a tear was at his circumcision, when a guy really has a reason for tears, not just because some skinny twerp gets a little bump on the noggin, but she was gone again.

CHAPTER
SIXTEEN

When we got to the bottom of the stairs, Billy opened the back door and we cautiously peered out. The Chevy was parked at the curb directly in front of us. Its motor was running. There was no lurking guard awaiting us. The street was almost deserted. Everything was ready. Only thing was, there was no Benny.

Fine time to take a leak, Benny, I thought. Fine start, I thought, to our carefully orchestrated getaway in which every moment was precious.

Billy sauntered out casually and opened the rear door for us; I was pleasantly surprised Benny had remembered to unlock it. No one seemed to be paying us any attention, so I crossed the few feet of sidewalk, deposited Sara in the backseat, and hopped in after her. Billy got in the front.

"Now what?" he inquired. "I don't want to be an alarmist, but we are in a sort of hurry."

"If I knew what to do I'd be doing it already," I said. "You got any bright ideas?"

Luckily, Benny ambled around the corner just then and headed our way. He jumped in beside Billy and we took off.

"And may one ask what you were doing?" I said. "Aside from giving us heart failure? Maybe you just couldn't tear yourself away without a farewell kiss from Ethel."

"Sorry," he said cheerfully, taking a brisk left turn onto 56th. "Thought it might be a good idea to tell the driver that the lieutenant and party would be another half-hour at least, so why didn't he get himself a quick bite somewhere. That way he won't get antsy and come looking for us for a while."

"Oh," I said, somewhat mollified.

"Also wanted to go by a mailbox," he said.

"You could have mailed your postcards earlier, Benny, like we did."

"It was a letter to Fred," he said, taking another left onto 55th.

"I didn't even know you were pen pals."

"I asked him to call the furniture rental people to take back their goods and told him to keep all the office supplies and other stuff for his trouble."

"Oh," I said. "Are we going fast enough?"

"I'd say so," said Billy. "We don't want to attract too much attention. Where're we going, anyway?"

"South to Cancún," said our chauffeur, "after a change of vehicles."

"Then what?"

"Then Puerto Morelos, down the coast, I hope," I said. "Then the good ship *Lollipop*, unless something comes up. Then Belize Island, if we're still afloat. Then a ferry 'cross the Mersey to the mainland. Then some shenanigans with the U.S. consul. Then a checker cab to the airport. Then home, sweet home. How does all that grab you, you old Panther, you?"

He gave a tired smile and shook his head.

"Fuckin' incredible," he said. "I still can't believe we've got this far. I never really thought I'd get out of that place. After nine months, if you've had a good record, you can earn a few cents a day in the jute plant. It took me another nine months to save enough to pay a guard to get that letter out, and then I was never sure it'd get to you."

"Try writing direct the next time," I said. "I'm in the L.A. phone book."

"How's Sara?" Benny asked.

"Seems to be holding her own," I said. "She'll need a couple of stitches in there sometime, but I'd sure hate to stop and hunt up a doctor now."

Billy cleared his throat.

"Eh, Vic," he said, turning around to face me. "You're not going to like this, but I have to make a quick stop before we leave town."

"What do you mean, I won't like it? I love it," I said. "I think it's a great idea. Let's all stop for a couple of hours and have a fucking picnic on the grass in front of that Memorial de la Patria. Are you nuts, Billy?"

"Over a quarter of a million bucks," he said, "is how nuts I am."

I whistled.

"So?" he said.

"So I'm thinking," I said. I had Sara's head on my shoulder, and I said to her, "Sara, help me think."

"Vic, I need five minutes, that's all. You're going south anyway, I'll just hop out at like Eightieth and Eighty-fifth and be right back. Hell, that can't hurt. And I want to get something out of all this except jaundice and new dentures."

"Who doesn't?" I said. "Listen, Billy, what were you in prison for anyway?"

"You could call it contraband."

"Contraband," I repeated. "Rolls smoothly off the tongue. What kind of contraband, Billy? You can trust me. I'm only the guy who saved your ass."

"You could say, illegal contraband," he said.

"That clears that up," Benny said, taking another left onto the street behind Jorge's shop.

"I'll give you this much, Billy," I said. "Let's make it to the truck first, then we'll see how it goes."

"Sure, Vic," he said. "Anything you say."

A minute later Benny pulled up in front of the old wooden gate that barred the entrance to the alleyway that led to the rear of his friend's hammock emporium. Billy opened it, then closed it behind us after we'd passed through. The Jorge family transportation was parked right in front of us. A ragged tarpaulin had been stretched over arched metal supports and then lashed down over a load of hammocks. Benny beeped his horn twice. Jorge and one of his boys, Carlos, I think, immediately emerged from the small warehouse behind the store and beckoned us out. We got out, me carrying Sara. All available manpower then unloaded our luggage. The son backed the Chevy down the alley in preparation to dumping it somewhere a long way away. Jorge gestured us toward the truck.

The truck's interior was piled high with close-weaves and a few hundred not so close, but a tunnel of sorts had been left on one side. Jorge, Benny, and Billy pushed the luggage in first, and then I followed it, with Sara awkwardly on my knees. Jorge & Co. had prepared a hollowed-out section up front, walled by strong cardboard boxes; it was surprisingly roomy, and enough light was filtering through so I could make out the floor was covered with blankets, and also spy a long rubber-covered flashlight and, in one corner, a box of provisions. I couldn't make out where the portable TV was; it dawned on me that perhaps this wasn't the first time Jorge & Co. had done this sort of thing.

I made Sara as comfortable as I could; although it was far from chilly in there, I wrapped a blanket around her to try to reduce the chance of shock. I could hear Benny, Billy, and Jorge arguing about something outside; then in came Benny up the tunnel. Jorge plugged the tunnel entrance from the outside with a leftover plastic bagfull of hammocks, then the cab doors slammed and we were off, and it was Cancún or bust.

"Where's Billy, and why?" I asked Benny, as if I didn't know.

"He's up front where he can jump out easier," he said.

"Oh, God, that's all we need," I said.

"Cheer up, amigo," Benny said. "So far so terrific."

"Yeah," I had to admit, and we slapped palms a couple of times and grinned at each other in the gloom.

After a moment I said reflectively, "That was a fun time, when the guard came through the door bringing the door with him."

"Sure was," he said, switching the flash on and off a few times to see if it worked, which it did. He shined it on Sara.

"Sleeping like a babe," I said. "Dreaming of Gorgeous George, hanging on behind him as they cruise off into the sunset at a hundred and twenty miles an hour." I rummaged around in the smaller of my suitcases until I found the fake leather bag in which I kept my toiletries, and rummaged in that until I came up with a vial of aspirin and some Band-Aids for Sara when she woke up, which I hoped she'd do soon, because when people who've bumped their heads don't wake up soon, then you worry.

A few minutes later the truck swerved to one side then stopped. A door opened and slammed shut.

"Billy," I said bitterly. "Gone to see how his contraband that is illegal is making out. He'll probably come back with half of Chichén Itzá, including the well."

We waited.

"He was a fascinating character," Benny said after a while, keeping his voice low in case of passersby who might be justifiably startled at the spectacle of talking close-weaves.

"Who was?" I said, doing likewise.

"Georgeous George," he said. "The original one."

"Wasn't he a wrestler?"

"Was he ever. He more or less invented the wrestler you love to hate. He was a practicing psychiatrist who'd wrestled in college, and he figured out that back in those days the guy you'd most love to hate would be some long-haired, dyed-blond, highly effeminate sissy type all in gold kitsch who went into an absolute snit if anyone dared to muss his golden tresses."

"I, too, get fairly aroused if anyone messes up my tresses," I said. "Except Evonne—she can do what she wants with them, including a perm for all I care." Funny what you talk about sometimes, like when you're waiting for the *federales* to collar you and throw you in solitary for the rest of your days.

"What happened to him finally?"

"He became a professional wrestler, he made a lot of money, then he went mad."

"Me too if Billy keeps us waiting any longer," I said.

We heard the cab door open, then close again.

"Thank God," I said. "Jorge, do your stuff, get movin'!"

We bounced off.

"And so we say good-bye to exotic Mérida," Benny intoned dreamily, "where the old meets the even older, land of the deer and the puma, the pheasant and the dove."

"You've been reading Rod McKuen again," I said.

We bounced onward. We laughed a lot. It was beginning to sink in that maybe we had gotten away with it after all, and it was a heady feeling. Sara woke up about a half-hour into the trip. She wanted to know why it was dark. I told her. She claimed she felt fine, aside from a headache, so I gave her three aspirins with some water and a piece of chocolate I found, and convinced her that no matter how fine she felt, she should take it easy for a while, and if she felt at all faint or started seeing double, to let me know. She said I'd be the first in line, and stop fussing. I said I wasn't fussing, I was merely showing the compassion due to any human being I ran across who was bleeding all over the carpet. Then I applied a couple of Band-Aids as best I could over her cut.

I filled her in on what had taken place while she was sleeping on the job; she of course wanted all the details, and as we had nothing but time, I gave them to her, trying successfully, I believe, not to take too much of the credit for the success of the operation for myself. I asked her how she got KO'd. She said she'd tell me if I told her how we got phone calls meant for the real Cul. Ass.

"There is a state of mind," I said to her with appropriate solemnity. "We in the Zen Buddhists' hierarchy have a name for it, but we are not allowed to speak it aloud in front of neophytes."

"Baloney is the name I call it," she said.

"Feeling your old self again, I see," I said. "This state of mind, of semitrance, achievable only after years of vigils, self-flagellation and meditation—"

"And shootin' the shit," she said.

"—is one wherein one is able to pluck brilliant and imaginative ideas out of a sort of information ribbon, an ethereal data bank circling above our globe just this side of the stratosphere. Or—take your choice, it's up to you, darlin'—I got the idea from an old caper movie I saw on the box with Mom just before we left. What the plot hinged on was getting the sucker to phone a number he believed was that of a famous museum, so what the con men did was replace the phone book in a busy café with one that had been doctored so it listed a different number for the museum. Well, we couldn't get to Joaquín's phone book, if he even had one, or his switchboard operator's, so we did the next best thing."

"We got to the switchboard operator," Benny interrupted rudely. "Or rather I did. I took a drive back out to the prison Tuesday, remember, and by no coincidence got there at lunchtime. Then I had a short but fruitful chat with a poverty-stricken clerk, name of Ernesto Byass. I gave Ernesto our phone number. All he had to do to earn himself two and a half million pesos was to dial it any time Lt. Esparza asked to be connected to the Cultural Association. And Lt. Esparza, you remember him, he's the one who thought you were so pretty, as indeed we all do, my dear, he couldn't dial it himself because all calls at Febrero Segundo, we noticed, went through a central switchboard manned by none other than Sr. Ernesto Byass."

"Naturally," I interceded smoothly, "Ernesto only got half his *dinero* in advance. He gets the other half after a month or two if he keeps his mouth shut if anyone ever asks him about it, which is highly unlikely because they'll blame it all on Ethel. It is perhaps needless to mention that Benjamin impressed on him the necessity of not flaunting his new wealth by suddenly going out and buying six new twenty-six-inch color TVs for his hut, which doesn't have electricity yet."

"Ernesto thought that perhaps in a year or two his wealthy uncle up in Monterrey might sadly pass away after a long and painful illness, leaving the Yucatán branch of the family a tidy and completely unexpected windfall."

"I hope I don't get so busy that I forget to send him the rest of his money," I said. "Ah well, time will tell. It's not as if he can go to the cops if he doesn't get it because he's already taken half."

"Pretty crafty, guys," Doris said from her bed of pain. "I'll give you that one."

"Thank you," I said sincerely. "Now it's your turn. What happened with you and the sarge? Did you show him a little too much leg so that he got all excited and leapt at you like a wild beast?"

"So I'm typin' away," she said, "and singin' away when you guys goof up and there's this god-awful racket from your office. Sarge heads for the door, what else? All I knew is if anything like that happened, I was supposed to try and delay him as long as I could—good luck, Doris. I could've torn off all my clothes, I guess, but what I did was scream *'¡Raton!'* like I'd seen a mouse, and I jumped into his arms. How was that for quick thinkin', guys?"

"Terrific," Benny said.

"Lucky for you the one word of Spanish you knew wasn't chocolate chip cookies," I said.

"So I hang on as long as I can, but the guy's a big mother and he finally peels me off and chucks me across the room like I'm a bag of laundry. I must have caught my head on the corner of the desk is all I can think of," she said. "What's it look like back there?" Sara made a move to explore the damage with one hand but thought better of it.

"Ah, it's just a scratch," I said. "You'll need a complete head transplant, but that's all. Maybe we can arrange to get you a head with hair already grown on it. Any particular color you like? You used to be partial to frosted magenta, as I recall."

"Piss off, Prof," she said, with a grin I could just make out in the half-light.

On we went. We nibbled at cheese sandwiches, apples, and biscuits. We sipped water. We bounced. We felt good; we were halfway home. Suddenly we really started bouncing; we'd turned off the highway. After a minute we pulled up, and Jorge cut the engine.

"More than likely giving us a chance to stretch our legs and water the greenery," I said.

We heard Jorge or Billy or both get out, and then the sack of hammocks hiding our tunnel entrance was removed and we gratefully crawled in the open air. As I had thought, we had turned off the main road and parked out of sight of it behind a clump of stunted bushes Cap'n Dan undoubtedly knew the Greek name for.

Jorge beamed at us and asked us if everything was all right. We said it was *maravilloso* and asked him the same thing. He said *igualmente,* but there was one little thing—he hoped it was all right—but we'd lost Billy.

"Lost?" I said incredulously. "You mean like mislaid? Did you look under the seat? How about the glove compartment?"

"All I know is I stopped where the señor wanted me to and off he went, and ten minutes later some child opens the cab door, hands me a paper bag, says the señor's taken off and I better do the same, which I did," said Jorge.

"I can't believe it," I said.

"After all we did for that mother," Doris said.

"Wonder what's in the paper bag?" Benny said.

"Probably his fingers," I said.

Jorge got the bag from the truck and passed it to me. I looked at it with unfathomable dislike.

"Go on, open up," Doris said. "It won't bite."

"Unless it's his teeth," I said.

I opened it. Inside were a note and a souvenir. I took out the note. It was scrawled in pencil on a second paper bag that had been torn down one side and flattened out. Sara and Benny gathered around and we all read it together:

> Vic—sorry as hell but I got no choice with this much money involved. Don't worry about me, I got friends, I'll make out. Take care of yourselves. I'll be in touch when I get back and explain all. DO NOT LOSE THE ENCLOSED IT IS ONE GOOD LUCK PIECE THAT WORKS.
>
> Adiós, abrazos, and muchas gracias, yore ol' pal
> Gray Lobo.
> Kisses to Doris. Happy landings.

I looked at Benny. Then I looked at Doris. Then I looked at Jorge. Then I took out the souvenir, a heavy statuette about five inches high, painted black, portraying some Mayan deity, I guess, a goofball with protruding ears, squatting on his heels. I'd seen a million similar in the windows of souvenir stores in Mérida. I placed its value optimistically at $2.99.

I hefted it—or is it him?—in one hand and wondered if I could throw it far enough to hit the cactus Jorge had modestly retired behind to commune with nature. I finally pocketed the damn thing, I could always give it to someone I didn't like for Christmas as a paperweight. Then I started feeling around in the bag again and finally turned it inside out.

"Now what are you looking for?" said Doris.

"I just thought there was an outside chance my old pal Money No Object might have included a blank check."

Jorge came back and asked us the equivalent of Now what, folks? As if we had any choice. We could hardly go back to Mérida and track down Billy and then massacre the little fucker, could we? So we climbed back into the truck, and Jorge replaced the hammocks, and off we went again.

After a while I simmered down somewhat.

After a while I surprised myself by dozing off for an hour.

More hours passed, about three of them.

We stopped for gas somewhere outside Cancún, then drove into and then straight out of town. I wanted to stop and let a doc or a vet have a look at Sara, but she insisted she was all right and it would be foolish to take the chance and anyway she could have it looked at in a day or two. Jorge stopped again, this time for twenty minutes or so, as we were leaving Cancún. About twenty minutes after that, the truck started jolting again. This time when it stopped and when we'd all emerged stiffly, we found ourselves in a deserted, peaceful grove of trees deep in the rain forest somewhere. It turned out Jorge's last stop had been for more provisions. Since we had over three hours until we were due at the rendezvous with Dan, we got to have our picnic after all. I was the only one with the intelligence to even think of keeping a close eye on the encircling underbrush for any herd of starving pumas who might want to share our ham sandwiches with us, or us with the ham sandwiches.

Afterward we lay around on the blankets we'd stretched out, and Jorge snored and Doris wrote in her diary and Benny stared at his chess set and I rued the day and counted killer ants and watched it get dark and then watched it get darker.

It was just on eleven when we started off again, with Sara in the front this time as there didn't seem to be any reason for her to face the discomfort of tunneling back into the womb again. For me, it was no discomfort; not only is a womb a nice place to visit, but it's not a bad place to live in either.

The moment Sara had climbed up into the cab, she rapped loudly on the partition separating us and called out, "Everyone comfy back there?"

"No," I said. "And keep it down, will you? I've started a diary of my own and I'm trying to concentrate."

After that she kept it down except for the occasional comment, like "This is your friendly tour guide. Puerto Morelos comin' up straight ahead," and "Puerto Morelos Hilton, next stop," and "Hang on, creepy crawlies ahead."

We bounced. We lurched. We jolted. We jarred. At last we stopped, this time in a clearing just big enough to turn the truck around in. I took a look around with the flashlight. We were on one side of a sluggish-looking river some thirty feet across. A decrepit, mossy, slippery gangplank only a couple of feet wide extended out from the bank to two uprights sunk in the river.

"That'll be fun too, with all the baggage," I said to Benny.

"Don't worry, we'll carry you, Prof," said Doris. "And crocs don't feed at night unless something large, with a lot of fat, falls in."

We had a half hour to wait, so we sat and waited. There were a lot of stars high above and a lot of mosquitoes lower down. There was the occasional unforgettable cry of the lesser Cancún vulture.

Twelve o'clock came, then twelve-thirty, then one, with no sign of Dan—or maybe he'd arrived in a submarine.

By two o'clock, we had to face it. Something must have come up, and I'm not talking about that old devil moon.

CHAPTER
SEVENTEEN

Now what, o wise one?" Sara asked, popping the last chocolate-covered marshmallow into her greedy little mouth. We had decided to give Dan up until three o'clock to show, which time it undoubtedly then was. "We could always do like Huck Finn did and make a raft," she offered.

"Keep your bright ideas to yourself, will you?" I said. "It's easy for you to be funny, no one's looking for a bald tomboy in sneakers and hip-huggers, are they? They're looking for Doris the dumb blond secretary. Even the lieutenant wouldn't recognize you if he saw you, and how's he going to see you? He can't be everywhere. And as for Benny, he could kiss Benny's hand for an hour and not recognize him—in fact, I hardly recognize him. I'm not sure I'd want to."

Benny had passed part of the time while we were waiting changing into baggy, knee-length yellow shorts; long socks; sandals; a T-shirt that read 1986 Hang Gliding Nationals, Riverside, Ca.; a cap that had Isla Mujeres written on it, the visor of which was painted to resemble a shark's gaping mouth complete with teeth, yellow-tinted sunglasses, and a false upper plate that fitted over his own teeth and completely altered the shape of his mouth.

"But what am I supposed to do if we have to beachcomb for a week," I said, "find a lighthouse to hide in? Maybe I could bury myself up to the neck in sand like those statues on Easter Island they forgot to put eyes in."

"We gotta do something pretty soon," she said. "I'm gettin' bit to death."

"Me too," I said. "And there's more of me to bite. But you are right, darlin', we sure gotta do something, and I sure wish I knew what it was. However, let us look at it logically. Right, Benny?"

"Right," said Benny.

"One. We decide to wait a week. You and Benny could rent a place in the morning, then I sneak in later and stay snuck in. But it can't be a hotel room because there's no way I could stay hidden in a hotel room for a week, what with maids and the food problem, so it would have to be a house somewhere, preferably isolated and preferably without a live-in maid, gardener, or cook. But it could be done. Or a boat, why not? The problem with that is, if Dan doesn't show up next week either because something's come up, then what?"

"Then we're in the same mess as now," Sara said.

"Exactly," I said. "Benny, do you think Jorge could put me up for a week somewhere and then bring me back down here again next Friday?"

Benny glanced over to the truck where his amigo was dozing.

"He might," he said. "I can always ask."

"If so," I said, "then he can drop you two in Cancún in the morning on the way back, and you can do what you will for a few days, have a holiday until the heat's off, and then fly home. I'll sort things out down here in a week one way or the other. That way at least you two are out of it all."

"Yeah, but you just finished saying we were out of it all already," Sara said.

"Except if you're with me," I said. There was a squawk from a spider-eating great tit in the nearby jungle.

"We could have a word with What's-his-name, Alfredo, at the hotel, to see if he knows anything," Sara said.

"We could," I said. "If he's not on the high seas with Long Dan Silver. And if he knows anything. And if he'll tell us if he does know anything." I looked gloomily downriver one more fruitless time.

A deep silence fell.

"Edgar Allen Poe," said Benjamin after a while.

Doris looked at me and tapped her forehead significantly. "Swamp fever," she said. "Drives men mad."

" 'The Purloined Letter,' " he said.

"Totally round the bend," she said. "Tragic, really."

"The problem Mr. Poe posed," said Benny, in a lecturing tone, "was how does one hide something of value in a fool-proof manner. His solution? Do not hide it at all."

"Taxi!" said Doris. "Take this man to the funny farm."

.   .   .

It was a quarter after eight in the evening of that same day.

The Mérida bullring, which held just under eight thousand spectators, was filling up fast. There were a surprising number of children, the girls in party frocks, the boys in long pants and white shirts. Vendors of all shapes, sizes, and ages sped up and down the aisles hawking ice cream, beer, soft drinks, *caramelos*, peanuts. A mariachi band high up in the stands played a lively ditty. The occasionally undecipherable announcement blared over the loudspeaker system. Pretty señoritas flirted with passing gallants. Matrons fanned themselves. Children hopped up and down in restless excitement.

At eight-twenty precisely there came over the loudspeakers the clarion call we were all awaiting—no, not the lonely bugle solo that heralds the start of "La Macarena," that chilling paso doble that is the signal for *toreros* to cross themselves one more, final time, and then set their satin-covered feet on

ANGELS IN HEAVEN

the still-warm sands for the traditional opening procession, but the stirring strains of "Sweet Georgia Brown," signature tune of the clown princes of basketball, the world-famed Harlem Globetrotters.

And from the large tunnel next to the smaller one aptly named the gates of fear, out of which *toros bravos* hurtled during bullfights, out pranced the Globetrotters to a roar of applause, tossing basketballs deftly to one another. Leading the team was a fetching miss, the next-to-newest addition to the side: bringing up the rear was the latest addition, V. (for Very Visible, Vulnerable, and Varicosed) Daniel.

Thanks again, Benny, I thought as I puffed my way to "our" bench and subsided onto it gratefully. There you are—you'll be leaving the Rocamar now after happy hour, wending your way down the hill, carefree and gay—and here I am, got up like Othello in warm-ups, being invisible in front of eight thousand Méridians.

Out on the wooden court that had been laid on the sand, the Globetrotters swung into their well-known warm-up antics, to the delight of the crowd.

Then a strange thing happened. Despite the fact that I was wearing on my head a six-foot-wide sombrero, had one arm in a sling down to and including the hand, attired as I was in Globetrotter warm-ups, outsized sneakers, and wraparound sunglasses, with a towel slung around my neck, I began, in a weird way, to feel invisible. I was so visible as an object, as a curiosity in a group of, to the locals, similar curiosities, that I felt invisible as a person, much like, as Benny had explained to me, the crucial letter of Mr. Poe that one of his characters hid, or unhid, by leaving it in a group of other letters tossed casually on a desk.

I was also black, of course, which did a lot to alter the face V. Daniel usually presents to the world. And I do not mean paper bag brown; I do not mean high yellow; I do not mean cordovan brown; I mean your basic black. When my ex-friend

193

Benjamin, long may his nefarious schemes backfire, first suggested the idea back in the swamps, I had to admit it did have something going for it, but I didn't see why I couldn't be one of the Washington Generals instead, that hapless white team who always played the Globetrotters and whose record was then something like Won − 0, Lost − 11,242.

"You're too old to be a white basketball player," Benny said cruelly. "Also, you wouldn't be noticeable enough and thus you'd be more noticeable." Sure, sure, it all sounded good on paper, but I couldn't help thinking that Benny would come up with any excuse to have a cheap laugh at my expense. He probably had one of his hammock-weaving amigos up in the stands taking pictures.

Anyway, while I was fretting, fussing, and fidgeting by the river trying to come up with a plan B that made sense, that little rascal had all the details of his own plan B already worked out. He'd seen, as I had, the announcement in the newspaper that the Globetrotters were in town. He figured they'd be staying at the most American hotel in town, the Holiday Inn just off the Paseo Montejo, phoned up, and they were. So he dropped by one afternoon when he was supposed to be by the pool—didn't he?—all on his lonesome, without telling his best friend in the world, who at that very moment was wracked by disease, and tracked down the road manager, name of Happy, whom he found in the outdoor bar by the pool. Benny drew Happy aside. Benny said his pal V. Daniel was in Mexico doing a chore for one of Happy's basketball brethren, none other than power forward J. J. Hill, for confirmation of which all he had to do was phone up J. J. at his hotel, number on request. Benny said in the course of my duties I'd had a minor altercation with the local fuzz, the specifics of which Benny had neglected to inform me. He offered Happy a lot of money (mine) if I could mingle with the team for a few hours, and that was all. Benny had a stroke of luck here, as Happy came up with the good news that the teams were taking a late flight out Saturday night after their last game—Mérida to Mexico City to Monterey to Houston.

Whatever line Benny spun, Happy bought it, and they shook on the deal. It was the twerp's idea to have a fake broken arm, that way I'd have a reason for not warming up with the others, let alone playing, God forbid, and also that way I'd only have one hand to blacken.

So when I got back to Mérida after some more soothing hours in the womb, I called Happy from Jorge's back room and made the necessary arrangements. Later I sent Carlos out shopping for a gigantic embroidered silver-on-black sombrero, a pair of flashy shades, one large souvenir scarf, a jar of cold cream (any brand), a box of tissues, one pocket mirror, several corks, and finally, an extensive supply of food and drink. Then there was nothing to do but wait and practice my lay-ups.

To the great delight of all Jorge's neighbors, the hired bus containing both teams plus Happy plus the two refs who traveled with the entourage pulled up in front of his shop just after seven. A half-dozen Globetrotters piled out and invaded the store. Happy followed Jorge out back and handed over the warm-up outfit and a pair of canoe-size hightops he'd brought along as arranged. The road manager was, as one might guess from his moniker, a totally harassed, permanently worried, short, black bundle of nerves with round glasses and a highly creased forehead; I suppose my pristine forehead might pick up a wrinkle or two if I had to baby-sit that busload of sports all around the world.

I was already made up and had been for some time, and I am here to state that burnt cork really works, as Benny had assured me it would. I do not care to speculate how he came by that information. What you do is cream your visage thoroughly, wipe off all the surface cream, burn some corks, and rub the charred bits on. Then one either pats the face gently all over with a tissue or powders lightly, my dear, with a soft puff.

I climbed into the warm-up outfit, slipped on the boats, put on the sombrero, then the shades. I slung the towel casually around my neck. I inserted my broken wing into the sling. Happy took one look at the finished product and shook his head slowly.

"Thought I'd seen it all," he said. "How wrong I was." I handed over two grand in traveler's checks, which failed to significantly cheer him up. He led the way to the door into the shop, opened it a crack, and called out, "Hey, Peanuts, Snowy, come here a minute!"

In came Peanuts and Snowy, already in costume, like me, but with Globetrotter shorts and vests underneath, as bullfight arenas don't have changing rooms and all personnel involved in a bullfight show up in their appropriate attire, be it suit of lights or the more mundane costumes of the ground crew, the horse handlers, and so on.

Peanuts was a skinny bald gent about my height. Snowy was a hefty afroed gent so black he was aubergine.

"This is the guy I told you about," Happy said.

"It sure ain't Sammy Davis, Jr.," Peanuts said. We slapped palms a couple of times. "Hey, babe. I'm Peanuts and this holy terror here is Snowy. Sorry to hear about your trouble."

"Thank you, Mr. Peanuts," I said. "Mr. Snowy, nice to meet you."

"Love the lid," Snowy said.

I'll get you for this, Benny, I vowed.

"OK, OK," Happy said agitatedly. "Let's get this show on the road, what d'you say? We're late already."

We trouped out into the store where Happy rounded up the others.

"Stay cool, Pops," I said to Jorge as I passed him. He seemed to be choking on something; perhaps he hated good-byes.

Thanks, Benny. I felt as invisible as the Empire State Building on a clear day. I shuffled outside and we clambered onto the bus to a smattering of applause from the onlookers. I slunk into the first unoccupied seat I came to—as chance would have it, beside an extremely pretty black girl who took one look at me and burst into an uncontrollable fit of giggles.

"If that ain't the creature from the Black Lagoon, I don't know what is," a wiseacre from the back called out. I slunk even lower in my seat. The bus took off. After a minute the girl next to me quieted down enough to say her name was Joy and don't mind her and she was sure sorry to hear about the trouble I was in; then she started giggling again. I began to wonder just what kind of trouble I was supposed to be in.

"I didn't know they let girls play now," I said after a while.

"Sure," she said proudly. "There's two of us but I was the first."

I took a close look at her, which wasn't hard.

"I know you," I said. "I saw you play on television. A couple of times. You were terrific. I saw you win the college championship."

"You got it," she said. "That was us. Now I'm broadening my horizons, I think they call it, seeing new countries, meeting new people, but mostly keeping my door locked." She took out a compact and began to inspect her makeup.

"Maybe I better do the same," I said. "My nose feels shiny."

She giggled again.

All of which, aside from a lot more catcalls, one-liners, and jibes from the cheap seats at the back, which I won't bother to report here, pretty much brings us up to "Sweet Georgia Brown" and me sitting on the bench getting splinters beside Happy, watching the boys and girls warm up.

When the game started, it proceeded along the well-worn and well-loved Globetrotter lines, and although most of the faces were new to me, the gags weren't. We were treated to the lopsided ball, the ball on a long elastic, the piggyback dunk, the forty-yarder thrown from the hip, the smallest Globetrotter dribbling through the entire other team before scoring, the player rummaging through a lady's handbag and holding up various items for the world to see while taking a breather in the audience, and all the other old favorites. And all the while their straight men (some of whom, I may say, Benny, looked almost as old as me) were careful not to score too many baskets or do anything remotely flashy. The Méridians lapped it up, and quite rightly too.

I wondered vaguely, a-sittin' there, what kind of life it was for those involved healthwise, travelwise, hotelwise, diseasewise, foodwise, and girlwise. Could be worse, I decided. I once knew a young lady, Mary Lou Kempsky—this was back east in my younger days—who spent half the year touring with the Ice Capades and the other half in Florida with a water ballet and acrobatics show. She said she loved the life, but after a few years, who knew? Who knows anything about a few years from now? I say. Mary Lou Kempsky. If you so much as touched the back of her neck, she fell down on the floor and purred, and that is all I have to say about Mary Lou, not being a kiss-and-tell, except she had a twin brother in Tahoe who gave snow skiing lessons in the winter and water-skiing lessons in Sarasota in the summer. I sometimes wished my life was arranged as neatly. I wonder if water ballets hire people my age. Maybe I could black up again, all over, to hide the wrinkles and saggy bits.

To the enormous surprise of no one, the Globetrotters hung on to win, despite a late rally by the Generals. Then as the mariachi band struck up again, we trotted off into the wings and straight onto the bus and then straight back to the Holiday Inn, where we stopped just long enough for folks to shower, change their clothes, and finish packing. I neither showered nor changed clothes because I wanted to go on looking like a Globetrotter and also because I only had one change with me and I'd be needing that later. I'd left all my luggage except for one oversized carry-on at Jorge's for him to air-freight up north with the hammocks. The last thing I needed was for some custom zealot at the border to say, "Open, please, señor," and out tumbles my collection of FBI paraphernalia, amongst other goodies.

I hung out in Happy's room till we boarded the bus again, and glued myself to Mr. Peanuts and Mr. Snowy when we got off at the airport, which wasn't exactly crawling with cops but it was certainly seething with them, all armed, all jittery, all watchful. One of the things they never tired of inspecting was the Generals, us folks they just smiled at or waved at every time we passed, so I took back my evil thoughts re Benny's intentions, for the nonce.

Then we were blessedly at thirty thousand feet straight down again, and I was opening my first but far from last libation and regaling the delectable Joy with amusing anecdotes from my daredevil juvenile days when I was the possessor of the most unstoppable hook shot in the history of American penal reform.

There were plenty of cops about, too, in Mexico City, where we had a long stopover, but again my crafty disguise, coolness, and powers of mimicry foiled the boys in blue (only in their case, gray). The only remaining danger point for me was at Monterrey, where, as it was our last stop in Mexico, we all had to deplane, with luggage, to go through Mexican customs and immigration. I was in line behind Happy, hoping that I wasn't sweating all my tan off.

When it was my turn, the official took a half-hearted look at my entrance permit, tossed it in a box of the same, then asked me where the rest of my luggage was.

I said the carry-on was all I had.

He asked me if I had any livestock with me.

I said I didn't.

He asked me if I had any fruit, vegetables, plants, seeds, flowers, bulbs, or dirt.

I said I hadn't.

He waved me through. Through I went, with the merest touch of a skip in my step. Onto the plane I went. Up into the atmosphere we went. Down a lot more beer went, despite the time of day—exceptionally early. Down, down onto the friendly tarmac at Houston we went. Toward U.S. customs and immigration we went. On the way, I ducked into a men's room and, with the help of a lot of cold cream, a lot of tissues and a quick-change act, metamorphosized back into my true persona, the one and only V. (for Victor) Daniel, white, unmarried, forty-four, and considerably grayer of hair.

I caught up with Joy and said good-bye. She said she'd love to meet me sometime and get the real story out of me, but it would have to be somewhere awful crowded, given my awful reputation. I goggled. She giggled. I said good-bye to Mr. Peanuts and Mr. Snowy and slipped Happy a two-hundred-buck tip when I shook hands with him.

They went off to wait for the carousel to deliver their luggage, and I went off to check up on flights westward. Was I a different man, a changed man, mayhap, as the result of my having been, for however short a time, not only black but visibly invisible? Amigos, you know what foolish questions get.

I had time for a quick breakfast before catching a TWA flight direct to L.A., during which I slept the whole time.

At LAX I hopped the free shuttle bus that went to a certain hotel's parking lot where I'd left my car for nothing. Ignoring the jealous glances directed at my souvenir sombrero, which I was toting, I found my chariot, dusty but otherwise untouched, and homeward we went, at least one of us with a song on our lips, except for the time I spent trying to add up in my head how much the whole venture had set me back. I stopped when I began grinding my molars.

L.A. was hot, muggy, smoggy, ugly, dirty, and oh, was it good to be back. Mañana I'd worry about Mom and going to work for Mel The Swell's old boss. Today I'd think about other matters, pleasanter matters. Evonne. Wouldn't she look darling in the sombrero. And we had sprung Billy, after all, and gotten back with a whole skin, after all.

" 'I took a trip on a plane, and I thought about you,' " I sang as I tooled northward up the freeway.

" 'A tinkling piano in the next apartment,' " I sang as I cruised down the far side of the Hollywood Hills into my beloved San Fernando Valley.

" 'Pardon me, boys, is that the Chattanooga choo-choo?' " I sang, turning into my driveway and cutting the motor.

"Mom! I'm home!" I sang out as I opened up the front door. "Yoo-hoo."

No Mom.

I checked her room.

No Mom.

I checked my room and the bathroom just in case.

No Mom.

I'd noticed something different about her room, and went back in. What was it? . . . Her quilt, a patchwork made by her aunt Someone, wasn't on the bed. None of her personal belongings were on the table beside the bed. The picture of me and Tony as kids and Mom and Pop that was always beside her bed wasn't beside her bed.

All right.

Maybe she took them all with her when and wherever she went with Feeb, although they hadn't been in the bag I'd helped her pack and had carried downstairs to Feeb's for her. But a quilt? Not even my mom would take a quilt on holiday. I checked both closets, both were as bare as the proverbial baby's buns. So were all the drawers in the dresser. Being a highly trained and skilled detective, it took me no time at all to come up with the answer: Mom had done a moonlight flit on her little boy.

CHAPTER
EIGHTEEN

I checked the top of the small bar that separated the kitchenette area from the front room, because that's where we left notes for each other, on a memo pad I'd been lucky enough to find in my stocking the Christmas before and which featured the old Dutch Cleanser lady holding a broom, the handle of which was the pencil. There might be a note saying Mom had run away to join the circus. Or maybe she'd found another man. What the note I found did say was, "Feeb knows all, Feeb tells all." I knew Feeb was home, as I'd seen her battered old heap downstairs in the drive when I'd parked mine, so I lumbered down to my landlady's. She had her door open waiting for me.

"OK, Feeb, tell all."

"Sit down first," she said. "Want a cup of coffee or something? I got some fresh."

"Don't mind if I do." I sat down in one of the two recliners that faced the fake fireplace. Feeb poured out two cups from her automatic coffee maker, added the necessary, then brought them over. My cup had a picture of two insipid children holding hands on it. Underneath was written in a kid's scrawl, "Love is . . . sharing your last jelly bean."

"All right, jelly bean," I said after taking a sip. "Out with it. Where's Mom?"

"In a home," Feeb said. "Want a brownie? Made 'em myself."

"Later, maybe. What home?"

"It's called Hilldale. It's in the hills between Glendale and Pasadena. I get there in about half an hour."

"How come she's in a home all of a sudden? When did you two come up with that idea? How come she didn't wait till I got back?"

"Now hold your horses, Vic. Your mother knew exactly what she was doing. We've been talking about it for months."

"Oh, you have, eh?"

"Yes, we have and don't get snitty with me. It's a fine place, my girl friend Shirl's father is there—you know Shirl—and I go visiting with her sometimes 'cause she hasn't any other family. It's run by a really marvelous man, Dr. Donald Fishbein. Everyone calls him Doctor Don."

"I am looking forward to meeting marvelous Doctor Don," I said.

"So let's go, soon as we finish our coffee," Feeb said. "You can visit any time out there up till eight-thirty."

I finished my coffee, went back upstairs, changed into visiting clothes—a clean Hawaiian shirt, cream cords, and tan moccasins—then got a lightweight blue fake-suede windbreaker out of the closet. I had three fake-suede windbreakers of assorted colors, which I—the great expert, the canny, street-smart know-it-all—got conned into buying; so if anyone wants one, size XL, cheap, you know where to come. It's called the Italian scam, for some reason. What happens is you're walking along the thoroughfare minding your own business, and a guy in a car perusing a map hails you and calls you over. His story is he's a salesman on the road with his samples and he's just lost all his dough either at Vegas or the races and he has to peddle the last of his samples dirt-cheap for gas money to get home. You, being so street-smart and all, know the guy's lying, but you probably figure, like I did, that what he's really unloading are hot goods that fell off the back of a truck somewhere. And of course the samples look pretty good in their new cellophane wrappings, but I will tell you three things about fake-suede jackets, or at least my three fake-suede jackets: do not get them wet; do not get them dry-cleaned; and do not use the zippers more than twice in any direction.

I threw mine over a shoulder and called my pet.

"Guess who," I said when she picked up the phone at her end.

"I guess my heartthrob, V. Daniel," she said. "Where are you, honey?"

"Just got home," I said. "Guess what I found—no Mom."

"I know," she said. "She called me."

"Weird," I said. "I feel weird without a mom."

" 'Course you do, dear. It must be pretty strange for her too."

"Yeah, sure. Feeb's taking me out to visit her, then I've got to sleep for a couple of hours, then can I drop by? I've got the chic-est little surprise for you."

"I'll be counting the minutes, precious," she said. She blew me a kiss and hung up.

When I got back downstairs, Feeb was ready and waiting, a scarf tied around her blue rinse and an angora sweater draped over her shoulders. Following her directions, I took the Ventura Freeway all the way east till it intersected with the Foothill Freeway, then headed north and then northwest on it, exiting at Berkshire, then doubled back into the hills for half a mile until I found a sign by the road that read Hilldale—Drive Slo.

I turned in, driving slo. The joint looked respectable enough, I had to admit. The drive wound a leisurely way through well-kept lawns dotted with flowerbeds, in one of which an elderly gentleman in a floppy hat was working. Two equally elderly joggers, taking it steady, gave us a wave as we passed them. We parked in front of the central building of a group of three. An elaborately made-up lady of a certain age and then some, with bandaged legs, who was sitting in a rocking chair on the porch of the main building said "Hello, dear" to me as we passed her. "Want a date for the dance tonight?"

"OK, but no jitterbugging," I said. "I don't think I could keep up with you."

She grinned. We passed inside, and Feeb led me up to the reception desk.

"Thought you might like a word with Doctor Don first," Feeb said, "if he's free."

He wasn't free right then, the lady at the desk informed us, but he should be in a few minutes; so I took a pew while Feeb took herself off to visit a spell with Shirl's father. A few minutes later in bustled Doctor Don. He had a quick word with the receptionist, who pointed in my direction, and he trotted over to me, hand outstretched.

I arose. "Victor Daniel, Mrs. Daniel's little boy," I said.

"Don Fishbein, Mrs. Fishbein's trial of strength," he said, and we gave each other a manly shake. Doctor Don was a man of some six foot nothing, dressed in a baggy maroon and pink sweatsuit. He sported a full brown beard, round tortoiseshell glasses, expensive Adidas, and one discreet gold earring. Energy poured out of him like he was plugged into an electricity generator at the base of Niagara Falls. He whisked me off to his office, a small, unpretentious, cluttered room behind the receptionist's desk, threw himself into an old leather swivel chair, and waved me into its equally battered mate.

"You must have a question or two," he said, "so fire when ready, Gridley."

"How's Mom?"

"Mrs. Daniel is somewhere between as well as can be expected and better than can be expected and not as well as can be expected," he said, "depending."

"On what?"

"I only wish I knew," he said. "No one seems to know why patients switch so suddenly from normal to aberrant behavior, what connections get cut. There are theories, but that's all they are as far as I'm concerned." He pawed through a pile of disorganized-looking files, found the one he wanted, looked pleased, then opened it. "You and your brother have been taking care of her for five or six years now, that right?"

"About that," I said, "ever since she was diagnosed. She would have been sixty-eight then."

"Young, young." Doctor Don sighed. "Sometimes it happens even earlier, again no one seems to know why. Hell, it can even strike in the forties. Black, white, rich, poor, smart, dumb, anyone. Mrs. Daniel told me you were out of the country when she moved in, what do you think of her being here?"

"Hell, I don't know, Doc," I said. "I don't know how I feel about it. Mixed up. Awful. Surprised. Guilty. Relieved enough to feel guilty about that too."

"What else is new?" he said, dismissing my whole confused emotional state with one contemptuous wave. "That's only normal, that is. That you can live with, to be frank, given the brutal alternative. You know the symptoms by now of Alzheimer's as well as I do. It is incurable and progressive, and the patient usually dies within three to eight years more or less, often from something like pneumonia. Your mother knows this. We have seen over and over what a devastating effect watching a loved one die of Alzheimer's has on the immediate family. While the patient is still sane, he or she worries about their effect on the family. Later, the patient often gets paranoid and has delusions of persecution by his or her family. Try living with that. Try living with a mother who doesn't even recognize you anymore."

"Yeah, yeah," I said. "It's already started."

"It's better she's here, for everyone involved. At least she's in an environment where she's continually monitored in case of accident. Wait till you see her flat. Obviously there's a medical staff always available—and a pretty good one too. I oughta know, I chose them. She's got company when she wants it and can handle it. And there's a million things to do here if she wants to. We got a terrific place—the food's even edible if you don't want to cook for yourself. Look around. OK, it's not Club Med, but a swimming pool we got, horses we got, tennis, squash, volleyball, bridge, canasta, poker we got. Nature rambles we got. Bingo. Dancing. Lawn bowling." He glanced at the wall clock. "Anything else? I don't want to rush you, but I got a croquet game to referee in five minutes."

"I didn't even know croquet had referees," I said. "OK. I might as well come out with it. There is one thing. I feel like a shit talking about my mother and money in the same breath, but what's it all cost?"

He scanned down one page in my mom's folder.

"It's all paid," he said. "Two years in advance."

"It can't be," I said. "So who paid, my brother?"

"Mrs. Daniel," he said. "Now if you want to see her, at this time of day she's usually playing pool with that little hustler Erwin, so tell her from me to look out."

"Are you sure we're talking about the same mom?" I said. "Mine doesn't have a Mexican dollar, and as far as I know, she's never had a pool cue in her hand in her life."

"See for yourself," he said, "pool hall's one building over, next to the card room." He stood up, so did I.

"What can I say?" I said. "I could start with thanks, I guess."

He waved it away and ushered me out.

"That way," he said, pointing. "Gloria!" he shouted at the receptionist as he strode past her desk. "Hold all calls! I'm in a vitally important conference over at the croquet court." He stopped outside the front door to gaze down at the lady in the rocking chair and say sternly, "Mrs. Lily Putnam, why do you rock your life away when the sun shines and the gardens beckon? Arise and walk and see and touch and smell, or you will waltz alone tonight. I have spoken." He helped the old lady to her feet and gave her a gentle push toward the ramp leading from the porch down to the gardens.

I located the building next door without too much trouble, went in, passed through the card room, which was empty except for a lady in a shawl who was laying out some complicated-looking solitaire, and went on in to the poolroom where that gray-haired mother of mine was standing by one of the two tables chalking her cue professionally and pursing her lips as she surveyed her next shot.

"Four ball in the side," she said. The tiny geezer she was playing with, most elegantly attired in a tight-fitting tan suit and a narrow-brimmed brown fedora, looked my way and slipped me a wink.

"Hi, Mom," I said. She glanced my way briefly.

"Hold it down in the peanut gallery," she said. She bent over, lined up her shot, and then missed it by a mile.

"Damn!" she said. "I can never make those damn cuts."

"There's a trick to it," I said, taking a seat at the side of the room. "I'll show you sometime."

Erwin polished off his last three balls smoothly, then turned to Mom and said, "That makes it a cool eighty-five cents you owe me, babe."

"Try and get it," Mom said, racking up her cue. She came over to me and we gave each other a kiss. "When did you get back, dear?"

"Just now," I said. "Is there someplace we can go and have a word?"

"Sure," she said. "Erwin, same time tomorrow and I'll give you another lesson. My boy's going to buy me a drink in the cafeteria."

"Anytime, toots," said Erwin.

"Lead the way, toots," I said.

She led the way briskly back outside and then into the central building and through a lounge into the snack bar—ca-

feteria. When I had gotten her a decaf and me an orange pop
and we were sitting at a table for two in one corner, she gave
one of my hands a pat and said, "Now, Vic, it's done and it's
going to stay done and I'm glad for everyone I did it."

"Mom, you're something else," I said. "I like Doctor Don."

"What's not to like?" she said.

"How's your room? Do I get to see it?"

"If I don't get tired," she said. "And it is a self-contained
flat, not a room. That makes it sound like I'm living in a
cheap fleabag somewhere. It's like our place but smaller. Tiny
kitchenette but big enough. Tiny bedroom but big enough.
Nice colors. Nice curtains. Rails to hold onto everywhere.
Bath a lot easier to get in and out of than ours. Buttons to
push every two feet in case of emergency. We can bring in
any of our own furniture, within reason. That reminds me—
next time you come, I'd like a few things. I'll give you a list.
You look tired, Victor."

"I am tired, Mom, is why," I said. "How about you?"

"Ah, you know," she said. "Comes and goes, darn it."

"Mom," I said, "it may be none of my business, but where'd
you get the money, hustling pool?"

"Very funny," she said. "Give me a couple of weeks, that's
all. I got two thousand five hundred dollars in insurance from
your father's union when he died. After paying the funeral
expenses there was just under two thousand left, so I put it
in a savings account for a rainy day. I never did have to touch
it, what with what I made working, and then thanks to you
and Tony and Gaye."

I tried to figure out just how much two thousand smackers
in a deposit account would accrue in thirty years but soon
gave up. Mom stopped talking the middle of her next sentence, as she was more and more wont to do, and sat there,
hands folded neatly on the table in front of her. Then she
shouted something and swept her plastic coffee cup off the
table. When she'd come back from wherever it was she went,

DAVID M PIERCE

I delivered her to a nurse at the reception desk who walked her to and then into the elevator. The last thing I said to her was, "Move your bridge hand closer to the cue ball, Mom. That way you'll get a smoother stroke."

"You got it, hotshot," she said, from which I deduced that Erwin had been teaching her some outdated slang along with how to shoot Eight Ball.

All right.

None too emotional a parting, but we were never a demonstrative family, the Daniels. It didn't mean we didn't love each other—hell, I even almost loved Tony sometimes occasionally.

I was hunting about for Feeb outside when Doctor Don intercepted me.

"How's the big match going?" I said.

"They're knocking the hell out of those balls, and each other once in a while too," he said. "I dunno why croquet is considered a sissy game. Listen, I saw on Mrs. Daniel's file you're a private investigator?"

"That I am," I said. "Why, got a problem?"

"That I have," he said. "Got a minute to take a small stroll 'crost the sward?"

I allowed I did, and so we strolled 'crost the sward, Doctor Dan not only stopping to have words with every patient, nurse, gardener, and visitor he passed, but also pausing to exchange greetings with a mangy black cat he called Fred, who was sitting under a tree pretending it had no interest at all in the slightest, perish the thought, with the family of squirrels who were frolicking overhead.

After a while we parked ourselves on a newly painted green bench and I said, "What's up, Doc?"

"Petty pilfering is what's up," he said, rubbing his beard vigorously. "A dollar here, a dollar there, never a lot, but it is annoying."

"From the patients' rooms?"

"Yep."

"Do they have locks on them?"

"Nope, in case we have to get in quickly. What they all have is a sliding thing that says 'I'm in but please do not disturb,' or 'I'm in and please do disturb.'"

"Do your patients sometimes keep real money or valuable valuables in their rooms, or do you keep them locked up in a safe somewhere?"

"Both," he said. "But like I said, nothing's ever been taken but a few bucks cash."

"Hmm," I said. "Let me reflect awhile."

I sat in the sun and reflected. Doctor Don closed his eyes and stretched out his legs and once sighed deeply with pleasure.

"I don't think it's staff," I said after several peaceful minutes had ticked past. "I can't see a staff member who's already making good money risking his job for a few measly greenbacks, although I must admit it's been known to happen. A lot of petty pilfering and shoplifting is motivated by needs other than financial ones."

"Boredom," the doc said without opening his eyes.

"Like boredom, like wanting to shock a spouse or a parent out of his or her real or imagined neglect—same as a very mild suicide attempt. There is something cheap and easy— and cheap and easy is what I have founded my reputation on—that you might try. What you do is buy an ink pad and a stack of filing cards at the stationer, and then you dream up some reason—I don't know what, some new law, a new requirement for old age pensioners, some new red tape, maybe even a game—for having to fingerprint all the mobile patients and maybe lesser staff, like any cleaners who have access to the patients' rooms. I don't expect the thief to go all white and break down sobbing and confess when you try to print him or, more likely, her, nor do I expect the thief to make a big deal of standing on his rights and refusing to let you take his prints, which would be a little obvious. But most civilians place great trust and belief in the power of fingerprinting, unlike most pros, who rarely find them useful for anything but identification purposes. Chances are your amateur crook will be scared stiff, thinking you're already closing in for the kill, and will lay low. If that doesn't work— and I can think of a lot of good reasons why it might not, so spare me—give us a call and I'll see what else easy and cheap I can come up with."

"Worth a try," said the doc, getting to his feet. He walked me back to my car, my '58 pink and blue Nash Metropolitan beauty. Feeb hoisted herself out of the rocking chair and came down to join us.

"Take care of Mom," I said.

"What else?" he said. He watched us drive away.

I drove back to our part of town, Studio City, thanked Feeb for all she had done, went upstairs to the empty apartment, showered, then went into my bedroom for a snooze. I realized I had a spare room now. Maybe I could use it as an office and save on my office rent. Or rent it to someone else's mom. Or get a large dog or start growing mushrooms at home—the possibilities were endless. I could move to a smaller place. Or move to another town even. Jesus, there was an idea, another state even. There was nothing keeping me in the San Fernando Valley anymore, yippee. I could visit Mom every other weekend, say, from anywhere almost. Paris, Venice, Rome in spring, Bangkok anytime ... suddenly the world beckoned. Of course there was my business, such as it was. And there was Evonne, such as she was, which was sensational. Plus a pal or two or three. Sara I could probably just live without. Fancy old Mom having all that money all that time, amazing. The last thing I did before visiting the Land of

Nod was to blow a loud vulgar raspberry in the general direction of downtown L.A. and in the specific direction of Mel The Swell's ex-employer. V. Daniel, of the Davenport Daniels—no forelock-tugging, servile, flunky, door opening yes-man he.

At least not yet, amigos.

CHAPTER NINETEEN

$4,752.15.

That tidy sum, my computer had just informed me, was the cost of that imbecilic paperweight adorning my desk—and that only to date. Still to come were whatever millions of pesos Benny and Doris squandered on riotous living back on Isla Mujeres, where they were headed when we parted company, plus doctor bills for her, no doubt, and probably plastic surgery for her later at the Mayo Clinic.

It was latish Monday morning, and I was in my office sorting through the pile of mail that had accumulated and also sorting through the pile of memories I had recently accumulated, with the accent on the particularly aggravating ones, i.e., those in which a large outlay of funds was involved. I sent a silent message to a certain switchboard operator south of the border telling him not to hold his breath while he waited for the rest of his dinero.

I was somewhat soothed to find a couple of checks in the mail: one was for the successful tracing of a missing person, a husband, whom I'd found living with a dental technician three blocks away from his former home; and the other was a final payment for a surveillance I'd carried out for a local bank on one of its employees who was about to be promoted. There was also a note from J. J. saying he'd called a couple of times getting no answer and what was going down, was I making any progress? No, was the answer. The fall catalogue from Remington & Co. I put away for later, the latest junk mail from *Reader's Digest* I chucked out immediately, figuring my word power didn't need increasing all that much and even if it did, *Reader's Digest* wasn't going to help.

When I was halfway done with the mail, I thought I'd better put a modicum of energy into assisting J. J. with his predicament, so I gave his hotel a ring, but he was out. I left a message saying V. Daniel had called and was expecting positive results any day now. Then I tried Lt. Carstairs again, down at South Station, and he was out too, but if I left a number, he'd call back. I left a number. I checked on my three long-term security clients, John D. (Valley Bowl), Arnie (Arnie's New & Used Cars), and Mrs. Beloni (Star Family Grocery); all were pleased to hear from me, but none had any problems for once.

I turned the face of the world's most expensive paperweight to the wall. I answered a query from an ex-client in Carson City who wanted to know if I knew anyone trustworthy in my line of work in London, England. No, was the answer. Not only didn't I know anyone at all in London, except the queen, I was hard-pressed to think of anyone anywhere in my line of work who I would deem trustworthy.

A lady from Palos Verdes, which is south of here, out past LAX, wanted to know my rates per hour, day, week, and month. I told her, adding that in some special cases they could be subject to moderation, i.e., I was willing to make a deal if it was a slow day.

Lt. Carstairs called back. He sounded busy. I explained briefly who I was and told him I needed a fast line on Goose Berry, if he would be so kind.

He didn't want to be so kind.

I mentioned my brother's name, current duty, station, and rank. The lieutenant unbent enough to tell me as far as he was concerned, quote, Goose is nothing but a piker and I only roust him when I have nothing more important to do, like chasing kiddy-car thieves, unquote. I asked him if Goose had any heavy connections. Carstairs said I had to be kidding. I asked him if the LKA down on East St. in Anaheim that Sneezy had given me for Goose was still correct; the lieutenant told me without looking it up it was, and was there anything else, as he had four hours of paperwork to do before noon and it was already eleven? I said no, thanked him, and hung up.

I got back on to John D., lanky prop. of the Valley Bowl, to ask him if I could borrow his office for an hour someday soon. He said what was the matter with my own. Termites, I said. In that case, he said, be my guest, as long as it's for something illegal or fun or both.

I looked up Goose's phone number in the book, tried him and found him home, which didn't surprise me all that much, as lowlifes like Goose are more familiar with night owls than early birds.

"Mr. Berry," I said in my movie gangster voice. "You don't know me but my name is Ace. I'm a friend of J. J.'s and let me tell you, pal, you sure put the fear of God into one poor fish with that postcard you sent him."

"J. J. who?" Goose said guardedly in an accent that in a pinch I'd say was Chicago, East Side.

"The J. J.," I said, "who is a friend of mine and who would be calling you himself if he didn't have to be extra careful these days about the company he keeps."

"Oh, yeah?" the Goose said.

"If I wasn't a pal of his," I said, "how would I know about you?"

"So?"

"So how about setting up a meet, you and me, in a couple of days, to come to some kind of suitable arrangement? The last thing J. J. needs right now is someone bringing up all that old shit, and he's willing to put his money where his dentures are for a one-time-only buy-out. He's no fool, he's got a chance for some really big bucks. What does he care for a couple of thou to get you off his back?"

"In that case," Goose said, "I probably could find a little free time later in the week. Just tell me where and when, friend, but let us make it somewheres reasonably public, you know what I mean. I'd feel better about things if we didn't meet up like in the middle of some desert at midnight."

I said I caught his drift and I'd get back to him in a day or two with the details, maybe some afternoon in a park or a bowling alley or whatever.

"OK by me," he said. "Thanks for calling, friend. Say hello to J. J. for me."

"Will do," I said, and we both hung up. All right, amigos, from the sound of him and from what Carstairs had to say about him, it didn't look like the Goose would be any match for the likes of V. Daniel in full swing. I suppose I could have met up with him that afternoon and had a go at him, but it would give me more of an edge if I had Benjamin with me and it was remotely possible Benny might tear himself and Doris away from their tropical idyll (on me) in a couple of days. Also, if I gave Goose more time to get his hopes up, he'd have even farther to fall when we lowered the boom on him. Finally, I needed a day or two to prepare a surprise package I had in mind for Peter "Goose" Berry, something I knew he'd adore.

I reached for the phone book again and began working on that aspect of the venture by turning to the Fs, F for finger. Under "Finger" I of course found nothing helpful, nor did I expect to—I was merely amusing myself, if you must know—what a card. I turned then to the more likely entries—hospital and medical supply companies.

Ever tried to buy a couple of fingers? Or a thumb or two? It's not as easy as one might think. Too bad Billy hadn't kept his and slipped them to me in the paper bag along with Shorty, my little paperweight. I started by telephoning something called the Cal. West Hosp. Sply. & Equip.

"Hello," said a lady's voice. "Cal. West. Can I help you?"

"You don't happen to sell parts of the human body, do you, m'am?" I said. "Fingers, specifically."

"What are you, some kind of nut?"

She slammed the receiver down.

"Thumbs would do," I said into the dial tone. Finally a nice, helpful girl at Morgan Med. Ltd. told me what I was doing wrong just before I phoned up Blades and asked him to see what he could do free-lance. What I ultimately got on to was a medical laboratory supplier, and did they have human bodies and all parts thereof, to say nothing of animals, ditto. Arms, hands, torsos, everything including complete skeletons, although those were now plastic, the man I was talking to informed me. He quoted me a price for two adult fingers, which I found steep to say the least, but he explained I was paying for the whole hand, as they had no call and thus no price list as such for individual digits. I said I understood completely but really had no need for a whole hand, and perhaps someone there might be kind enough to hack off a couple of fingers for me and wrap them up separate, and they could keep the rest on me for the trouble.

He said sure, no problem, but then wanted to know which medical facility I was calling for.

"Eh, none," I said. "I'm doing private research."

No sale, he said, without an order form from an accredited medical school, research center, or the like.

"How about an M.D.?" I said.

"Sure, no problem," he said. I said I'd get back to him.

My own doc had just retired and was on a year's cruise around the globe, spending (partly) my money, and I didn't want to bother Mom's regular specialist for something so seemingly foolish, so I bothered Doctor Don instead. He owed me one, did he not? When he finally came to the phone and was done laughing, he of course wanted to know what I wanted them for. I told him—to frighten the five o'clock shadow off a two-bit chiseler who was leaning on one of my clients. I gave him the name of the company I'd just talked to, and he said he'd get a note to me in the mail immediately that should do the trick, which he did, because it got to me by Wednesday, in the evening of which, as it happened, Benny and Sara returned.

They both promptly phoned me up at home, where Evonne and I were sipping strawberry daiquiris, holding hands, and watching TV, to tell me they were back safely and how tanned they were and what a good time they had on the island and that they went sailing one day with Big Jeff and turtle watching another day and Doris had two stitches put in her noggin and she told her folks she'd bumped her head when she slipped on some rocks skin-diving with a bunch of Aussies. Sara, needless to say, wanted to know when I was going to cough up all I owed her. I said it was already in the mail and I was glad they were home safely, as was I, after a few adventures en route, about which I'd tell them all someday if they were lucky.

Evonne switched channels about then to the highbrow one, as she wanted to catch Laurence Olivier's *Hamlet* again. I said OK, but the last time I'd seen it I'd been disappointed as it was mostly quotes, and jokes don't come much older than that. She wound up spending the night, and not in the spare room, either, gossip lovers. She helped me wash off the last lingering traces of black from the back of my neck first. Sharing a bath with a blonde and a rubber duck does make it crowded, but there are compensations.

I forget what I did all day Wednesday after I drove my American Beauty Rose to work, so it was probably even less than usual.

Thursday morning, armed with the doc's letter, I took the

Hollywood Freeway, then the San Bernardino, to Monterey Park and picked up my digits, which were awaiting me at the front desk. I handed over the note and some money, and they handed me my fingers, neatly wrapped. I, being the sentimentalist I am, still have the receipt tucked away somewhere safe: "(1) ml. adlt. rt. hand – $119.00." I unwrapped the package back at the office, took a peek, and wished I hadn't. Looking at two nasty, gray, peeling fingers with uncut nails bobbing about in a slightly cloudy glass of formaldehyde is not recommended right after a late breakfast at Mrs. Morales' Taco-Burger stand.

I scraped the company label off the jar, strolled around the corner to Mrs. Martel's, purchased some colorful Christmas wrapping depicting Santa's elves hard at work, and then back at the office again, rewrapped the jar.

I phoned John D. He said OK to three o'clock at the Valley Bowl.

I phoned Benny. He said OK to three o'clock. What did he have to do and what should he look like? Just sit there, I told him, looking rich, powerful, and scary.

I phoned Evonne at work just to say I adored her and she could wash the ring off my tub anytime. She said something about her mother having warned her about men like me.

I phoned Goose. Goose said OK to three o'clock at the Valley Bowl. I told him where it was and to ask for the manager's office.

I phoned Mom to see how she was settling in and getting on; she dictated a short list of what she needed, and I said I'd get them to her that weekend if that was OK with her. She said sure, and guess what? She'd just been fingerprinted in the cafeteria and that the whole place was abuzz with rumors. I said I'd always told her that crime didn't pay and they'd get her in the end.

After a late lunch at Fred's—cream cheese on toasted raisin and a glass of buttermilk—and after laying down a modest wager with Two-to-One Tim, the house bookie, on the Dodgers against the Giants that night (easy money), I returned home, donned my prescription sunglasses, strapped on my shoulder holster, tucked one of my Police Positives in it, practiced my slow draw a couple of times in front of the mirror, put on a sport coat, added the worst tie in my collection, which is saying something, then finished off the ensemble with a garish tie clip in the form of a (fake) gold horseshoe.

I attacked the traffic again, arriving at the Valley Bowl around two-thirty, parked around the back and went in. I exchanged friendly hellos with Sal at the Snack Bowl, accepted her offer of a speedy cup of java on the house, declined deftly an offer to go to a wrestling match with her some night, made my way past the line of pinball and Space Invader machines to John D.'s office, where I found my friend tapping busily away on an adding machine with one hand and rubbing the top of his crewcut with the other. When he'd finished up whatever it was he was doing—checking out the bar totals, it looked to me—we small-talked until Benny showed up some fifteen minutes later, at which time John said, "OK, it's all yours, boys, but not too much gunplay—it disturbs the bowlers' concentration," and then discreetly withdrew.

I looked Benny over to see if he looked scary. He sure did, in the way that a combination of Baby Face Nelson, Buddha, and a tax examiner might look scary—expensive one-button mohair suit, lizard shoes, narrow tie with a diamond stud, gray gloves (a nice touch), gray homburg, steel-gray mirror shades, black leather attaché case.

We exchanged moderately emotional greetings, as we hadn't seen each other since early one morn in a swamp. Then I said, "Benny, my boy, thanks for everything you did down south, we would have been in deep shit without your brilliance, foresight, and everything else."

"Victor, my man," he said, "my pleasure. You must tell me some sunny day how you got on with the Globetrotters."

"Let me sum it up this way," I said. "I don't think they're going to renew my contract. What did you tell Happy my problem was anyway?"

"Double paternity suit," he said.

"Is that all?" I said.

"With twin sisters," he said.

"Is that all?" I said.

"Just going on sixteen," he said.

"Is that all?" I said.

"Yes," he said.

"Thanks a million, pal," I said. "It will not be forgotten."

I handed over the jar, which he put in his briefcase, outlined the action, then took the seat behind the desk, leaving the one facing me free. Benny besat himself carefully in the corner on the one remaining chair, underneath a framed photograph of our host just after he'd won the $50,000 Phoenix Open back in '76. The rotter hardly looked a day older now. I unbuttoned my jacket so Goose could spot the cannon in my holster, and wondered how John D. had managed to spot that I was carrying it with the jacket buttoned up. Remind me to ask him about that sometime. Maybe it was just a lucky guess.

A little after three there was a knock on the door. I let a long minute go by before calling out, "It's open."

In, warily, came Goose, who surprised me because he didn't look like I thought he would, like a racetrack tout or a West Coast version of some Damon Runyon character. Goose was a short, pudgy, tired-looking man who walked like his feet hurt and blinked his eyes a lot.

"You Ace?" he asked me.

I nodded and pointed to the vacant chair across from me. His eyes glanced nervously toward Benny, in his corner. Benny looked impassively back.

Goose took a seat; his legs were just long enough so his feet reached the worn carpeting.

"This your place?" he said, looking around. "I usta bowl. Looks like a nice operation."

"Turns a buck," I said. "Just like you're trying to do."

"Everyone's gotta make a living, right?" he said with a grin.

"OK, Goose, let's cut the shit," I said, slamming one fist on the desk under his nose and letting my jacket flop open so he caught a good glimpse of the .38. His grin went somewhere and didn't come back. "J. J. Hill. Not the smartest dude in the world—what jock is?—but smart enough to know who to call when some little shitass starts puttin' the squeeze on. Right, Mr. G?"

Mr. G took a cigar out of a leather cigar case, rolled it between his fingers briefly, licked one end delicately, then put the other end in his mouth. I almost tripped over myself getting across the room to light it for him. When I was back at the desk, I said, "So here it is, Goose. We got plans for J. J. that do not include some two-bit jerkoff from Anaheim, for God's sake."

"Come on, you guys," the Goose protested. "Why jump on me? What have I done?"

"Nothin'," I said. "And that's the way it's gonna stay. Hey, I dig that, it sort of rhymes."

"Ace," said Benny, which was to be his entire contribution to the dialogue. He held up his briefcase.

"Oh, yeah, sure, Mr. G." I crossed to Benny with alacrity, took the case from him, opened it up, took out the gift-wrapped digits, and put them gently on the desk in front of Goose.

"Here," I said. "Birthday present from Mr. G. He gives terrific presents, you'll like it. I did the wrapping," I added bashfully.

Goose looked at the parcel like a committed vegetarian eyeing a plateful of fresh steak tartare.

"But it ain't my birthday," he said.

"So happy Labor Day," I said. "Open it, it won't bite. If you open it careful, you can save the pretty paper."

He opened it . . . *gingerly*, I suppose, would be more accurate than *carefully*. With extreme gingerliness. When he took in what was in the jar, he went green and dropped it on the rug.

"That's no way to treat a gift," I said. "Are you lucky it didn't break. So pick it up, asshole."

He bent over and picked it up.

"So put it away," I said. "It's for you. What would I want with a couple of fingers sawed off some chiseler's hand?"

"What do I want with them?" Goose muttered.

"You want them to remind you," I said, "that you got one week, which is seven days starting today, to mail to me, Ace, here at the Valley Bowl, Olive and Alameda, every picture you got, any film you got, every negative you got stored away under your dirty socks, of J. J. and his old teammates. Otherwise, what happens is me and a friend of mine take a drive out to East Street and you lose one finger per day you're late with the mail. And when they're done, we start on something you only got one of. And I don't mean sliced neatly off under anaesthetic with a nice sharp scalpel in a nice clean operating room. I mean sawed off with a crosscut rubbed with dog shit in an alley somewhere. Do you hear me, Goose, am I gettin' through at all, did I use too many big words?"

Poor Goose didn't know whether to shake his head no or nod yes. Mr. G snapped his fingers once in my direction. I hurriedly took him over an ashtray, one purloined, I noticed, from the same piano bar that supplied several of mine.

"Say it, Goose," I said on my return. "Say I'm gettin' through all that dandruff."

"You're getting through," he managed to get out.

"Now beat it, creep," I said, "if you can figure out where the door is. Go home. Get out the Scotch tape. Start wrapping—it doesn't have to be neat like mine. Then go stand in line at the post office. Make sure you put enough stamps on, Goose, even if you got to get someone else to lick them for you. Now fuck off."

Off he fucked.

"I love doing Sheldon Leonard," I said when he'd fled.

"Primitive but effective, I would surmise," said Mr. G, stubbing out the cigar. "Ptui. I hate those things. Did you know if you rub cigar ash in your hair, it makes you look ten years older?"

"No," I said, opening the door to air the place out a bit. "And I don't need cigar ash to make me look ten years older, going along with your insane schemes in foreign countries has already done it. But it was a nice touch, as usual, the cigar. If you paid more than a quarter for it, I'll add it to J. J.'s bill. Remind me to phone him up later with the good news."

"Don't forget to tell John D. you're Ace and you're expecting some mail," he said.

"Already taken care of, pal," I said mendaciously. "What do you take me for, anyway?" P.S.—I phoned up John later. The next day a package arrived by courier service. I glanced through the contents, then burnt them.

Bits and pieces ... all that remain are fluttering bits and wind-tossed pieces scattered through time and space....

Bit one (one week A. G., i.e., After Goose): Postcard from Big Jeff. I'd left him my address so he could mail me anything there was in the local papers about our escapade to add to my meager collection of clippings, but I guess the authorities down there hushed everything up to save themselves considerable embarrassment. The card had an advertisement for his pizza joint on one side. The other read: "No press. Alfredo in hospital. Dan disappeared south after someone torched his boat. Selling pizzas like mad. Having wonderful thirst. Big Jeff. XXXXX to Sara."

Piece one (two weeks A. G.): Who should drop by my place of business but my old pal Mr. Lubinski, Family Jeweler. He'd had a minor heart tremor while I was away, and as a part of his recovery program, he was supposed to take a brisk walk an hour a day after his nonfat, nonalcoholic, nontasting lunch, served up at his store by his vigilant wife. So what he would do was stride off purposefully, wave to the little woman, then pass the hour out of sight around the corner with pals like me and Andy the dentist and, if his wife wasn't watching like a hawk, Mrs. Martel across the street from him.

The first time he dropped in on me after lunch, I was computing away, and he was across from me puffing on a forbidden cigarette when he spied Shorty, which he picked up and hefted.

"What's this, Vic?"

"The only five grand paperweight in the universe," I said, trying to concentrate on which I was doing, which was to see exactly how much money I could save if I did work out of home, if Feeb would let me.

"What's it made of?"

"Money," I said. "Lead, granite. How would I know?"

"It feels like gold," he said.

"You, Mr. Lubinski," I said, "have my undivided attention. How can you tell?"

"It weighs like it," he said. "You could make sure by liquid displacement."

"Liquid? What liquid?" I said. "Name it. Have I got liquids."

"Jewelers' scales you won't have," he said. "You could also maybe find out like this."

He took out a tiny one-bladed silver penknife that was on his key ring and carefully scratched a small bit of the black paint off the base. He showed me the result, a glint of gold, or gold color anyway. I remembered Billy's words and felt like I'd discovered the Comstock Lode.

"Of course, unfortunately, all is not gold that is golden," he said. "Stick it in a mild paint solvent and see what happens."

I dunked it in a jar of turps the painters had left behind a while back when my office was being redone after the fire. Then I rinsed Shorty off under the hot water tap in the bathroom, paying particular attention to behind his jugged ears. When I took it back to Mr. Lubinski, he screwed a loupe in one eye and gave Shorty the once-over. After a minute he winked at me with his nonlouped eye and said, "This I can tell you: copper it isn't."

Bit two (five days A. G.): Postcard from Doris, sent from Isla Mujeres. On one side was a picture of a ruined garden in which there was a large tombstone. On the other: "Tomb of a pirate we saw who died here of love. Tombstone reads: 'What I am, you shall be. What you are, I was.' Neat, eh? XXX Dumb Doris. P.S.—Lost a *fortune* of your money gambling last night at the casino. Ha-ha!"

What a twerp. Even I knew there was no casino on Isla Mujeres. But wasn't there one in Cancún?

Bit three (two months A. G.): Postcard from John Brown, aka Gray Wolf, aka Billy Baker, aka slickest escapologist since Zsa Zsa Gabor. The card pictured "El Rey Motel, U.S. Highways 60 and 70, Globe, Arizona. 24 units, Air Conditioned, Fully Carpeted, Tubs, Garages, Room Phones & Patio."

"Had any good luck recently? See ya afore too many wanings of too many moons, Gray Wolf."

Piece two (ten days A. G.): Discovered on the floor of my office with the rest of the junk mail but delivered by hand:

Extract from a soon to be published diary
By
Sara Silvetti, Poetess Extraordinaire
... purple bougainvillea 'gainst a white-washed
wall ...
one-eyed chameleon frozen by cruel history's
pace ...
chameleon speak with forked tongue also,
Running Deer.

DAVID M PIERCE

I am aware
Of my body tonight as hummingbirds hover like
minute helicopters
In the lukewarm air.
I have never really been anywhere
Till now. Studio City isn't anywhere.
Davis CA isn't anywhere. They are but wounded
moles,
They pain but do not soar.
Nor, as yet, as yet, the painted whore
in the graffitied door.
Bald is beautiful. Hair is for the bears.
Let's go a-wanderin' agin sometime, Prof,
Let's take off
Let's shake off the sandaled shackles of
afternoon duties,
Herbal teas and nonfat cheese,
Diet life and designer blah,
The freeway leads nowhere but to the grave
Of some unknown brave.

Well! Not too bad, the twerp was actually improving. Listen,
I was glad. After considerable thought, I gave her a D minus.
I wondered briefly what her next metamorphosis was going to
be—Hare Krishna, maybe; she was already bald. And nothing
could be worse than punk.

Piece three: If you would all please put your specs on—
mine were already starting to scratch up, I noticed, because
I refused to pay ten bucks extra when I bought them to have
a nonscratch treatment—and then retrieve from the coffee
table your Sotheby's (the auctioners) winter catalogue for
1987. Turn to page nine, item 192. You will read the following: "Mayan statuette [aka my Shorty!] circa 1100. Gold.
Height, 10 cms. 48 mm. Unique. Believed depiction of a wor-
shipper of 'God Deer.' Estimate − $25,000 to $27,000."

Benny, who knows about such things, informed me that an auction house's estimates are generally well below the final selling price. I did not argue the point. I wondered how many more contraband Shorties Billy was sitting on patiently in Globe, Arizona, not that he would still be there. I hoped he had the sense not to flood the market. You know what that does to prices in the art world.

Bit four (twelve days A. G.): Postcard from Milwaukee, of the downtown area seen by night. The message read: "Hey, babe, whatever you did, it's still working. Your bread's in the mail. Cut by Lakers, but front seats here any time you pass thru. J. J." And which would arrive first, I wondered, my visiting Milwaukee, J. J.'s check, or the Second Coming?

Piece four (five days A. G.): I was at the bureau (as in office) doing this and that when Willing Boy and the twerp putted up on his bike. It was the first time I'd seen either of them since I got back. Sara looked ... awful. Like an old maid, but older. No makeup. She wore a nothing scarf around her head, knotted under the chin, a long Mother Hubbard dress, and flat shoes. Willing Boy was not only out of his biker's leathers for once, but I'll be damned if he wasn't wearing a wooly brown robe, with a hood even, like a monk's.

Sara knocked politely on the door.

I shouted, "It's open, for Christ's sake."

They came in and stood, holding hands, in front of me. Sara said, with excruciating meekness, "Please do not blaspheme, Victor. Brother George and I have been born again, and we walk with Jesus now."

There was only one thing to do, and I did it, fast—

I swooned.